# THE RED DUST

## Phillip Aughey

BLACK COCKIE PRESS

The Red Dust
Published by Black Cockie Press
Copyright © Phillip Aughey 2019
The moral right of the author has been asserted
Cover design © Natalie Muller 2019
Distributed by IngramSpark
Printed by IngramSpark
ISBN:978-0-6481366-9-9

*To my parents, Ruth and Fred.*

# CHAPTER 1
# LORRY'S DAWN. FEBRUARY 1965

There is a moment when the night loses its potency and awaits the first sign of the approaching dawn. The timeless peace which the night has created is about to be interrupted by the emergence of a subtle silvery light from the east. The night creatures, having moved carefully not to disturb the calm, look for their hiding place to protect themselves from the day's light. Soon the sun will signal the beginning of the day's events. Soon light will enter the scene to reveal the open plains, the parched landscape, the red dust, the waterless dams and the starving sheep. It is the view of a drought.

It is usually the coolest part of the day. The vibrant heat produced by the previous day's relentless furnace has had time to diminish its intensity. Country reluctantly waits for the sun to rejuvenate the inferno. Sometimes in the winter there is a frost, but on this day, in late February, to be cold is a fantasy too far into the future to be contemplated.

Sparrows began to chirp on the gum tree outside Lorry and Marg's bedroom. Their noise was enough to stir Lorry from a restless sleep. He opened his eyes and saw the first glimmer of light coming through the window. It was enough to move him from his rest. He moved carefully so as not to disturb Marg. He yawns as though in protest against a night that did not yield much rest. It was either the intense heat which lingered, or the concerns he still held from the previous day's dilemmas, that has led him to be still weary. Whichever, it was now history. The thought of the latter drove him urgently to find his clothes. They were in the usual place, piled in correct order, washed, ironed and arranged neatly. Marg's doing, of course. The clothes, comprising baggy blue trousers which already held the scars of Marg's needle work, a green tee shirt which had now been pulled, unshaped and uncoloured and a blue woollen jumper although when bought fitted him well now fell off him like dead wool of a sheep's hindquarters, if needed. The socks are at the bottom of the pile. There was no need for fashionable garments in this place.

Now attired, with socks in hand, he moved out of the bedroom and into the tiny kitchen leading to the door outside. He moved quickly, almost with military precision like a serviceman on a solo mission. He knew what had to be done and there was urgency in his movements. The enemy was out there, it had always been out there, it was never going to be defeated. It was a war against the elements, the drought, the floods, the heat, the isolation and the toil. It was an enemy that always held the initiative.

Once outside the house he was met by much cooler air. The house tended to keep the day's heat in for longer. The nights were always too short to gain parity with the temperature outside. He was greeted by the two kelpie dogs, Flight and Sergeant, who had been very patient in their wait for his appearance. With Lorry's appearance their greatest joy was now realised. Named after the rank

Lorry had attained whilst enlisted in the RAAF during World War Two. Being from the same litter they worked well as a pair and their love for their human master was equally shared. Their enthusiasm was in direct contrast to the worry on Lorry's face. Appreciating their loyalty Lorry rewarded them with a pat each.

Immediately outside the house there was a covered space, a landing. Created at Marg's insistence to serve as a point where the outside doesn't get into the inside. That served to keep the house cleaner. There was a steel chair which stayed in the usual position with Lorry's boots always placed in front of it. The chair bit into the cement flooring under the pressure of Lorry's weight. Lorry was by no means a fat man. Not quite six feet tall, he was heavy, but his bulk comprised of muscle and bone. Basically a quiet man, but when he did speak it was to the point. He was typical of a man who had lived his life on the land, strong and sturdy. Although now in his forties his capacity for work had not diminished with age. His hair was black and his face bore the results of a lifetime facing the wind, the rain, the sun and the heat. His descendants had arrived from Ireland in the 1870's and settled on a block in Clare, South Australia. In 1920, when Lorry was five, the third child in a family of at that stage, five, his father heard of blocks opening up at Talimba in New South Wales. Deciding to make a go of it for himself, he loaded up the family onto a horse and dray and traversed the Hay plain in summer. He found his thousand acres of thick Mallee scrub, set up a tent and with the help of his sons cleared it for wheat. The only tools available were axes, shovels, a horse and plough. Hard work was no stranger to Lorry, he was brought up on it.

To Lorry work was a matter of course. It had to be done in the best way possible. There was never a thought of the hardships involved. It was his lot and he must deal with all that he came up against with never a thought of why. His time as a Flight Sergeant in a Dakota crew flying supplies into Papua New Guinea was merely a variation upon the theme of what he had been used to. The job had to be done, the orders had to obeyed, no need to wonder why, just do. That war may have been completed, the victory attained, but this war was on going.

He noticed the extra weight on his boot when he lifted it to place on his foot. He saw the dried mud which was caked onto them from the previous day's efforts of dragging sheep out of an empty dam. The poor wretches desperate for water had been trying to find it in a dam which only held mud. Conscious of Marg's insistence on a clean house he picked up both the boots, moved to the closest space away from the landing and with his arms crashed them against each other. This cleared the mud off them and the chair took his weight again.

Boots on, broad brimmed hat, with distinct sweat marks, placed on his head, the dogs jumped with excitement as he arose to face the day. He could feel his boots crackling on the dry leaves of what was, in a good year, green and vibrant kikuyu. The gum trees, which lined the house yard, gave a faint sound of air passing through them. It was a good sign. They hadn't been stirred by any breeze for days. The forecast was for a southerly change to come through this evening. There might be the possibility of rain. As he moved up the path towards the gate he felt the air on his face. It was coming in from the north-west. It is a definite sign of a possible change in the offering.

The dogs had reached the gate out of the house yard well in advance of Lorry and had impatiently jumped it before Lorry could open the gate for them. As he closed the gate after himself, he paused to look at the view through the growing morning light. All was red. The ground, devoid of any vegetation, was red to the horizon. The redness of the ground corresponded directly with the red now filling the sky from the approaching dawn. It was difficult to detect the straight lined, western horizon of a perfectly flat landscape against a sky of a similar colour.

He accepted what he saw with little expression and moved towards the corrugated iron shed to the west of the house. He picks up a shovel, some wire and a knapsack of tools and headed south, on the tractor, to the furthest paddock. That was where the trouble had been. That was where he had spent the previous evening trying to repair a bore until he couldn't see what he was doing. That was where the sheep, now in the adjoining paddock, had got bogged in the waterless dam. This was where today's battle was to be conducted.

# CHAPTER 2
## MARG'S MORNING. FEBRUARY 1965.

Ascending the eastern horizon, the sun's ray pierced through the bedroom window and struck Marg's face. Her eyes squinted at the unwelcomed light as she rolled over to escape the vicious rays. She soon realises that the body which had lay beside her all night was no longer there. She could feel the wet sheets from Lorry's sweat had turned cooler which could only mean that he was long gone.

She had had trouble sleeping until a partial coolness from the night outside eventually crept into their bedroom. Now she felt as though she had only just gotten to sleep before she must rise again. Then she felt the wet, warm sheets underneath her body. It gave her a feeling of being unclean, which she never liked. That was enough for her. No more feeling tired and lethargic. There were things to do. Why? She could not answer.

Quickly taking off her damp nightie and replacing it with a frock which was quite fashionable a few years ago now. Now it was best served as a garment to be used whilst doing domestic chores. It was clean and only ironed the previous day. It still fitted her slim and tall body. Despite her early greying hair, which was a genetic attribute, she had still kept her beauty, which added substantially to her charismatic demeanour.

She stripped the bed and placed the linen and bed clothes in a pile to be washed. Her eyes were now used to the sun's glare and she chanced a peek outside towards the east. Beyond the gum trees she could see the straight lined horizon. The colour of which was obscured by the sun's brilliant white, as though to give a positive illusion upon what she really knew was there. There was nothing, except for a waste land which had been created by this seemingly endless drought.

It was a completely different view to what she knew as a child. That was spent in the Upper Hunter Valley near Gungal. There, there were hills, lots of them, plenty of trees and flowing creeks. There, there was family, sisters, cousins, aunties, grandparents. Her ancestors had come out from Northern Ireland in the 1860's and settled on rural holdings around Denman, NSW. As the family grew the siblings also bought land in the district. Her greatest memories were of Christmas at "Minnie Vale", the original family property, when the entire family would assemble. The youngest child of four sisters, she was lucky, she had attained a substantial high school education. She was the only one of the four sisters who had. She then proceeded to teacher's college in Sydney.

After the war she was teaching in Parramatta where she met Lorry at a dance in the Town Hall. Directly after the war Lorry had stayed in the forces, not being sure what to do next. He was stationed at Richmond on the outskirts of Sydney. Marg was always attracted to a uniform and to her Lorry represented all that she was looking for in a man. He was dark, tall and strong with a magnificent physique. Their respect for each other was however founded more upon the fact that they had come from similar rural upbringings. They shared similar values, similar cultures and held similar ambitions – to bring up a family on a property of their own.

Some soldier settler farms came up for ballot soon after they were married. Available at a place called "Coolagy". Somewhere near a place she had never heard of. Lorry applied and won a property. That was the start of their current life. It was a long way from the Hunter Valley. It was a long way from her sisters whom she missed dearly. It was a long way from their two sons, Ken and Tim, who were now at boarding school. It was far from what she had envisaged all those years ago, but must now make do with what they had.

Sometimes she would ask herself Why? Not often. She never felt as though she was a part of this landscape. She had difficulty in associating with the harshness of this outback existence, the isolation, the loneliness, the hardships. The question was always quickly answered by the call of duty, the stoic resistance, the sense of family, the will to succeed. Marg was a woman who wanted more from life, but had to be content with what she had.

As she looked out the window she hoped that she might see a cloud. A change in the weather had been forecast, perhaps rain. First there needed to be a cloud. She could not see any. Although she could hear the wind as it passed through the gum leaves creating a rustling noise. This was better than the previous day's endless silence. They gave off a different pitch as the wind gusted through at different intensities. This was also a good sign.

# CHAPTER 3.
## THEIR HOUSE. FEBRUARY 1965.

A cup of tea was always the first item on the agenda. There was water left in the jug from last evening. She opened the lid and smelt the water. The drinking water supplied from the rainwater tank outside was running low. They do that in a time of drought. As a result the water was starting to get an unwelcomed odour about it. Perhaps the boiling of it last night displaced the demons. She resolved herself that it was safe and waited for it to boil. As she let go of the jug she noticed grit on her fingers. The feel of grit she knew only too well. It was the red dust.

She glanced outside to see the gums were voicing an increasingly higher, erratic pitch. The gusts were intensifying. It was a good sign of a change on the way, but a warning of the red dust that would find a way into the house. By the feel of the jug it was already happening. Although, during the night, it was preferable to have all the windows open, with the red dust now moving, it was time they were closed.

There were many things that Marg did not like about this fibro house. Yes, it was better than the two rooms at the end of the corrugated iron machinery shed. (These sheds were standard and the only building on all the farms when they were settled). But since it had to be built in haste due to the eminent arrived of Ken, their oldest, it was more practical than fashionable.

First and most importantly, the dining/living room which was really only used when they had guests. This room housed her most treasured possessions, their furniture. It was a belief adopted by her family that good furniture represented class and taste. She could not bear to have the red dust covering her objects of fine cedar. To Marg having dust on the furniture would be betraying her parent's standards. Unfortunately this room had two louver windows, one to the south and one, which pointed west, viewed the landing. With this wind today, guarded by these windows, the furniture was in peril.

The windows in all the rooms were louver windows. Designed to regulate the airflow, but when closed as tightly as possibly the red dust would always find a way through.

She made sure they were closed as tightly as she could make them. This was also the only room that had carpet. A long piece of plastic, just wide enough to walk on, protected the carpet and provided a walkway from the door leading outside to the kitchen.

All the other rooms had lino floors. The kitchen was small. There was just enough room for a fuel stove, a sink, the refrigerator and a small table where the four of them would eat. The fuel stove, although handy in winter, was a curse in summer. The fuel stove also supplied the hot water, thus it needed to be going regularly. A new electric stove had been on the wish list for quite some time. However Santa kept forgetting to bring one. Perhaps when the drought was over and the good seasons return he will have enough room in his sleigh. A radio sat on top of the refrigerator. This was their only form of external entertainment. Lunch was always ready by one o'clock each day and silence would have to be kept whilst the day's episode of Blue Hills was heard. The bedrooms, two of them, were to the east of the kitchen. The boy's room was off Marg and Lorry's. The bathroom, toilet and laundry were outside through a door off the landing.

Meticulously she proceeded through the whole house closing each window. This time she was going to keep the red dust out. By the time she had closed the windows in the boys room, which was adjacent to their bedroom, the kettle had boiled. She stared sadly at the two vacant beds and wished that she would have had to make them. The insistent whistling of the jug broke her trance of melancholy. She hoped the house was now safe. Except for the heat which, with all the windows closed tightly, would only increase. She felt like a roast waiting for the oven to be switched on.

# CHAPTER 4
## TODAY'S TASK. FEBRUARY 1965.

Having had her cup of tea and some toast Marg was in the bathroom when she heard the tingle of the front gate into the house yard. It is a slight noise, which could only have been made by the dogs jumping over the fence and having their tails bump the top rail as they passed.

Their arrival pre-empted Lorry. The different tingle from the gate was the proof. Anxious to know the situation she entered the landing to be greeted by two very excited dogs, happy to see her. She rewarded their joy with a pat each. She could tell by the concerned demur on Lorry's face that all was not well.

"What's wrong?" she asked, as Lorry walked down the path.

"The windmill's really had it this time, I can't get it to work without that part. I've had to put them into the next paddock. There is nothing in that paddock at all and there are five hundred ewes without water."

This was the last paddock where there was any water. This was the only paddock where there was a bore. The dams in the other paddocks were filled from run off when there was rain. There had been no rain for quite some time so they were now empty.

"I'm going to ring Mr Kelly up and see if that part's arrived yet."

Marg could see he was heading for the door into the dining room where the phone was. She could also see a lot of red mud caked onto his boots.

"If you're going to ring him, take your boots off first, please."

It was obvious that in his rush he had forgotten, but he gave a glance to suggest that he really was about to take them off. He sat on the chair in the landing and soon his hands were covered in the soil that would've finished up on the carpet.

"Marg," he said in a tone that could only mean that he had something in store for her to do. "Fancy a drive into Wallabra?"

"Now?"

"If that part's there we need it right away. It just won't be fixed with wire anymore. I'll have to try and get water to them from the bore here."

With this his boots were off, his direction was towards the door. The bathroom was in a different direction.

"Wash your hands before you go in, please," she said, confident of an affirmative response.

This time he could not rely upon the thought that he was going to.

# CHAPTER 5
# JANET ARRIVES IN WALLABRA.
# FEBRUARY 1965.

The heat from the sun's morning acceleration had already made the tar soft on Main Street, Wallabra. In this tiny village, this was the only road that was sealed. It was the only road in Wallabra. The only other roads were tracks that led to houses and there weren't many of those. There was only a mile of it, just enough for the buildings and a few hundred yards towards Worthton. The closest other bitumen road was three and a half hours drive away towards Worthton in the east.

During the night the road had remained silent and unused as the inhabitants hid in their houses. Now, as it approached eight o'clock, an earlier model Holden approached from the Worthton end which signalled the day's beginning. Gleaming white when it was new, it had lost its lustre through years in an unforgiving environment and several previous owners. It was now freckled with the red soil that invaded everything. It was driven by Janet Baker who was making her way towards Kelly's Agricultural Supplies and Real Estate building where she worked.

The first building, coming from Worthton, was the service station, situated on the left. It also doubled as the local mechanic. Jack Clements and his wife June ran this business and the locals had learnt to always count their change. He was a tall and thin man with shifty eyes. At first he gave the impression of one that could not be trusted, but after listening to him that opinion usually changed. His uniform for his vocation were overalls, a clean pair every Monday. He had a few cars for sale with no guarantee that they would go. The two petrol pumps stood like mechanical warriors under a flimsy shelter near the one roomed shop. The diesel pump was further along, open to the elements. The shop was always full of stuff not much of which was usable. Pieces of junk and parts that Jack always maintained someone might need one day, cluttered up the shop. They lived in a couple of rooms off the shop which had a kitchen and a bedroom, similarly cluttered. The shower and toilet were out the back. To the left of the shop and pumps was an old, put up in sections, shed which served as the mechanical shop. It was also cluttered up with stuff. Except that the stuff in this room, Jack wanted for himself. Jack and June pretty well kept to themselves. It was not as though they were anti-social. On the contrary Jack was always most welcoming and liked to talk. Mainly about old wrecks that he had come across, the parts he could get from them and how he could adapt them to other models. June however was rather shy and felt uncomfortable in the company of too many people. Unlike Jack she was not thin. They both had a fascination for mechanics.

Jack had heard the approaching car and emerged from the shop in hope of an early customer. Disappointed to see Janet's car passing he gave a friendly wave, in recognition to which, Janet responded out of habit.

On the left past Jack's place was a small paddock with a tumbledown wooden shed in it. This paddock used to be where the horses would rest and be stabled whilst their owners did their business in the town before heading back out to their farms. The beginning of cars had changed the role of this paddock to nothing.

Spear's general store bordered the paddock. It was a long building constructed out of fibro and timber. It was supposed to sell everything for the home, including groceries, clothes, library books and furniture, however the locals knew that it was best to always shop on Tuesdays after the supplies had arrived on the Monday otherwise they would just have to wait for more supplies to come in from Worthton, the next Monday. Mavis and Harry Anderson ran the business. Being the main shop in town, it had become the town crier as it were. If there was anything going on, the general store became the herald. There was no need for a local newspaper, Mavis, in particular, could deliver any happenings live and with expression. Besides running the store Mavis and Harry saw their "community noticeboard" role as their primary task.

They were ably supported by Helen and John Davidson who ran the Post Office. Given the fact that the general store and the post office were next door to each other, information flowed readily between the two buildings.

John had been a PMG technician, installing phone lines to all the soldier settler farms and when the position at the post office came up, he jumped at it. They have been a part of the town's fabric ever since.

There was a small gap between the Post Office and Mr Kelly's building, filled up with stuff, to be sold from Kelly's. Opposite this was the Royal Hotel, the only business on the other side of the street. It was not a big building as hotels go. There was a bit of a veranda in front with a few steel tables and chairs where patrons preferred to drink in the hotter months. Inside there was a small bar and a large room with steel tables and chairs. It was cooled in summer by a small fan in the ceiling and open doors. It was very basic, without much need for an elaborate decor. Out the back there were a few rooms where in the old days workers could stay during the harvest or shearing. Now they serve as living quarters for Peter and Betty Dunn who owned the Hotel.

About three hundred yards behind the Hotel was the railway station with the silos and the sheep yards. Since there were no more passenger trains coming to Wallabra the station itself had been left to neglect. The only things to visit the station, which consisted of a small waiting room with wooden benches, now broken, were mice, birds and plenty of red dust. The silos, which stood as beckons to a successful season, saw plenty of use in early summer then lay dormant for the rest of the year, like a church which is only opened for blessings after a good year. Similarly the sheep yards were only used when Mr Kelly organised a stock sale. Wallabra was the last stop on this railway line from Worthton. The authorities must have deemed that there was nothing much after Wallabra. They were right. Heading west the soil and the climate were not conducive to much agriculture.

The bitumen continued past the hotel for a few more hundred yards. Along this stretch was an entrance on the right and on the left. On the right it led to a shed made of corrugated iron, standing out like the last symbol of civilisation before the flat expanse of an endless plain heading west. It appeared stark, bare and out of place, certainly not welcoming. This was the community hall. To the locals, however, it was the most welcoming of all the buildings, since their best memories were formed in this anomaly of a structure. Next to the shed was the most important of all the focal points in this little town. A small tower made of bricks which reached twelve feet high with a cross at the top. This was the war memorial and was held in great reverence. Directly to the west of these constructions were a line of gum trees. In a good season they would actually grow, but in the dry times the new growth would wither and die, leaving dead branches, which in time would eventually fall down.

There was no church. God through his representatives, namely a priest of any denomination that was available to come out on that date, only made his presence felt for weddings and funerals. If no one from Worthton could attend Mr Kelly, who had a copy of all the right things to say, would officiate. The community hall would be used for these occasions, as well.

To the west of the hall, at least two hundred yards, was the cemetery. Where the white people were rested was closest to the hall. Then further along was where the Aborigines were buried. There were no stones to mark each grave as the flat plains didn't quarry any rocks, usually small wooden crosses. In the Aboriginal section, there was only a mound to mark each place.

The stretch of land between the War memorial and the railway was used as a sporting oval. It had no boundaries. The lines were made up as needed for each occasion. A lawn mower was all that was needed to make the cricket pitch.

On the right of where the bitumen ended was the

entrance to the school. It currently had sixty five students, ranging from kindergarten to the higher school certificate. Of course this number would fluctuate depending upon the number of Aboriginal children who bothered to attend. It stood as a symbol of hope for another, better life for the next generation. The children could learn that there was a world outside the district of Wallabra. It comprised of four classrooms occupied in age groups. One teacher was in charge of each classroom, thus the teachers were multi skilled in different subjects and ages. At least that was the plan. It may not have been ideal, but it was a school and the locals were very proud to have it.

From here the road became a track. Potholes ensued that the path was not straight. To the left, about a mile out of town, there were some scrubby gum trees. They lay in a depression in the land and therefore, when it did rain, water would lay in this place for longer. Thus these trees could survive the dry times, just. Because of this occasional water, this area was where the local Aborigines lived. There was no structure or planning to the buildings that were constructed in the settlement. They were pieces of corrugated iron held together with wood, wire and a few nails, all of which had been sourced from whatever was available. The mob were left alone, ignored, by the white people. The cultures did not mix. They were worlds apart. Where the bitumen ended acted as a sort of boundary for the whites. To go to their camp was to go beyond into another existence. During the day, however, many of the mob would cover the gap. They would spend most of their time sitting around the town studying the white people going about their activities. The Europeans didn't take to this very well and it caused a lot of dissent.

The Aboriginals were happy just doing nothing. They wanted for very little and for the most part were content. The Europeans were the ones that wanted and spent their lives in need.

Unbeknown to the white people at Wallabra, the mob at the settlement had been in disarray for a number of days. Charlie, the main elder of the group had gone missing. It was not uncommon for him to go off on walkabout, but in this heat and this drought, they were a little concerned. Charlie, being the elder, had tried to assimilate the mob with the white man's ways. He could see no future in trying to continue the way his people had lived for thousands of years. Without country anymore their culture had become severely restricted. He wished that they would continue their beliefs and saw it as his role to pass down the knowledge, but also he wanted to encourage the younger ones to go to school. His bet each way had not been paying off. Rather apathy dominated. This would make him depressed and he would have to go back to country for a stint, seeking guidance. His presence was missed however, as without him, purpose was lost.

The track that headed west past the settlement was only used by people who lived on the stations out that way. There weren't many of them so the road was never attended to. It was not a through road. It only led to properties. No one went out that way without coming back to Wallabra.

The truck that usually came on Mondays was the true lifeline of the town. It brought supplies to all of the shops and businesses. It served as the umbilical cord to this small community on the edge of the great expanse.

The town would not survive without the supplies coming in on the Monday.

It came from Worthton which was the main regional town. It serviced the smaller towns within about five hundred miles, more especially to the northwest. In distance it was about two hundred miles away, but to drive it, depending on the weather and conditions of the road, could take five hours. In the wet it was near on impossible. In the dry you could get stuck about half way along at the sand hills. The closer you got to Worthton the better the roads became. The only bitumen was fifty miles short of Worthton. One time they didn't see the truck for three weeks because it had broken down near the sand hills and the driver, due to the phones being down at the time, had a hard time getting back to Worthton.

# CHAPTER 6
## KELLY'S STORE. FEBRUARY 1965.

The sun's reflection off the freshly corrugated iron roof of Kelly's store served as a lighted guiding path to Janet as she approached. There was never any need to look for a park there were plenty to choose from. She could hear the stones crackle on the tyres, loosened by the melted tar, as she stopped.

As she alighted from the car she could feel the wind through her hair which instantly destroyed her neat appearance. She was certainly a country lass well inducted into the culture of the squatters. She was young, bright, attractive and well thought of. Janet was always the first to arrive at Kelly's store thus it was her job to open the place up. She knew the routine she had been working here since she left school two years earlier. Her father, who owned a property twelve miles out along the Worthton road and Mr Kelly had always been the best of mates. Hence the job at Kelly's was virtually waiting for her when she left school. She was lucky to get this job, the best job in town and possibly the only one for a bright young woman.

Jill Armstrong, who had the job before her, married Brian Morris who was the eldest son of one of the biggest landowners around here. It was what most of the girls who worked at Kelly's did. They could check out all the cockie's sons as they came into the shop and have their choice, there wasn't much competition. Since Janet had no brothers or sisters she sometimes wondered if her father had this thought in mind. After all he needed a man for her to marry to keep the farm in the family. Janet, however, yearned for a life outside this rural enclave.

Upon opening the door the wind followed her in and brought life into the space where the air had been still over the weekend. Mr Kelly's business was the biggest in Wallabra. The town was too small for two similar such stores so Mr Kelly was the sole supplier to all the farmers in the district. Not only did he sell produce, hardware, fertiliser, shearing gear, etc., he also sold larger machinery like tractors, ploughs, etc. As if that wasn't enough he was also the stock and station agent and the wool broker. Some say the town was run by Mr Kelly. He was certainly very popular.

He was the type of man where even if you didn't see his arrival, you knew he had arrived. When you did see him you would tend to not take your eyes off him. He was on a good thing with his business and he wanted it to keep going that way. His father had owned a similar such business in a bigger town east of here. Mr Kelly was the younger of the two brothers and thus the original business would go to the older brother. He set up this one and had probably done better.

He knew very well how to relate to farmers. Although to look at him for the first time you might think him pompous and arrogant. He did carry that air about him, but in reality he wasn't. That sort of attitude wouldn't go down well with rural people and once you got to know him you discovered he had a real empathy for the rural community. He genuinely wanted to help people and his advice was well sought after. You didn't have to count your change when you'd done business with him, but you could be assured that he's made his cut out of it. He knew that to be a successful businessman in a rural community you had to treat people with a lot of respect. That way the clients respect you and your business thrives.

One of the drawbacks to his life was that he was always, always very busy. It showed on his face, he always seemed to have something else on his mind. Sometimes Janet would wonder if what she was saying to him was getting through, but he would always come back with the right reply. She would also sometimes wonder how much he really did see of Mrs Kelly, he always seemed to be off seeing this person or trying to fix up some machine that had broken down or off to some sale somewhere buying or selling sheep. They lived in a nice house three miles out of town to the east, on about three hundred acres, only a small place, but enough to put stuff and to have a few sheep.

The small door entrance was beside a much bigger door which was opened and closed by chains. Mr Kelly always liked to have this door opened as soon as possible in the mornings to let people know they were open for business. Janet also knew that as soon as that door was opened the heat and wind would come flowing in like unwelcomed strangers. She decided to leave it for a bit. It was a Monday morning and a hot one. She wasn't expecting a busy day. The space inside was large as it had to contain as many products as possible. There was no ceiling the corrugated iron roof was plain to see. There were a lot of windows along the walls and this let in plenty of light and air. To the left of the entrance was the counter and behind it, the office. The office was a closed room, locked at night. When Janet opened this door she could feel the residue heat left over from the weekend strike her like an unpleasant memory. Best to leave this door open for a while she decided.

She sat at her desk, waiting for the motivation to start. She could feel the heat being generated by the outside and given that this was still rather early in the day, contemplated just how hot this day would become. The moment's silence was welcomed until it was disturbed by the appearance of Kevin. Kevin also worked for Mr Kelly. He saw to the customers and made sure all the products were in the right place. School did not agree with Kevin. His father, who didn't go to school, had been a shearer and general handyman all his life and had done all right out of it. Although Kevin didn't want to be a shearer, he did have a fascination for parts and how they worked. At the age of fifteen, Mr Kelly took him on as he could see the boy was self-motivated and wanted to get ahead in his place. He figured that the boy would probably learn more at his place than at the school.

They looked at each other in recognition and the common thought of, this is going to be a very hot day and it is Monday with nine hours to go before knock off time. It was not a pleasant thought.

"Would you mind opening up the big door please," asked Janet resigned that this day must begin.

"It's going to make it even hotter," Kevin protested.

"I know, but you know what Mr Kelly is like about that door."

Kevin proceeded to pull on the chains and the light, wind and heat entered with abundance. The two looked at each other bracing themselves for the big acceleration in the heat. They waited in silence.

The inertia was broken by the sudden and compelling sound of the phone ringing. Automatically Janet answered it.

"Good morning, Kelly's Ag Supplies."

"Is that you, Janet?" replied a voice.

"Yes," she replied not sure who it was she was talking to.

"Lorry Stirling here......"

She now recognised the voice. She had met Lorry and Marg Stirling on numerous occasions. He had been a client of Mr Kelly's for a long time and she knew that he was well respected in the community.

"...I'm wondering if you can tell me if that part for this bore has arrived yet, please."

She was stumped. What part was he talking about? They received so many orders for different things it was sometimes hard to remember them all. Trying to remember she stalled for time.

"Which part was that Mr Stirling?"

Occasionally her job came down to guess work. Although Mr Kelly usually made it a point to keep Janet informed he sometimes forgot to tell her everything. She often found herself in this position of having to guess what prior arrangements Mr Kelly had made with the client. These usually happened when he was with the client in a pub or in a paddock somewhere. The decisions made in the office she would know about either by him telling her or figuring it out from the one sided conversations over the phone. In the past two years she had been working here she had learnt how Mr Kelly thought and that did help with the transfer of information. Her usual response was to say that she would go and have a look. She did recall a part being ordered for Mr Stirling some time ago and naturally assumed it had been already sorted. Fortunately this time Mr Kelly made his appearance right on cue. She now had a ready response for Mr Stirling.

"I'm not sure Mr Stirling, but Mr Kelly's here just hold on and I'll ask him."

Mr Kelly entered as though the worries of the world were upon him. Certainly he had things on his mine that did not involve a part for Mr Stirling. Janet could sense this and wondered how she would present this enquiry to Mr Kelly. He surveyed the shop and moved towards the office.

"Good morning Janet. Have we had a phone call from a bloke called Des Wykes yet?"

"Good morning Mr Kelly" she replied, "No..."

"Funny. He said he'd ring early, I..."

Even though Mr Kelly didn't like it Janet felt compelled to interrupt him, as she knew Mr Stirling was waiting.

"But I do have Mr Stirling on the line waiting to speak to you."

"Oh," he said.

He glanced at the phone to see if Janet had her hand over the mouth piece. On her first day here he told her to always do this when there was someone on the phone, especially when he was either talking to her or had someone else in the room. She never forgot it.

Satisfied that her hand was in the right position he asked, "What does he want?"

"Something about a part for the bore, I thought he already had that?" she said.

Mr Kelly stood silent for a moment.

"Is this the same part that he ordered about a month or more ago?"

"I think so. I haven't ordered any other parts." Janet wondered if this was developing into another one of those incidents where she had not been properly informed.

"Well it should be here by this. Did the truck from Worthton come last week?" he asked.

"No, it didn't."

"Why?"

"Apparently it broke down."

"Again. It's always off the road. Has he got enough money to get it fixed? Get in touch with him will ya? If he hasn't got enough money tell him I'll help him out, again. No don't say again, but we must have that truck coming to Wallabra regularly."

He hesitated for a moment as though he had something else to say, but had to think it through first.

"Did it come the week before?"

"Yes."

"Much stuff amongst it for us?"

"Yes,"

"Then Lorry's part must be with that lot, get Kevin to look for it. It must be here by now. Here, I'll talk to him."

Janet took her hand away from the mouth piece.

"Sorry to have kept you Mr Stirling. Mr Kelly will talk to you now." She passed the phone to Mr Kelly.

"G'day Lorry, having a bit of trouble out there, are you?"

"Little bit," Lorry began. "I can't do anymore to get this

bore going without that part."

"Have you done what I recommended?"

"Yeah, but the wire has worn through the holes. I can't attach it to anything now."

"Got any water left?" Mr Kelly asked.

"None at all, all the other dams are dry. This is the only one that has a bore and I've got five hundred ewes without water, in this heat. Has that part arrived?"

"You ordered it some time ago didn't you?

"A month or more ago."

"Then it should be here." Mr Kelly replied.

Janet, who had been listening without trying to make it obvious that she was, became instantly concerned. She had not seen any such part with Mr Stirling's name on it. She was always very diligent when stuff arrived as she knew clients would be waiting and took it upon herself to inform them of any arrivals. Had she not done this with this part? Had the part not arrived at all or had Mr Kelly some prior knowledge to which she was not privy?

"Good. I'll get Marg to come into town and pick it up right away," said Lorry.

"Right oh. What time do you reckon she'll get here?"

This reply from Mr Kelly made Janet even more concerned. Obviously someone was going to come into town to pick up this part that she wasn't even sure was here. She also knew that it was probably a two hour drive into Wallabra from where they lived along a pretty rough road and in this heat. What would they say if they arrived and the part was not here?

The conversation concluded, Mr Kelly turned to Janet and asked, "Janet will you give them a ring in Worthton and see if that truck's coming out today."

This request did nothing to allay Janet's fears. She lifted the receiver and waited for a dial tone. Sometimes it took a while to get a dial tone, but this time it seemed to take longer. Mr Kelly sensed the delay.

"What's wrong?" he asked.

"The phone's dead Mr Kelly," she replied trying it again.

"It can't be I was just using it."

They both waited impatiently for a response on the phone line.

"There's nothing, Mr Kelly."

"Bloody lines down again, must be this wind," Mr Kelly said.

"What about this part for Mr Stirling?" Janet asked.

"Yeah, Marg Stirling is coming in to pick it up, probably be in after lunch,"

"But is it here Mr Kelly?" Janet asked with some urgency.

"Should be, get Kevin to look for it, probably came with all that stuff the other week, it will be here somewhere."

Janet was not convinced. If it did turn out to be a wasted trip for Mrs Stirling hopefully Mr Kelly would be here to do the explaining, she consoled herself.

Their attention was suddenly drawn to a well-dressed man in his fifties who looked like he had driven some miles. Although he was a stranger to Janet, Mr Kelly had obviously made his acquaintance.

"Ah, there you are Des," greeted Mr Kelly.

"Sorry I couldn't ring, the phones are down out our way apparently," replied Des Wykes.

"Yeah, we've just found that they're out here too now."

"Must be the wind, it's getting up a bit out there now," Des said.

"Yeah, that's what I reckon too. So are we right to go?"

"Whenever you're ready."

"Janet, this is Mr Wykes. We're going out to Kandar to look at a mob of sheep."

"When will you be back?" asked Janet knowing that the Kandar station was about three hours west of Wallabra depending on the weather and the state of the track.

"Later in the afternoon, I suppose." Turning to Des he said, "We'll go in my car if you like."

With that they were gone. Janet soon realised that they wouldn't be back before Mrs Stirling was due to arrive. In the meantime she hoped that they could find this part.

# CHAPTER 7
# PREPARING FOR THE DRIVE.
# FEBRUARY 1965.

With Lorry now waiting on the phone, Marg had a lot to consider with regards to this trip to Wallabra. She looked out upon the deadened horizon and dreaded the fact that she must become a part of this great and threatening expanse of nothingness. It was a task that she was not looking forward to on this very hot day. She never liked driving alone on these roads. She was always worried that something might happen. That was why Lorry did all the driving. But the thought of all those thirsty sheep instilled in her some courage driven by the necessity of the situation.

For Marg it was simply not a case of hoping in the car and going. Such a trip had to be planned and more importantly, considerable thought had to be given upon what to wear, since she was going to be in public. It was most important to always look respectable when going into town. First consideration, though, was a cup of tea.

With the kettle boiled she handed Lorry, still waiting on the phone, a cup of tea and proceeded into the bedroom to sort out her attire. Something light and airy so she wouldn't become too hot. She came across the slight yellow dress Lorry had bought for her in Worthton when they went to pick up the boys from school in December. It was different to what was available in Wallabra and she deemed it to be fashionable. The brown stockings and the dark brown shoes always went well with this dress.

This done she could hear Lorry's voice on the phone and was anxious to discover the details of this day's journey. The conversation had passed by the time she entered the kitchen, Lorry was enjoying his cup of tea sitting at the table.

"Thanks for the tea," he said.

"That's all right."

"That parts there waiting for you, when you get there," he said.

"Is it?" she asked, not wanting to go all that way in this heat and it not being there.

"Apparently."

"I'm going to have a shower now and I'll be on my way. Could you check the car please?"

"Yes, I'll leave it outside the gate for you."

"Thank you."

He finished his tea and they walked out through the dining room door to the outside. Marg, to the bathroom and Lorry to the heat, the flies, the wind, stranded sheep, a thirsty paddock and a worried disposition.

"It wouldn't be nine yet. Better get anything if we need it, you should be home about three, do you reckon?"

"I suppose," she replied not terribly sure, as anything can happen on these roads and when you are in a hurry they usually do.

"Come and find me, I'll be down there somewhere." With that he gave her a peck on the cheek, as he usually did, turned and faced the elements.

The dogs were happy though. Replenished with their long drink and quick rest, the thought of some work and excitement by following Lorry quickly erased Marg from their memory for the time being.

# CHAPTER 8
# THE ROAD. FEBRUARY 1965.

Although a little smelly the coolness of the water from the shower gave some relief to Marg as she contemplated the fact that this was the coolest she was going to feel all day. As she was putting on her dress she could feel her body heat increasing. The joy of having a cool body under the shower had passed. As she pulled on her stockings she noted how dry they were and wondered for how long they would stay that way. Last of all was her makeup which was always a necessity when going out, even though it was so hot and she might not see many people at all, it was still an essential. Nothing too elaborate, a bit of lipstick, some powder around the face, but enough to show a determination to still look beautiful even in the extremes that nature had presented.

All done, time to go. Not before checking all the windows again and collecting the library books. Hopefully there might be some new books in, perchance an interesting book to show her of another world outside Coolagy. Out of habit she would normally have found her watch so she would know what the time was. However her watch had been at the jewellers in Worthton for months being repaired. When it was finished it was supposed to have been sent out to Wallabra. Hopefully it might now be in Wallabra and she could pick it up too.

Then she would know what the time was on the way home, but the trip in was going to be timeless. Handbag in hand she ventured out the dining room door to be hit by the wind which seemed to act as a warning of the day's extreme. Grit and bear it and never complain. That is the way it was out here.

The car was at the gate beckoning to her. She looked at it as though she was putting all of her trust into something she didn't properly understand. Like riding a newly broken horse, the trust would have to be confirmed if they were to return safely.

It was a green FJ Holden. Its green was a little ironic since the landscape it was traversing was anything, but green. She noted that it hadn't been washed for a while because of the lack of water and felt a little embarrassed to be taking it to town. The red stains of dirt speckled across the metal work gave an indication of the environment it shared. The only consolation was that all the farmer's cars would be just as dirty. Marg was now well conversant with the column shift, the poor suspension, the spongy brake pedal and the lack of any heating or cooling. Windows up or windows down were the only tools to regulate the air inside the car.

The wind that she felt as she stepped outside was only a pre-curser to what she was expecting once she got past the shelter of the gum trees that lined the house yard. She braced herself as she neared the gate with good reason. The searing heat hit her face like tiny needles and hastened her to get through the gate and into the car. She could now feel grains of the red dust, which was being picked up by the wind, striking her legs through her stockings and sticking to her makeup. The clip on the gate became abstinent in its mechanism. This only happened when she was in a hurry.

Fortunately there wasn't far between the gate and the car door, but far enough to ensure that her hair had lost its shape. It had been so delicately designed at the dressing table only minutes previous, now a victim to the merciless wind.

The car door now in sight she hurried inside, out of the blasting heat and into the oven. The interior of the car had not wasted time in accumulating a heat greater than outside. She closed the door behind her quickly so as not to let in the red dust, but to no avail as there was plenty inside which had been stirred up by the door opening. She could smell it and feel it as it began to settle on her clean attire. This was not on, best to open the window a little in the hope that the red dust might venture outside.

It was always Lorry's job to check the car before a drive, such things as water, oil, tools a spare tyre and jacks etc. to change a tyre. In the wet a shovel was always included in case they had to dig their way home. There was no need for that shovel today. Marg had no need to doubt that Lorry would have done all these things. A glance at the back seat revealed the esky. This would be handy to bring any groceries home. He had even thought of that.

"But he might've cleaned the inside of the car," she thought.

Handbag placed beside her, fingers on the ignition key, let's get going was the prevailing thought. Ahead of her lay ninety miles of a basic dirt road. Due to the layout of the original stations a straight line to Wallabra was out of the question. Wallabra was south of their property, however firstly she must travel east for fifteen miles till the boundaries of the old Coolagy and Wymere station, (to the north of Coolagy), finished at a main intersection. Here she would turn right and head south for sixty miles. This stretch done she would meet the railway lines from Worthton and the main road to Wallabra, another fifteen miles to the west.

Their driveway was a little over a mile long to the main road. As she drove off she could already see gusts of red dust passing in front of her where the wind was moving the plains, like ocean waves of dust with no shore to stop them. Even the crows were having trouble in this wind. There seemed to be a lot more of them around lately. It may have been lean times for the farmers, but boom times for the crows with the number of dead sheep.

The road was rather basic, a track wondering through a paddock. She was grateful that, since there were no sheep in this paddock, the front gate could be left open. This meant that she didn't have to get out of the car and risk getting the red dust on her. The main road displayed evident scars of greater use. The track that everyone uses, because there is only one lane, had lost so much dust over the years there was always that risk of bottoming out. That is hitting the underneath of the car on the gap between the two tyre tracks which was not so eroded.

If enough of them complained the council would sometimes send out a grader and they would all rejoice. The graders appearance was as spasmodic as the rainfall. Not only did it even it out so they didn't hit the bottom of the car, for a while, it would also get rid of the wretched corrugations which felt like they would shake the fillings out of teeth.

On this day it had to be noted that the grader, like the

rain, hadn't made an appearance for quite some time. No sooner had she turned onto the main road, Coolagy road, but she could feel the corrugations jarring the car and her body. She clenched her teeth and resolved to try and travel a bit faster and hopefully just skim over the top of them. It always works for Lorry.

She was now travelling east and time for some readjustment of the car's interior cooling system. Since the wind was now coming sort of behind her on the passenger's side, it would be best to open the passenger side window, just a little, and the window behind her, just a little. She hoped that this would create a current of air passing through the car and more specifically past here back. She noticed as she leant over to open the window to her left that sweat had already started to collect on her clean, relatively new dress. The coolness on her back as the dress separated itself from the vinyl seat covering was the tell-tale sign. She definitely didn't want to arrive in Wallabra with sweat marks.

She had learnt that it always paid to be vigilant on these roads. They appeared to be long, straight, flat, and repetitious, but one never knew what might suddenly appear. Emus, kangaroos, birds, stray sheep all could appear at any moment. The other lives to look out for were Aboriginals on walkabout. They would appear in the most unusual places. Most of the farmers would frown upon them. They were worried that they would be up to no good. Marg didn't see it that way, sure they might steal the odd sheep, but after all this was their land, they were used to wandering around. Some of the ladies felt threatened by them and would warn about some bad encounters with them. Whether they were true or not,

Marg was never sure. As Marg saw it they were a passive race of socialists who had been taken over by a tribe that had made an art form out of capitalism. She often felt inclined, when she saw them on the edge of the road, to stop and see if they needed help. She never did though. She figured they were doing what they have always been doing very successfully, they didn't need her help.

Now on the straight stretches she peered well ahead. Straining to see the cloud of dust an oncoming vehicle would make. At this point it was understood that, since it was only one lane, a detour into the scrub was imminent. There was, however, an unwritten law that courtesy was the best defence. When the actual passing occurred both parties would find a mutually considered line to avoid each other, wave, and the journey would continue. Fortunately, out here, there weren't that many vehicles.

# CHAPTER 9
# SWAMPY. 1964.

The trees around their house yard had now descending beyond the horizon. Mirages impeded the view and they were gone. To the left was the great expanse of Wymere station. Five hundred square miles of next to no trees, barren land, perchance the odd windmill to bring water to the sheep. Besides the fence lining the boundary, the windmills were the only human structure. They stood out like a claim to the land. There were a few out houses where the stockmen would live a very basic, isolated existence. The main homestead was further north on a river where there were plenty of trees.

The sight of this great empty space would often frighten Marg. The idea of isolation, stuck alone amongst this endless nothingness, drove her to constantly hope that the car would not fail.

To the right was the consolation of a greater human influence. Coolagy station was originally about the same size as Wymere. It was owned by a Mr Draper who had two sons who both went to the war. Neither of them returned. Faced with no heirs to take over the property and out of respect for the soldiers who did return, he donated some of his property to soldier settler farms. Fifty one farms all of approximately 2000 acres. A community had been established from a common cause.

As she looked to the right she could see more fences, the evidence of crops, buildings and homes, all of which she felt easier with, the view gave the element of hope.

The road stretched before her in a combination of parallels. The road, with its edges outlying a pair of straight lines, the tyre tracks, vaguely running equidistant from each other. The boundary fences, identically apart and the telegraph poles, even with the loop between the poles, all the same. As if the humans, in their effort to bring civility to an untameable landscape, had created structures that by their sheer repetitiveness copied the savannah they occupied.

She had settled herself into the pattern of toiling with the path and all its minor adjustments to ensure one didn't just stay still. There was always a hole, a rut, shifting dirt and on this day the fierceness of the wind to keep her focused on the job at hand. Soon the first milestone was traversed. The boundary fence on the right was broken by the driveway into the neighbouring property, a track that, on this day, only led to a mirage hiding everything, but leaving the possibility of company.

This property used to be owned by Thelma and Bob "Swampy" Pond. He got his nickname in the army apparently. He was in the division that the English surrendered into the hands of the Japanese at Singapore. A lot of them never even got a chance to fight. If they knew what they were going to be in for they would've preferred to fight rather than be betrayed by the English. He was sent to the Burma Railway. At the end of the war he was lucky to be still alive.

Marg often wondered if, in fact, a part of him had already died. There was a vacancy in his eyes as though there was something there that wanted to come out, but couldn't because it was not the done thing to do. On the surface he seemed just like all the other diggers in the community. They all got on very well. They were obvious comrades who had seen the worst of this life, but still displayed a facade of victory and a joy to be alive. They would only talk about the funny things that happened during their service. Marg would often think that they liked to glorify their experience in an attempt to hide the obvious, to her, painful realities. They would never talk about the horrors that they saw. One learnt very early never to ask. It was as if they didn't want to remember the tragedies that occurred every day during that time. Now they had a block of land and this was, apparently, compensation for their nightmares. A land fit for heroes. Heroes who had lost their youth and now had been commanded to make some form of peace with the lost years. Only to now have to battle with a different type of enemy which was called the weather. Anzac day was the only time Marg and the others who didn't experience their horrors, could see the pain on their faces. As soon as the ceremonies were over they would all adjourn to the hotel in Wallabra and make themselves forget the nightmares in the company of their mates who also had their hidden dreams.

Lorry and Swampy shared a great rapport. Not just because they were neighbours, but by being neighbours they saw much more of each other. Both of the men would drop everything to assist the other when needed. What's more, by the time the job was finished, would've totally enjoyed each other's company. Marg sometimes wondered if they would find an excuse to be with each other. Lorry alluded to this one day when he said that the job only took five minutes and could've been done alone. The talking afterwards went on for a couple of hours.

"I think he just wanted someone to talk to," Lorry would say when questioned by Marg.

At the end of the day they were a great help to each other. Sometimes, when Lorry had been asked to help Swampy, Marg would come along as well to be company for Thelma. They never had any children and Marg was not sure if either of them wanted children. At the social evenings neither took much interest in the children of the other families, Swampy in particular. Therefore their house needed only to suit themselves. They still lived in the side of the shed provided when they took on the place. There seemed no need for anything better. Marg often felt Thelma must have been very lonely and she was always happy to visit her. Thelma too knew that she was always welcome in the Stirling house.

In their tiny living space two photos stood out. Not because they were larger than the other items, on the contrary there were quite small, but it was the gravity of the subject matter that gave them emphasis. One photo was of Swampy going to war. He struck a very proud, physically outstanding, strong willed figure with the ship in the background. The other was of a stretcher bearer being brought down from the ship with the skeletal figure of a man, too weak to raise a smile, desperately clinging to life for reasons he did not know. It was obvious both these men were Swampy. The presence of these photos emanated throughout the room. They imposed a gloomy mood.

Marg was always curious about these photos. It was

obvious what they were, but her curiosity was more aimed at the impact these photos had upon their relationship. She could sense an underlying problem and out of an effort to help, asked Thelma about them one day, very politely of course. There was a silence before replying and Marg was worried she had touched on a subject that should have been left alone. However, after a time, Thelma did answer.

"I want Bob to see them always. It's a bit hard to talk to him about it all. I have tried desperately for him to open up about what had happened. Sometimes he wakes up in the night shouting and crying like a little boy. Often I feel him sweating in bed on a cold night even. I ask him about it, but when I do, up come the walls and I'm left feeling helpless. I keep the photos there, I guess, in a way for him to remember the man I married before the war, the man who came back, and the man he is now – much healthier – and hope he can see that things have moved on. We have a nice property, a sturdy living, we have each other and we are both on the land as we always wanted to be. I hope one day that it will work."

She then looked at Marg with a surprised expression which turned to worry as though she had said something that she should not have and was worried upon Marg's reaction and confidentiality. Marg had broken a wall that was never meant to be broken. The horror tales of the war and its aftermath were never to be discussed, but locked away to fester. Marg took her hand softly, looked deeply into her eyes without saying a word and she knew this conversation would go no further. Marg could see that she looked resolved and at the same time, grateful for the chance to talk about it.

"When do you think we will get another visit from the grader? Aren't the roads getting bad again?" It was the usual response when wanting to change the topic. The roads were a constant topic of conversation. Marg respected her wishes and felt grateful that her presence had helped even if it was just a start.

They found Swampy Pond dead on a dam bank at the far end of the property. Thelma rang the Stirlings up one evening and said that he hadn't come home. Lorry and Marg organised all the neighbours nearby and off they all set out with their car headlights for vision not knowing what they would find. He lay with his back against an old drum, his head bowed and his legs apart. His arms lay at his side with a flagon of cherry wine in his left hand. Remnants of the wine still soaked his shirt. Scattered around the bank were dozens of empty wine flagons. This was obviously the only place he could find some solace, a place to reflect on his unpleasant memories. He did, however, look the most peaceful Marg had ever seen him. She hoped that he had found his peace and would dream no more.

Poor Thelma was distraught. Perhaps she somehow felt a little guilt in that she couldn't help him. The community all gathered around, worked the farm, organised the funeral and the wake. The funeral, which was held in Wallabra, was one of the most moving moments the community had ever witnessed. All the returned servicemen and women, and there were many of them, lined the pathway to the grave in true RSL tradition.

Thelma finished up selling the place and went to live with her sister in the city.

She kept in touch with Marg and seemed much happier.

# CHAPTER 10
# BOGGED. WINTER 1962.

The road continued in its never ending sameness on a path to nothing very much at all. The sturdy car kept going and that was of never ending relief to Marg. The horizon now had become a shimmering blue on all sides with the mirage now filling the entire scene. There was no line to distinguish the horizon since it was now all blue like the sky. It was as though the mirage was disguising any destination into an illusion. She was stuck in an all encumbering, never ending cauldron of heat.

She could feel the sweat on her back soaking into her dress. It was a feeling she did not like. Leaning forward gave her a sudden sense of cooling relief down her back and that proved quite consoling, until it became too uncomfortable to be leaning forward. At some stage a resignation of surrender would be reached and the dress would become wetter again. The air conditioning, provided by the windows, was not keeping up with the increase in the temperature. She could have leant over and let more air in, but then that would increase the risk of the red dust pouring in. Better to have just sweat marks and not sweat marks with stains, was her logic in avoiding the move.

Through the mirage she could now distinguish the next milestone. Not necessarily a giant banner with a congratulatory message, but rather a line of trees, just as improbable. They stood resolutely alongside of a gully which crossed the road. A natural depression enhanced during a rain event. It was certainly no major water system. It only held water after a substantial amount of rain. It started, for no particular reason, on the Coolagy side and ended in Wymere where the land rose up a little to impede any flow. As a result of the water laying in this place for longer a series of gum trees staked their claim to existence. To see them approaching gave a sense of distance travelled. They represented a welcomed difference from the normal. Sometimes, however it was not so welcomed.

Due to the erosion the traffic on this road created, where the road passed through the gully, it was much deeper than the rest of the gully, to the extent that during a wet it became impossible to cross. Council had been notified of this to no avail till out of desperation the community combined to collect rocks within the gully on either side and placed them in the depression. This gave a hard base to the section and stopped any further erosion. It was now able to be crossed in all conditions as the rocks gave the tyres traction. It did however mean that the crossing had become very rough and when approaching the gears came into use to slow down.

Perhaps because the gully was something different it had built up a reputation with Marg over the years. It was on a day that was quite the opposite of this day. It was a winter where the rain had forgotten to stop. Ken was already attending boarding school and it was to be hoped that Tim would follow the next year. In order to do so he had to pass a test. The date was set and it had to be done at the school in Wallabra.

The date arrived and fortunately the previous three days had been fine so the roads had had a chance to dry out, a bit. Marg was still hoping though that Lorry would be able to take Tim into Wallabra. She did not fancy trying to get the car through ninety miles, each way, of what would still be mud. Not to be, the three days of dry gave Lorry a chance to do things on the farm that he had not been able to do.

The sun did make an appearance early for a little while. Marg felt a little relieved as she felt it's warmth through the bedroom window. It was not to last. High Cirrus cloud quickly invaded the sky from the west. Sometimes, particularly in a drought, these clouds would appear, with hope, only to wander off again like the flight of the Black Cockatoos, aimlessly wandering. In a wet time, however, they were only a sign of more rain. Like a crow en route to a carcass, the result was inevitable. By the time they were ready to leave, it had already starting to sprinkle.

The car waited for her at the front gate like a key to impending trouble. She was well schooled for driving in the wet, she had watched and participated with Lorry in many such journeys. She knew what to do, but this was no consolation to the way she felt as she watched Lorry approaching down the path.

"You've got a shovel in there I hope," she asked him with a touch of cynical resolution.

Lorry could sense her sceptical mood.

"In the back seat," he replied. "You'll be right."

She had heard this line before and had recognised it as the pep talk.

"Just drive steady, don't stop and don't make the wheels spin in the mud."

Not to get bogged in other words, especially when he was not in the car. If he was in the car and they became bogged a routine had been established. That is where the shovel in the back became an essential weapon in the struggle. When they became bogged Lorry would start digging in front of the tyres until he told her to drive the car forward, slowly. Then back, then forward, then back, then forward, with him pushing the car each way until they reached firmer ground. Most of the time this got them home, but not without a few terse words being exchanged. This time there would be no Lorry.

Handbag and library books in hand Marg and Tim moved quickly towards the car so as not to get wet. She noticed the tractor parked close by, like a premonition of impending trouble it stood ready for action.

"I'll keep an eye on you till you get to the road," Lorry commented, tractor at the ready with a rope attached if needed. She wondered if this was an aspersion upon her abilities. This was in direct contrast to the, you'll be right, line heard reassuring earlier. She consoled herself that it was common knowledge that if she got to the front gate the worst was over since their road was the worst of the journey.

With Lorry watching dubiously the journey commenced. Going very slowly and getting it into a gear that would give some momentum without losing control on the slippery, sticky surface.

Fortunately the front gate was open so she didn't have to stop. She felt a certain pride in herself in getting thus far. She was brought back to reality as the back end slid out as she turned onto Coolagy road. The track through the slush, made by the other vehicles battling the road created a readymade path for her to follow. So deep were the tyre tracks the car could almost steer itself.

The rain was consistent, but only light at this stage. The sky was grey and gloomy as she viewed the western horizon behind her. She could see that the clouds were darker than what they were to the east. This was not a good sign. The rain did have a redeeming quality though. Since there was still water laying on the track and when it became deep enough it would splash up onto the windscreen leaving a thick layer of red mud. Together with the wipers, the rain would conveniently clean the glass to give her vision. This was most fortunate.

She approached the gully with trepidation knowing that there might be water in the centre of it, but more urgent was the sloppier mud either side of it created by clay being deposited from this and previous rain events. Fortunately with a greater speed and a rough progression in the middle through the rocks, she was able to transverse the gully. Of course the interior of the car was disturbed due to the roughness of the rock base. Tim, without being told, rectified the situation. He had learnt to stay silent as his mother battled the roads. Any question asked would result in a terse response.

Fortunately Lorry's concern about the paddock track through their property being the worst of the surfaces was correct. The closer they drove to Wallabra the better the road became. Marg was quite proud of herself when she could see the silos of Wallabra emerging through the greyness of the atmosphere. They arrived in plenty of time for Tim's test. Tim could sense his mother's pride and commented,

"Well done Mum."

The greyness of the clouds began to turn much darker whilst Tim was doing his test. Marg could feel the raindrops becoming noticeably heavier as she did the rounds of the post office, Joe Clement's place and the shop.

"Nice bit of rain Marg, "said Mavis, her face gleaming to see Marg entering the shop. Here was someone to whom she could unload all the news to.

"Yes, but I think we've had enough for now," replied Marg.

"We are going to get a lot more in this lot they say."

This was not what Marg wanted to hear.

"Polly Condon was on the phone a little while ago, they are out on Cumby, about hundred miles west…"

"Yes I know Polly…" Marg interrupted.

"Well she said they've had nearly an inch all ready and she said it's heading our way. And Maureen Hellier down south of here said it's even heavier at their place. She also said it's heading our way," Mavis continued.

"Have we got any new library books Mavis?" Marg asked trying to change the topic. The rain subject was making her feel a little anxious.

"I just don't know where it will all end. We get a couple of days of fine then down it comes again and for days on end. They reckon this lot will be the heaviest of the lot of them. I just don't know what going to happen. We'll all be just stuck here. And there will be a flood if it keeps going like this. Where's all the water going to go, that's what I want to know," she continued.

As she waited in the car outside the school reading a new library book her concentration kept being interrupted by the ever increasing frequency of the rain drops.

Fortunately Tim finished his test ahead of time. It was now nearly two thirty, the aim now was to get home while there was still daylight.

The puddles on the road were growing, as they set out. The tracks were already full and overflowing. The wipers were doing their stuff in keeping the red mud off the windscreen, excepting for the moment of blindness when the mud splashed up. Since the road closer to town was better she decided to use this and get as many miles done before the rain got heavier still. Lorry always told her to take the puddles steady, but on this occasion she was in too much of a hurry to get the miles done. The extra splash, created by driving through water too fast, gets water up into the engine, which in turn wets the points. This in turn brings the car to a sudden halt. To her great annoyance it did happen and they came to a sudden halt. Nothing to do, but simply wait until they dried out, being careful not to use up too much of the battery in trying to get it started again. After the second one of these incidents she had learnt her lesson. Of course no other cars came along as they waited. The time passed ever so slowly with the constant irregular beat of the raindrops the only audible stimulation.

The rest of the drive was much slower. So slow in fact, that by the time we were on Coolagy road it was quite dark. Two tiny headlights floating like a submarine on the water logged path. At least the corrugations had been levelled out a little by the rain, but that didn't stop the car from slipping around from side to side, whilst always trying to keep it going straight and not spin the wheels. What was really worrying her though was the gully which now appeared directly in front of them. Going down into it wasn't a problem, getting back out of the gully was. The soil for fifty yards on either side of the gully was also different. When the gully did flood it would deposit silty clay on either side. This soil, once wet, was even boggier. The other possibility was that the gully would have by now collected too much water in it thus making it impassable.

As they descended she looked for the bottom to see how much water there was in it. If there was too much it was going to be a long, wet, dark and infuriating five mile walk home. This was the main reason for hurrying home. If they got through it she could praise herself, if they didn't she would curse herself for the lost time waiting for the points to dry. The headlights, at last, showed a brief glimpse of the water level. It was all right she decided in an instant.

She changed into first gear as she entered the water to give them more power when accelerating out. She was hoping that her guess upon the depth of the water would be right. In the middle of the gully they could feel the water just reach the bottom of the door and they held their breaths hoping it wouldn't get any deeper. It didn't. Breathing again she slowly started to accelerate knowing the rocks on the bottom would give the car a solid base. Also realising they would need some momentum going up the other side. Soon they were out of the water and progressing up the other side, another one of these, do I take a breath or not moments.

In the slushy silt mud, going up the side of the gully, she could feel the earth grabbing hold of the car. She dare not try and accelerate too much least the tyres would start spinning. The car was losing speed at a rate that it would not make it up the side. She had to gently press a little bit harder on the accelerator. It worked for a bit until she felt the obvious sensation of the wheels spinning. She immediately eased off the accelerator, but still they kept slipping. Eventually she had to put her other foot on the clutch otherwise the car would've stalled.

She tried going back, to get up momentum to go forward over the track already created. It went forward only to the place where they were. She tried going back again, then forward, each time the tyres would spin at the same spot creating an even deeper hole whereby they would never get out of. This is where the shovel usually came into operation.

She hopped out to see, as best as she could through the rain and the lack of light, how deep the hole was that had been created. It was very deep. She had tried too hard to get the car to break out from the hole. Her efforts had only made it deeper. She couldn't really see how digging enough mud out would get them out of this predicament. One hole escaped from would only lead to the next hole to be shovelled. It was a job for a tractor. However, on this lonely section of road at night, there was no tractor.

The anger which she felt overtook any thoughts of vulnerability. She was angry that she was placed in this predicament, cursing this country of extremes that it decided on this day to unleash this down pour and she was cross that Lorry wasn't here to get them out of this.

Tim, who had been sitting quietly letting his mother concentrate on what she was doing, suggested.

"Do you want me to push the car while you drive, Mum?"

She had to admire his boyish enthusiasm and the belief

that he could actually push this car up this slope in this mud.

"Thanks dear, I think it is beyond that," she replied.

Stuck. Alone. Totally dark. No help. Desperate. Frightened. She now found herself in the middle of, a part of, in conjunction with, consumed by this wild country she had always tried to stay aloof from. But for the raindrops setting a regular pattern of beats on the car, all was still, all was calm. The timelessness of the situation only intensified the anxiety she felt. She could not relax and could not be consoled. She could not feel at ease with this spirit in this land of peaceful endurance.

Her anger, her anxiety, her will not to be beaten, her protest against this land of indomitable hardships and the fact that she had a cold, wet and hungry son with her led to the only decision that could be made. There was nothing for it, but to start walking the five miles home in this rain, through this mud, in this cold, defying the elements with eyes peering through the darkness. It would be better for Tim to spend an hour or so walking to get to a hot shower and food than to spend the night cold, wet and feeling miserable.

"What if someone else is coming along the road, the car would be in the road?" Tim asked.

It was a valid point although there was nothing that she could do about it.

She eased his concern by replying, "No one else would be so stupid as to use this road in this weather."

Leaving the groceries, her handbag, Tim's school bag and anything else that was not absolutely necessary, and putting as much clothing as possible, they set out.

It was going to be a long, cold, wet and angry walk

home. The rain was relentless, no point worrying about getting wet, they were soon completely saturated. In the dark it was difficult to see where they were treading. It didn't much matter where the shoes landed, puddle, flowing water or just mud, the main objective was not to slip over.

In the dark it was difficult to tell just where they were. The flat plain gave no dimension of length since it was all the same. She thought of counting the power poles manning the road, but since she had never counted them before and given that she didn't know which number was near the gully, there was little point. Beside it was so dark it was hard enough just to see them. All to do was to keep trudging.

If she had been anxious about joining this spirit of the land whilst waiting in the car, she was now getting the full initiation. She was now a part of it, she was in a space where she could absorb its timelessness, its vastness, its enduring survival, but she, like her fellow Europeans, still rebelled against it.

The tedium of placing one foot after the other without falling over preoccupied their thoughts. The initial shiver of water seeping down their backs had given way to acceptance that their bodies were now completely wet. They searched for the ground to give some indication of the best place to plant the next step. Time was being measured in footsteps. The only time to look up was to check that they may have been heading in the right direction.

One such glance up moment she noticed, in the distance, a light. Faint, but it was there. In this darkness any light was quite obvious.

Her first inclination was to now worry about where the car was stationed, certainly in the wrong place for anyone trying to get through. If it was a car and she was to warn them they would have to stop to hear her and then they would get bogged as well as they would've lost their momentum. The light grew stronger and closer, till they could faintly hear the noise.

"I think it's a tractor, Mum," said Tim, who had been very quiet for the whole walk. His quietness was possibly a learned reaction to a Mum's in a bad mood, scenario.

She listened carefully and realised he was right.

"Who would be driving a tractor on this road in this weather, they would have to be mad," she replied.

"I think it's our tractor," said Tim, excited that they might be rescued.

She was still apprehensive till it started to slow down and she could see the familiar shape of their machine.

"I figured you'd have to be along this road somewhere," Lorry called out.

"You took your time," she replied.

The tractor was open. There was no shelter on it. She could see the rain pouring on Lorry and the tractor. Excepting that it was pouring off him, as he had a thick raincoat on, a hat and gumboots, he was certainly more protected than they were.

"Where's the car?" he asked.

"This side of the gully," she answered.

"Climb aboard, we better get it."

They clambered onto the tractor as best as they could and they now got another chance to re visit the territory they had just walked over in the dark, visible now by the lights of the tractor. She was surprised by the distance they had walked.

*The Red Dust 62*

Back at the car, Lorry positioned the tractor. Marg and Tim got back into the car and were grateful not to have the rain torturing them. Lorry crawled under the car and hooked it up for the tow home, climbed back onto the tractor. He gave the signal, a look back at her and a nod, to say make sure the hand brake was off and it was out of gear. All of which she knew anyway.

On arriving home Marg and Tim enjoyed their respective hot showers.

# CHAPTER 11
# FIRE – THE WOMEN. NOVEMBER 1958

Now, in the gully, only the bare rocks, worn by the constant pressure of tyres on them, were exposed. No water, no rain on this day, just heat and a raging north westerly. The shadows from the trees gave a very brief respite from the sun's glare as she descended into the gully. Remembering that night, in the cold and the rain, and wondering if it might not have been better than this very hot day. The extremes in conditions were difficult to debate, let alone accept. The trees stood resolutely against the wind now tormenting their structure. They remained unscathed and proudly no fire wounds. The gully's other notoriety, still fresh in Marg's memory, was another battle which was fought here, in this gully.

It was another hot day much like this day with a cool change predicted. The wind was coming down from the northwest. It was common procedure that on such a day as that day, all the community would keep a constant visual vigil on the horizons for clouds, not rain, but smoke.

And so it was on that day. It was after lunch, Marg was in the house, doing chores that kept her indoors, out of the heat, when she heard the phone ring.

"Hullo," she answered.

"Is that you Marg?"

"Yes Swampy," Marg recognised his voice.

"There's a bit of smoke coming up from the northwest."

Knowing his language she knew that a, "bit of smoke," was more than likely to be a lot of smoke. Whatever the amount of smoke on a day like this it was not good. She felt her heart beat louder as the anxiety of a bushfire set into her thoughts.

Lorry suddenly burst into the room. It was obvious that he saw what Swampy had seen.

"Swampy, Lorry's just arrived. I will put him on."

She could tell by the worried look on Lorry's face that the threat was serious.

"Swampy," she said to Lorry passing him the phone.

This had now become a *drop everything* situation. Nothing is more important than a bush fire. A little flustered, she contemplated what to do first. Change her clothes to something a bit more practical, trousers for a start. They will need water, not just for the fire, but for themselves. How much tea did she have? And food, they'll need something to keep them going. She did have some of that sponge cake left and there were those scones. Best to get that picnic basket out and whatever cups and plates she could muster. What about the house, was it in danger? She couldn't tell as she, at this stage didn't really know where the fire was.

She had changed into the trousers by the time Lorry had gotten off the phone to Swampy.

"I'm going to get the tractor and hitch it up to the carry all with all the fire stuff on it. I'm pretty sure the tank's got water in it, but I'll check. Can you ring Wymere homestead and tell them. It is coming in from their place. Swampy's ringing up the ones around here. Then can you come over and help me get everything ready."

With this he was gone. It is always urgent when there was a bush fire. She went to the phone to find Wymere's phone number. The boys were at the Coolagy School at the time. She wouldn't be able to pick them up so she also rang Sally Hunter, whose boys also attended the school, if she would look after the boys.

Every year, around spring, the men of the soldier settler farms at "Coolagy" would meet at the community hall for their annual bushfire brigade meeting. The women never seemed to go, it was a men's thing. However the amount of beer consumed by the end of the meeting always left them a bit cynical. At this meeting they would elect a Captain for the year, make sure everyone knew everyone else's phone number and decide upon who was going to get what equipment. Those along Coolagy road, got the better equipment since it was recognised that Wymere, because of its vastness and being to the northwest, was the greatest threat. Swampy had the big truck and the Stirlings had a carry all which fitted onto the three point linkage at the back of the tractor. This had a tank for water, a pump, which ran off the PTO of the tractor, and hoses. It was also common practice for all the farmers to plough firebreaks along their boundaries, in their case Lorry and the other farmers along this road would not only plough in their places, but also along the road side of the boundary fence to Wymere.

Given the urgency of a bushfire and the diligence of the farmers, the phones were running hot. Everyone dropped everything they were doing and rushed to assist. Thus was the case when Marg rang Wymere, they knew about it already and they were on their way. Trouble is they had a lot of miles to come from the homestead.

Phone calls done, Marg rushed out to help Lorry with the carryall. It could be done alone, but was always much quicker with two. She would back the tractor up and Lorry would fit the carry all onto the tractor. Not without, usually, some complaint upon her tractor driving ability to which she would comment on the hours she had sat on a tractor ploughing a paddock or relaying the bin at harvest time. This time however the hook up went very smoothly. Urgency brought out precision. Lorry had everything that he would need already loaded. He headed off and she went inside to finish preparing what would be needed.

By now being outside Marg could see for herself that Swampy's 'bit of smoke' had turned into a cloud that had darkened the western horizon. Like a great black mass of destruction it was engulfing the whole scene. The unmistakeable smell was now filtering into her lungs which made her feel anxious. Coming in from Wymere not only would it destroy a lot of Wymere's pastures, the sheep and possibly where the Gilmore's lived in an outhouse. If it got across Coolagy road it would also destroy their wheat crops which were only weeks away from harvest. Coolagy road was the key. The other worry in this strategy was the gully with its collection of gum trees and scrub lining its bank. Fire in timber is a lot more difficult to control than in the open plains. Once it got into the gully it then had a first class passage through to many of the farms in Coolagy.

There was no time to waste. Grabbing as much as she could, as quickly as she could, Marg loaded up the car with supplies. With the enemy approaching she was in too much of a hurry to get all that was needed. Cutlery and plates were not going to stop this inferno. There must be something more constructive that she could do. She glanced towards Coolagy road and could see the fire was almost upon it. It was time to go.

As she drove down their driveway towards Coolagy road she could see that the fire would hit the road near the boundary of Swampy's and their place, first. What was she going to find? Although she was confident the bush telegraph would have been used adequately and everyone would now have known about this new offensive, there was that delay, with the distance that had to be covered, in actually getting there. Were Swampy and Lorry alone in their defence of the road?

The smoke became much thicker as she turned onto Coolagy road to face the enemy. She was worried that at any moment she would see flames coming across the road in front of her. It worried her, but it did not stop her. The danger it posed to the people already fighting it and the damage it would cause resulted in no thought of self-preservation.

She found Lorry near Swampy's driveway spraying water on the Wymere side of the road. Swampy was further along in his truck with spray gun in hand. They had realised where the fire was going to hit the road and were dampening down the forage in readiness. It was as though they were setting a mine field against advancing tanks. Hand guns against cannons. There was a bit of bare ground in Swampy's place so she parked the car there. She was uncertain that this would be a safe place. Lorry was close by and came across with the tractor to ensure that this ground would be safe by deluging the area and car with water. This was to be the field headquarters, as it were.

Upon seeing Marg's arrival Swampy brought his truck back and the three of them faced the enemy now bearing down upon them like a disciple of doom.

"Marg, can you hop on our tractor and spray across to the Wymere boundary fence heading back towards our gateway. I'll need to go and help Swampy, it's a two man operation to use that truck properly," said Lorry seeing Swampy with his truck.

He didn't wait for a reply before he was gone, running across the road to catch up with Swampy. No more the idea that because she was a woman she would be incapable of such a task. The urgency of the situation made it necessary.

Marg had her doubts about using the hose and spray whilst driving the tractor, but was resolved to doing it. She had to.

She was just about to put the tractor in gear when she noticed Eddie Baker arriving on his tractor dragging a plough behind it. Shirley and Eddie were the neighbours to the west. They had only been on their place for less than a year. They had bought Joe Harrison's place. Further down the road she could see the approaching dust of their car.

She got off the tractor to meet Eddie. He was much younger than Marg, a short man, but with a stocky build. In his presence one could feel his overwhelming positive energy as though nothing was going to stop him.

"Lorry's gone down to help Swampy with the truck," she called to him.

"I think there are a few blokes on their way from that

end. I'll stay here and give you a hand with this end. Shirley's on her way. I'll get the tractor set up and do a firebreak next to the Wymere boundary fence, if you and Shirley can come along after me, in the furrow, hosing it down towards where the fire will be coming from."

With that he was heading back towards his tractor. Shirley arrived and parked at the designated headquarters and headed, almost instinctively, towards Marg.

A tall woman and rather thin, like her husband she carried an air of confidence. Although she was three months pregnant with their first child, she was ready for the task.

"Hi Shirley, we're to follow Eddie with our tractor and spray water into Wymere," Marg stated.

"You better drive it you know your tractor better than I would. I'll take the hose."

Marg's experience with the tractor had been restricted to directing the tractor along a trail or following along beside a furrow with an implement in tow. The pump which created the spraying water was operated by a lever beside her left leg. It was called the PTO. She had seen Lorry work this lever and when she had previously tried to operate it would shake in her hand. Shirley was ready with the hose, Marg was on the tractor and tried to move this lever. It began to shake violently. She could feel her hand vibrating to its erratic movement. With the fire now beckoning closer and Eddie already out of ear shot she could feel herself in a panic. The fire was now so close she could feel its heat and the smoke it created was clogging her lungs and watering her eyes. The flames were only now thirty yards from where they were stationary. If she could not get this lever into place they could be caught up in the inferno. Their calculation that the fire would hit the road at Swampy's gateway was correct they now found themselves stuck at that very spot.

Shirley could see Marg's dilemma and rushed over to help.

"This damn lever won't go into gear, Shirley," Marg said in a panic.

"Pull the throttle back and put it in neutral," yelled Shirley.

Marg looked at Shirley too much in a panic to comprehend her direction, until Shirley reached over and moved the throttle herself and the gear sticks.

"Now try it," she suggested.

With her hand still shaking violently on the lever she pulled as hard as she could and was relieved to feel it go into gear. With the fire now bearing down upon them, Shirley realised that they were going nowhere until they had stopped the fire at this place. The centre of the battle was now with the two women. There was so much smoke now that they had difficulty seeing anything.

"Let the clutch out Marg," Shirley commanded.

With this done water started flowing from the spray gun in Shirley's hand. Realising their immediate peril Shirley first sprayed water onto the tractor, Marg and onto herself, then faced the fire now bearing down upon the fence. Like helpless dwarfs against a seemingly unbeatable huge giant they faced the enemy defiantly. They had to hold their ground. If the fire got past them, all would be lost.

With the tractor compulsorily immobile Marg grabbed an old wet wheat bag lying under her feet, alighted from the tractor and started beating the ground between the fence and the firebreak created by Eddie's plough. Bravely they faced the foe now upon them. The heat was unbearable, the smoke intolerable and the visibility, except for the flames, was gone. But they held their ground.

Unbeknown to them Swampy and Lorry, as well as Eddie, had seen the enemy's thrust at the critical point of the offensive and had retreated with the reinforcement and heavy artillery. The ladies had not seen their approach, but were elated to see Eddie and his plough appear through the smoking mayhem between the fence and his previous firebreak, moving through the fire which had already broken through the fence. Behind them, between the road and the firebreak they could feel the water from Swampy's truck slaying the fire in its wake.

They had saved their headquarters, the cars were safe and the fire was now split in two. With the north westerly still aiding the enemy to the east was now where the battle would be at its most intense. Eddie kept his easterly progress with the firebreak hoping to be one step in front of the fire.

With limited wind assistance, to the west the fire would still persist, but not with the speed or intensity. Lorry alighted from the truck and approached Marg. The two ladies stood exasperated by their near defeat, but awaited further orders.

"Marg," he shouted through the cracking flames. "Get the tractor moving and go towards our driveway spraying the fire as it gets to the firebreak, Swampy and I will follow Eddie with the truck."

Marg glanced towards the east and through the smoke she could make out other human figures and machinery advancing down the road towards them. Reinforcements were arriving. She glanced to the west as she climbed onto the tractor and noticed only smoke and a barren road. This section of the battle was hers and Shirley's. Lorry, Swampy and Eddie were now lost in the smoke fighting the flames as they encroached upon the road.

Shirley, without being told, had figured out that the west, was up to the pair of them and wasted no time with her spray gun dousing the flames as they reached the firebreak made from Eddie's tractor. Marg had the tractor in gear and was following, occasionally alighting to beat flames that resisted Shirley's watery persuasion. There was no time to think of the heat, the smoke, the clogging lungs, their thirst and exhaustion. There was no stopping till the enemy was beaten. On and off the tractor Marg kept up with Shirley's progress. She glanced back occasionally to check if their efforts were successful and that no flame had escaped and crossed the fire break. So far so good, they progressed. She looked over into Wymere and could see the flames travelling west, much slower than those travelling east, but they still posed a threat. She wondered where it would all finish. There was nothing to stop it coming from Wymere. This conflict seemed to have no end. All they could do was to do their bit and hope for the best.

They both realised that at some stage Eddie's firebreak would end where he turned around to give assistance to where the fire first met the road. The old fire break that Lorry had done a month before would not be near as effective as Eddie's effort today. Also, as large as their tank was it would eventually become empty. They would have to refill at some stage. The fire wasn't going to wait for them to do that.

Without the assistance of the wind their section of the fire was beginning to fail. Their urgency and speed of attack had them almost in front of the flames. Worried about their method Marg glanced back again to see if it hadn't crossed their line. It hadn't. They were now in front of the advancing menace. However when she looked forward she could see where Eddie had stopped and turned around. This was going to be the next crisis. She tried to catch Shirley's attention to warn her of the situation. Shirley was looking into Wymere and couldn't be drawn to Marg's concern. Something out there had caught Shirley's eye. Marg looked into the great vastness of Wymere and noticed that there was no smoke rising from where the flames should be in the distance. She wondered why. Then she could just make out something moving through the open plains just in front of where the flames should've been. Behind the object there were no flames and no smoke.

The mystery could not be resolved as they still had to be alert to the flames still on their front and the concern of the ending fire break was now approaching. The road in front of them was still vacant, devoid of any human activity. They still felt alone in their sector. As for what was happening behind them they had no idea, but knew that that was where the most intense fighting was being carried out. While there was flame on their front in Wymere they knew their job wasn't going to end. The enemy had to be controlled on the other side of the fence, but from who or where they had no idea. The fence had no gates and therefore no access.

Shirley continued with the hose and Marg kept up with her. Their farms and properties were their responsibility and they were not going to cease their struggle while that danger existed.

Marg glanced over the fence into Wymere and could see that the flames in the distance were no longer. It was hard to fathom why since the flames and smoke closer to them hid the reason. She kept looking until she could see a different red moving differently from the flames. This red object had figures moving around it. She tried to gain Shirley's attention which was only gained when she stopped the tractor and Shirley ceased her toil to wonder why. Marg could now see that they were not alone in their struggle. She pointed into Wymere where upon Shirley could also see that they had company in their struggle.

The red object was a fire truck which must have come from Wymere. It was heading towards them along the path of the fire. The two women looked at each other with relief. With the help of this new reinforcement they knew the danger of the western front would soon be under control.

As they got closer Marg could recognise Joe Gilmore and his two elder sons, Kevin and Eric. Together with his wife, Marie and two other daughters they lived in an out house in Wymere. The children attended the Coolagy School and that is where Marg had gained their acquaintance. He was a wiry man who never had really much to say, but what remained unsaid said volumes about him. Tall, thin with a stern disposition he did not attract an immediate social interaction, but commanded respect by the toughness he projected. His two sons were also quiet being guided by his actions and discourse.

They met at the fence like the red army, if not in miniature, of 1942 west of Stalingrad. The flames were surrendered to the water from their tanks.

"I'm pleased to see there was someone here to protect Coolagy," Joe said.

"We're pleased to see you as well Joe", Marg replied.

"Where did it start Joe?" asked Shirley.

"The wind blew down some of the windmill on the way out to our place, created a spark and off it went. The wind has kept it away from the house, but Marie and the girls are watching it. I had to come down this side of the fire because I knew the sheep were on this side and I was worried about them. Is there anyone on the windward side?" he asked.

"Lorry and Swampy headed down that way, Eddie as well. I suppose more would have arrived by now," Marg replied.

"Marie was to ring the homestead at Wymere, I hope they would be on their way by now. Just as well old buff was a bit lame today otherwise the children would've been at school," Joe said. (Buff was the horse that pulled the sulky that took the children to the school).

"I rang them as well," Marg added.

There was an uncomfortable silence as Joe, uncertain as to what to say being socially insecure, was at a loss. The women were taking a breath feeling relieved that their section of the conflict was now possibly resolved. The next thought would be; what to do next. Joe was worried about the other side of the fire, the eastern front.

"Look me and the boys should be right with this end now. We'll just keep going around and make sure it's all out, if youse want to go down and see what's happening at the other end. I can't get down there from this end of the fire and I like to stay here to make sure the sheep are safe," he said.

The women realised that this was a good idea, besides they were worried about their husbands, their cars and the fact that they had little water left.

"Sure you'll be right down this end, Joe?" asked Marg. "Should be someone else arriving from this end at some stage."

"If we need help I'll get one of the boys to run down to that end," he said.

The women's anxiety decided the decision.

"All right Joe," Marg answered.

Shirley clambered aboard the tractor and they set off east towards where they knew the battle was now raging. Although still being frightfully hot they appreciated that it was not as hot as when the flames were all about them. They looked upon the ground they had just covered and protected, now strewn with ash.

When they got to where the cars were parked, Thelma was already there setting out tables, chairs and refreshments for the fire fighters. She was pleased to see the women as she had no idea upon who was winning.

"How's it down that end?" she asked.

"We've stopped it down that end. Joe Gilmore and his two boys are watching it," Marg replied.

"I don't know what's happening down that way," Thelma said.

"We think we better keep going and see what we can do. Will you be able to hold the fort here, Thelma?" Shirley asked.

"Oh yes I'll be right here. You better take down as many water bags as you can carry. They will be needing them."

The three ladies instantly grabbed the water bags available.

"You'll find a few things in our car Thelma," said Marg.

"And in ours too," Shirley added. "We're getting low on water....."

"Go into that dam of ours. It's only about four hundred yards up there in the next paddock. There's a gate you can go through," said Thelma.

Marg and Shirley set off towards a blackened horizon of destruction.

"Do you know how to pump water into the tank?" Marg asked.

"Not really," Shirley replied.

"I guess we'll just have to figure it out."

# CHAPTER 12
## FIRE – THE MEN. NOVEMBER 1958

At the other end of the fire Tom Patton stood on Coolagy road between the encroaching fire and the gully which crossed the road at right angles. In true military tradition, he had his binoculars around his neck and his weapon, a pair of pliers and a wet bag in his hands. He knew if the fire got into the gully, because of the trees that bordered it and their associated litter, it will have gained a first class ticket into the farms and their crops. The flames from this grass fire had been fierce enough, but if it feasted on the trees the result would be even more catastrophic.

Tom had been a Captain in the army during the war and now in this community he still held rank. He was also a little older than most of them. He had been in the army before the war and his and his wife Lizzie's, sons were born before the war started. Whether it was out of instilled customs from the war, or whether he had natural leadership characteristics, he was always elected the fire brigade captain. Everyone seemed to always accept that he was in command. He was also the president of the school's P and C Association. His participation in these roles were not without merit. He was always calculated in his decisions and was rarely rattled.

Of stocky build, charismatic, handsome, he exuded

authority. He had also been quite a successful farmer. He was not afraid to use his intelligence rather than his brawn on his patch. It possibly also helped that his two sons now both worked on the farm with him. He now had two relatively new tractors. His farm was a number of miles away from the fire, but he was one of the first ones there on this day with his fire truck.

He kept looking east along the road as if he was looking for the reinforcements. Already he had the two trucks and a couple of tractors with equipment attached in the front line. Given that one of these would be away filling up at any one time, he knew it was not enough.

It was fortunate that Swampy and Lorry were at Swampy's dam filling up when Marg and Shirley arrived.

"How did you go," Lorry asked.

"Joe Gilmore and his boys arrived with a truck from Wymere," said Marg.

"Is it under control?"

"Yes. They've stayed down there to watch it," Shirley replied. "We're nearly out of water."

"Marg, back it down the bank. Don't go too close to the water though."

"What's happening down that end?" Shirley asked as Marg carefully reversed the tractor towards the water.

"We are worried it will get in to the gully."

"What do you want us to do?"

"If you and Marg can keep an eye on what we've already done, just so it doesn't spark up again behind us. Swampy and I will go back to the front of it."

Although Tom's vision was clouded by the smoke he still searched for help. The wind was relentless and the fire seemed to be feeding upon it. Using its force the fire was trying to encapsulate the enemy, the humans and their little squirt guns. The smoke from the fire and the dust kicked up by Eddie's plough forging a fire break, was now engulfing Tom. The resources available were leap frogging themselves in an effort to be faster than the fire.

The men fought bravely, they had done this before, and together with Eddie's now substantial fire break were stopping the enemy from crossing the defensive line of the road. But they also knew that the gully would be a different proposition.

Tom realised that while the fire was in Wymere they had no real way of controlling it. It would just continue with even more ferocity once it reached the gully. They had done well so far just to keep it from crossing the road.

Now with his visibility of the road practically gone there was no point in waiting. The fence into Wymere had to be cut and he would have to send some of the machines into Wymere. A new front, defence line had to be created even if they didn't have the resources to defend it. He moved hastily towards the fence, pliers in hand, but had only gone a little way when he could see through the smoke, a truck approaching from the east.

He rushed over towards the truck to instruct them. As he got closer he could read "Wymere Brigade" on the door. He was relieved to see Stan McLean, the foreman at Wymere, peer out.

"What's happening Tom?" he called out.

"We've managed to stop it from crossing the road so far. It is the gully that we are worried about. If it gets in there..."

"I see a couple of tractor with ploughs behind them," Stan started to report.

"They would be my two sons. Where were they?"

"Not far back. We nearly run into them. Couldn't see them for all the smoke. Pretty fancy gear, bet ya that set you back a bit," Stan replied.

"Look, we've got to get into Wymere and try and get in front of it before it gets into the gully," Tom began to explain.

"We've got the other truck in there. They went in through the gate at the crossroads. They are heading to the top of this front," Stan explained.

Although this was good news, Tom was preoccupied with the problem at hand here.

"Do you mind if..." Tom began to ask.

"Don't know what's happening the other side do you?" Stan interjected.

"It's under control. Joe Gilmore's keeping an eye on it, I believe."

"I thought that is where he would be. Always thinking of the sheep you know is Joe ..." Stan continued.

"Look, I'm going over to cut the fence into Wymere, is that all right?"

"Yeah, go ahead," Stan replied.

"I'll send the boys down that way, can you follow with the truck?" Tom ordered.

"Yeah, all right," Stan replied.

As Tom, pliers in hand, was about to rush off, Stan remembered something else.

"Oh and, Mr Field is on his way he said to tell you."

"Righto," returned Tom.

Tom was not going to listen to any more and ran fifty yards east. On reaching the fence he wasted no time in cutting wires. Timely, as his two sons, Colin and Doug, having followed Eddie's fire break spotted their father amongst the smoke peeling back the fence. There were no words spoken, the boys knew instinctively what had to be done. They paused for a moment before going through the gap, changing gears and engaging the ploughs. More smoke, but of a different kind, exhaled from their exhausts. They didn't need the order to charge. Ploughs at full depth, throttles to a maximum they invaded the line that had to be protected. Great clouds of dust were thrust out as the tractors, groaning under the stress, gained momentum. Stan appeared with two men on the truck dousing the ground in front of the fire break. Soon all three vehicles were out of view, covered by the smoke. As they disappeared into this no man's land all Tom could do was hope.

To his right he could now make out the figures of the men and machines approaching, as that front was drawing closer to the gully. As there was nothing he could do at this spot, nothing he could do for his sons and Stan on his left front, he rushed over to help with the current conflict.

When they had reached the place where the fence had been cut, there was no time to gloat over the successful completion of the right front, the resources were turned onto the left front. Tom stayed at this place, the new headquarters, to command any new troops that might arrive.

The smoke near the road was now clearing. The trees at the gully were now revealing themselves to be only fifty yards from where the fence was cut. It had been a close call. The sunlight began to peer, considerably to the west from when they last saw it. The afternoon was getting on.

Marg and Shirley arrived relieved that their part of Coolagy had been saved.

"We've got some water bags on the tractor," Marg informed Tom who was preoccupied with his watchful vigil on the left front which now had ever decreasing smoke.

"Good oh," he replied.

"Do you want us to get some more?" Shirley asked.

"If you wouldn't mind. Leave the tractor here and go up in that Ute over there. Leave the bags, knapsacks and stuff here," Tom answered. "We'll make a camp near the gully."

They found Thelma still waiting anxiously near their gate. She had managed to get everything in order for the men, including food, tea and water, all set out with chairs and tables. She was pleased to see Marg and Shirley arrive.

"They've saved it from getting into Coolagy," Marg told her.

"I thought they must've. I could tell from the smoke. Did it get to the gully?"

"Not near the road, and hopefully not into it in Wymere, that's where they are fighting it now," Shirley replied.

"Thelma, they're going to make a camp on the road near the gully. Can we move all this down there?" Marg asked realising all the work Thelma had put in to make it all as comfortable as she could.

"I suppose so," Thelma replied studying her wasted efforts.

"We'll help you," added Shirley.

Back at headquarters Tom was studying the battle. Many tactical ideas passed through his mind depending upon what he could see. This is where the binoculars came in handy. The only indication he had upon the state of the battle was the amount of smoke and where it was coming from. Most of his troops were obscured by the smoke. However this was a good source of information. It was becoming quite obvious that the smoke was coming from further inland. None from the road or anywhere near it. The fire break had not been breached. Recognisance from the front, given by trucks returning for water, was also proving to be positive. The smoke cloud was thinning.

By the time the ladies returned to the gully the day's heat was beginning to diminish in its intensity. Evening was beginning to take over. The wind was dying and there were high clouds wandering in aimlessly from the south west, teasing them with the chance of rain. A sign the cool change was approaching. Mr Kincaid, the manager of Wymere had arrived and was in consultation with his staff and Tom. The only smoke to be seen was the smouldering ground that had already been burnt. Tom's tractors and ploughs, although covered in dust and ash had survived the conflict and the two boys awaited further instructions. The Fire trucks kept up a visual of checking for any new flare ups, but certainly the battle had been won. After this event the ladies were not so cynical about the annual bush fire meetings.

The ladies set up the portable kitchen and found themselves going backwards and forwards to their houses to get more stuff. Through the darkness of the night the road and paddock into Wymere was dotted with pairs of lights like the eyes of mechanical dogs waiting to pounce on any stragglers or in this case a flaming counter offensive from an enemy depleted of its force.

The cool change arrived before midnight. It was a subtle

difference. There was no great wind, just a gentle relaxing breeze which although brought no rain, did temper the day's heat. Tom had sent his two sons home with their machines. The danger had past, only Tom, Lorry and Marg, Swampy and Thelma, Eddie and Shirley, Mr Kincaid and some of his staff remained. The tales of the day's events began.

Marg had never met Mr Kincaid previously and was happy to do so. To her Wymere had always been this vast expanse devoid of human intervention. She wanted to see the face behind the wilderness.

Wymere, itself, was one of a number of properties owned by a consortium in the city. Although Marg quickly gained the impression, by his nature, that it was owned by Mr Kincaid. Certainly he carried a demeanour as though he did. He rarely smiled, but could be trusted to do the right thing, his good reputation had preceded him.

As they conversed, Marg pondered the thought of their isolation. If she had thought where they lived and farmed was isolated enough none of them had taken into account just how much more isolated they were at the Wymere homestead. He stated that getting staff to stay was the main problem and virtually impossible to get families.

"Why?" she asked.

"We have no schools," he replied. "There is only the school of the air, but it is not very good."

This hit a nerve with Marg as to her education was very important to her. It might be all right for the parents to battle away on their piece of dirt, but it was no reason for the children to be forced to do the same. She always kept this opinion to herself though as it was not necessarily shared by the others in the community. To Marg education was the key to the children's future.

 She would remember this conversation and it did come in useful.

# CHAPTER 13
# WHERE THE GILMORE'S LIVED.

The memory of that day made Marg look about when she had ascended out of the gully, on this just as frightfully hot day as it was then, for smoke. This was now a custom the whole community shared. By her reckoning, not having her watch on, it must've been after ten in the morning. The time of the day when all hope of the morning coolness had been burnt off. It was now hot to stay for the rest of the day and possibly into the night. She could feel the sweat on her back so she leant forward again to try and dry it before it left a stain on her dress.

As the trees at the gully diminished into the horizon behind her, she began to search for the next landmark to remind her that she was moving. Since the open plains held such a similarity it could often be mistaken for never ending inertia. Even the fence posts and the power poles ticked by in such a regular and monotonous manner it felt like she was watching a movie with the scenery being viewed on a screen while she kept still.

She knew she didn't have to wait too long. She knew where it was. She had seen it many times before. There was a time when she would look at it with curiosity. The mystery was eventually solved.

It was very subtle. If you didn't know of its existence it could be passed without notice. A small break in the vegetation on her left and the two wheeled trail that branded the barren dirt, were the only indications. The gate that broke the, up until now, continuous fence that was the Wymere boundary, was the only other clue.

Insignificant as it may have appeared it was the entrance to where the Gilmores staked their claim on domesticity. Seven miles through the gate, far into the obscurity of the vast emptiness that is the outback, Joe, Marie and their four children continued their existence in the hope for something better.

Their track was not used as much as it was since Buff no longer pounded the path. He made his presence felt before and after school. Buff, the old draft horse, had a purpose. His claim on existence was to provide the Gilmore children with transportation to the Coolagy School.

Each school morning Kevin, the oldest son, would harness Buff and adjust the sulky. Then each school morning the old horse would convey the children twelve miles into the Coolagy School and back again. Each school day whether it be raining, windy, hot, cold, dark or in blinding sun he would plod his well-known path. During the day he could rest in a paddock next to the school. He was a favourite within the community, the farmers would often bring him a bit of grain as a treat.

Marg had often wondered just what was at the end of that track leading into the great unknown. She wondered why a family would choose to live in such isolation. Her questions were to be answered in the autumn following the fire. In her capacity as secretary of the P and C meetings she had the need to visit the Gilmores so as they could sign a document.

It was a question of necessity as to why these out houses existed. The properties were so big, they needed people to be stationed at various positions to care for the stock in their area, make sure they had water and ride the boundaries. Usually performed by single men, no woman in her right mind would entertain such an existence. Yet Marie Gilmore was rearing a family in this situation. They did have a car, and although it was never discussed, it was common knowledge that it shouldn't be on the road. Everyone always turned a blind eye to it.

The Gilmores kept very much to themselves. They very rarely attended any of socials at the Coolagy Community hall. They knew that they were always welcome to come along. When they did come it was always a difficult conversation though. They were both very likeable people, but very shy. It was as if they had forgotten, or never knew, how to relate to people socially. Marg always felt sympathy for them, but was consoled by realising that was just the way that they were.

The autumn rains had not yet arrived, as Marg turned left into the Gilmore's gateway. The ground was barren, dry, mainly red with a touch of yellowed vegetation clinging on. It was a Saturday morning and the boys were home. She gained special permission from Lorry to bring the boys in preference to them doing chores on the farm, so as they could be company to Kevin and Eric. The boys had built a friendship with the Gilmore boys at the Coolagy School where, at the time, they were all attending.

Entering the gate Marg looked at the tiny little track leading off into who knew where. There was only the track and a single line of wire supported occasionally by poles, which served as the telephone connection, as a guide. The boys were excited about going somewhere different. To Marg it was all the same, this time even worse. What was this track leading into nothingness going to be like? This was not a public road. It had never seen a grader. She expected to find no one or nothing on it till she arrived at the Gilmore's where ever and whenever that would be. She felt a little anxious, compensated by the boy's enthusiasm and the knowledge that Buff had been doing this for years she took a deep breath and ventured on.

She expected it to be straight and to a certain extent it did head in a north westerly direction. The steering wheel, however, was in constant operation, dodging pot holes that were obviously a permanent structure. Some were so deep that Buff had been avoiding them and a little horse and sulky track, off into the great savannah, had been established only to reunite with the original.

Coolagy road had disappeared beyond the horizon. The only sign of human existence was the trail. Till on the horizon, in the general direction that the track was taking them, she noticed the unmistakable shape of tree branches looming. There were not very many, but enough to be noticeable. Now there was a bit of green between the blue sky and the red dust. The boys noticed them as well and became transfixed by the "something different" prospect. As they moved closer the trunks could be seen together with the outline of buildings. They were grey, brown shapes standing resolutely, some with leaves on top, some with rusted corrugated iron, blending together.

The car began to tilt downwards a little as they approached. The trees and the buildings were in a slight depression. When it did rain the moisture would be held longer in a depression. This then made the existence of trees possible. It was also possible for a house hold to exist as a bore could successfully obtain water. Fences could now be seen coming from different directions with the bore and the associated water troughs leading from it as their focus. The ground under the trees was completely barren from decades of being used as a shelter for the sheep.

When they stopped and after the dust, kicked up by the car, dispersed, the view revealed a house or shack totally made of corrugated iron, now rusting. It had that tacked on appearance as though there had been no plan. Build it as you needed it, seemed to have been the architectural design.

Beyond the house were a couple of sheds, one of which possibly would've been used to shear sheep though it was hard to say, and the other to store stuff in. There were a number of dog kennels, empty at the moment as all the dogs had rushed over to greet them, absolutely delighted by the arrival of strangers. There was another shelter near what was the horse paddock this had the sulky under it. Beyond these objects there was nothing to suggested human intervention. The complete horizon which was, looking away from the small clump of trees, truly one line, no trees, no hills, just open savannah for as far as they could see and beyond. Here, in the middle of this vast emptiness, this family existed.

She was expected and it was obvious that the Gilmores had been waiting for her arrival. The whole family filed out of the house with beaming smiles. The curiosity of visitors did possibly bring about a certain expectation in them. As soon as the customary greetings were concluded Joe became uncomfortable. His shyness and uncertainty in a social situation was becoming evident. He found an excuse to leave. With him their two boys followed as if trained like the dogs to be always with the man. Marg beckoned Ken and Tim to go with them.

There were two horses saddled up tired to a railing near the house. The two daughters, Dorothy and Martha, stood patiently, under the spell of polite behaviour, although it was obvious they had something else that they wanted to do. Marie could sense their yearnings.

"You can go back to the horses now if you like," Marie said.

The girls didn't need a second chance.

"Nice to see you Mrs Stirling," they added whilst leaving.

Marg appreciated the very old fashioned manners on display. The whole family must be present to greet visitors, pay their respects and, in this case, leave the women to have a cup of tea. It was obviously Marie who had insisted that this is what had to be done on this occasion. As a reward they could then go off and do what they were already doing. Marie had shown a sense of dignity, which for her, must prevail in this indignant landscape. It was a sign of defiance against an inhuman situation.

The two women proceeded into the kitchen where the tea had already been made, the best china was on display even though it was a mixture of pieces, and the scones buttered. The corrugated iron roofing was plain to see which gave the interior a feel of spaciousness which belied the reality. There were three bedrooms on either side of a hallway leading to the kitchen/living room. They were separated by corrugated iron. Small verandas shaded the front and back doors. Some of the wooden slats being used as flooring were broken, patched up with small wooden fills and nails. The limited carpet inside the house covered up some of the wooden flooring. There was not really any design or predominate colour to the carpet. Years of wear, stains, dust and ash had diminished the carpet to token status.

There was no elegance amongst the decor, practical considerations rather than visual appeal. It could have been seen as being untidy, but given the amount of items in a room much smaller than was needed, navigation through the room was quite logically devised. The fuel stove in the kitchen would have been handy in winter for its warmth, but a curse in summer. Although there were lights and an electric radio, there was no electricity supplied to the house. The only power was from a diesel generator. Given the openness of the whole house to the elements it was obvious that a perfect clean could never be attained. It was noticeable, however, that on this day a special effort had been mounted.

The two ladies sat at the kitchen table made of wood and covered with a clean white table cloth, obviously used only on special occasions. As they chattered it soon became apparent Marie had been looking forward to Marg's visit. It was as if Marg had been a life time acquaintance, but the truth was their relationship, prior to this, had been merely courteous and polite. Sometimes the uncertainties in a social situation where there are a lot of people will disappear in a one on one talk, where trust has been established.

Although Marie was dominating the conversation Marg

was happy to listen to her. Marg was like that. She always maintained that one doesn't learn anything whilst talking, but learns everything as a listener. She suggested that they come to more social gatherings, hoping that this conversation would give her the confidence to seek more interaction.

"Oh, Joe doesn't really like going out much," was her reply.

The conversation drifted, as it usually does, onto the children. It became obviously apparent that Joe and the children were her life. After all there was nothing else. It was her role. But in that role she did excel. A very maternal woman she saw it as her duty to provide Joe and the children with all that a mother was supposed to do. She played her role as had been handed down for decades to station hands and their families. It was a role based upon persevering through the elements of this relentlessly inhospitable environment and never seeming to want to attain anything better. It was their lot in life.

As the conversation continued Marg learned that Marie did want something different. To her the children's education was most important.

"Joe and I never went to school. On the stations we were at they didn't even have the school of the air. The only education we ever got was from our parents who also didn't have any schooling. The only things we were taught was how to live like our parents. I want a bit more for our children, that is why I am so grateful that there is at least a school that they can go to, where they can learn something different, where they can meet other people, so they don't necessarily have to live the life we are leading. This might be a bit rough living in this house on this property, but this house is near a school, so I put up with it."

Marie suddenly started to look anxious. It was as though she had been caught in such a different thought patterns, hypnotised by the novelty of talking to someone else, she had lost track of the time. She had duties to perform.

"Would you like to stay for lunch?" She asked not out of politeness in that she knew that she had to now prepare lunch, but more out of a genuine yearning for Marg to stay so she would have her company for longer.

Marg felt a touch of guilt when she declined, but it would not have been totally polite to have stayed for lunch as well. Document signed, it was time to bid her farewells. Lunch time beckoned and Marg could see that preparing their lunch was more on Marie's mind than the pleasantries of a conversation.

"I would like you to come over to our place for afternoon tea one day," Marg said as they parted and genuinely hoped that she would.

Marg felt a need to do something one day to help this family.

# CHAPTER 14
# WALLABRA. FEBRUARY 1965

The only thing moving along the main street of Wallabra was wind and the red dust it kicked up. Nor was there expected to be, all the farmers would be out on their patch and it would be deemed too hot for a drive into Wallabra. The town appeared to be in hibernation, waiting for this particular extreme set of the elements to pass. With each sudden gust of wind now occurring with increasing regularity, Janet could see the red dust coming in through the open door. She knew it was only a matter of time, with Kevin still out in the back room, when she could stand the collecting dust no longer and give the broom some use.

The telephone had become inert. It had not sounded since Mr Kelly left some two hours previous. Since it had been so quiet Janet was able to catch up with a lot of paper work, although her concentration was being disturbed by the concern she had over this part for Mrs Stirling. The longer Kevin stayed out in the backroom the greater her anxiety became. Finally her concern led to curiosity, she had to find out for herself what was going on down there.

Outside the office she could feel the force of the wind. Much stronger than when she had arrived. As it dried her sweat she could feel a touch of relief. But with the wind came the intensity of the heat that was gathering outside. The wind was now only going to make her hotter. As she made her way towards the backroom she noticed the red dust already collecting visibly on the products. The paper work would now have to wait.

The back room was on the left along the back wall. It was sectioned off with corrugated iron walls. There was a small window, which was jammed shut, facing outside into a usually untidy backyard, but none on the interior walls. Mr Kelly didn't want clients knowing what was in the backroom. Next to the backroom was a set of roller doors which opened onto the back yard. Similarly Mr Kelly didn't want clients knowing what was out there so it was usually closed.

Deeper into the building the wind had lost its intensity, but the heat it transported impacted on itself to multiply its strength. The only ventilation into the back room was through the entrance door near the closed roller doors. The only light, except from the permanently closed window, was a large single bulb dangling from the roof, which emitted considerable heat as well.

Janet found Kevin with sweat streaming off him peering at the hordes of boxes and articles strewn across the shelves and the floor.

"You must be boiling in there," Janet said.

"I won't be needing a jumper today that's for sure."

"I'll open this back door for you," Janet said trying to help.

"Mr Kelly doesn't ..." protested Kevin.

"He's not here and won't be till later this afternoon. Besides I'm just going to lift it a couple of feet."

As she pulled on the chains she could feel the air around

her become alive with the chance of escape. The draught it created had an immediate effect including forcing products off the shelves.

Although it was never really stated, it was understood that when Mr Kelly was away, Janet was in charge. Kevin understood this. Possibly because she was the one answering the phone and Mr Kelly spent more time with her being in the office, so she was the one who knew best what was going on. Besides Kevin was told very, very little of what was going on.

"You haven't found this part yet?"

His expressions gave the answer. Obviously not and it had not been from lack of trying. The room never looked tidy due to the amount of stuff it had to contain, but now with opened boxes, articles moved, bits of metal laying around in disorder, it now took on the image of chaos.

"Do we know just what it is?" asked Kevin out of sheer frustration.

"All I know is that it is for a bore and it should have Mr Stirling's name on it," she replied knowing her answer wasn't going to help much.

"Do you know much about bores?" she asked.

"Dad's fixed a few of them over the years," said Kevin.

"Do any of these things look like a part for a bore?"

"There are all different types of bores you see," said Kevin.

It wasn't looking good. Her curiosity had only led to more concern. At least there was more air movement as she returned to the office to collect a broom, replacing fallen objects as she went.

Before entering the office she could hear the approach

of Mavis Anderson from the shop. Janet didn't have to wonder who it was Mavis had a very distinctive walking style, loud, heavy and with urgency. The short, a little overweight figure of a self-assured woman in her fifties rounded the door. Her anxious eyes searched and found who she was looking for, Janet.

"Dreadful day Mrs Anderson."

"Absolutely dreadful, I don't know where it will all end, and this wind, it nearly blew me over just trying to get here," Mavis replied.

"There's supposed to be a cool change coming through later," said Janet.

"Won't be much in that, "she replied. "By the way this wind's getting up there will be more chance of dust than rain."

The formalities over the reason for her visit was about to come. Janet could tell by the worried expression which was now invading her face.

"You haven't heard anything about the truck have you?" Mavis asked.

This one stumped Janet, which truck did she mean? There were a lot of different types of trucks that come through this street.

"Which truck is that Mrs Anderson?"

"The one from Worthton with the supplies, I was expecting it through last week and it didn't come. I'm right out of a lot of things in the shop. I've tried ringing them, but I couldn't get through. I went and saw Helen Davidson at the post office to see if she knew anything about the lines. She's going to look into it. She said she hadn't had a phone call all day. I just thought you might've heard something."

"No I haven't," Janet replied. "I tried ringing them this morning..."

"Is your phone out too?"

"Yes it is, all of a sudden, before nine this morning. Mr Kelly was on the phone then when I tried just after him, it was dead." Janet said.

"That's you too then. I was talking to Suzy Budd, they live along..."

"I know," said Janet.

"Earlier this morning so their phone was working then. She said the wind was getting up at their place then, so I don't know if their phone's still working now."

"We had Mr Stirling on the phone..."

"Out at Coolagy?" said Mavis.

"Yes," said Janet.

"What time was that?" said Mavis.

"Before nine."

"And it's been out ever since," said Mavis.

"Yes," said Janet.

"So it must've dropped out sometime between eight and nine, then?"

"I'd say so, except a client of Mr Kelly arrived around then and he said that he had been trying to ring earlier, but couldn't get through," said Janet.

"Where did he say he was trying to ring from?" said Mavis.

"I don't know, but he'd come a long way," said Janet.

"They must be down all over the place then. This wind is all over the place and getting worse. Where will it all end?"

At this point Helen Davidson arrived. A tall, thin woman who carried an air of authority since, after all, she did run the post office. Her greying hair and expressionless face added to a lack of transparency.

"There you are Mavis," she said as she entered. "I thought you said you were coming here. Good morning Janet."

"Good morning Mrs Davidson," Janet said.

"Have you heard anything?" Mavis said.

"I can't get through to Worthton either, but I can get through locally. I just spoke to Harry on the phone so it must be working there." Helen said. "John reckons perhaps the wind has blown down a pole somewhere between here and there."

"Janet said that their phone is down, went out all of a sudden. One minute it was working and the next it wasn't," Mavis said.

"I haven't tried locally though," Janet added.

"What time was that?" Helen asked.

"Before nine," Janet replied.

"Must have gone out then, then," Helen said.

"That's what we think," Mavis said. "What are we going to do?"

"Won't they know in at Worthton?" asked Janet.

"Not if no one tells them," replied Mavis.

"With this wind the way it is there's probably more than just us out," said Helen.

"Janet said some bloke tried to ring them much earlier and said he couldn't get through," said Mavis.

"I was talking to Joe at the garage..." Helen said.

"On the phone?" Mavis said.

"His is working, though he can't get through to Worthton or anywhere else, he said."

"We are really cut off then," Mavis said.

"He said that if anyone drops in after fuel, going to Worthton, he would ask them to let them know in Worthton what's going on."

"That's a good idea," said Mavis.

"We just hope someone who's driving around might see the pole that has come down," said Helen.

"I doubt if anyone will come out on a day like this though. Did he say if he knew anything about the truck from Worthton?" said Mavis.

"He said someone who called in last week for fuel, who'd come from Worthton, said that the truck would be coming out, they've just been delayed," said Helen.

"Yes, but when. I bet that truck's broken down again. Did you see the tyres on it the last time it came out?" said Mavis.

"Virtually bald," said Helen.

"I know. And he was having trouble with the motor that day," said Mavis.

"Was he?" said Helen.

"Oh yes, it broke down on the way here that day. Joe had to patch it up to get him home," said Mavis.

"There's no telling when it will get here then," said Helen.

"If it is on its way today, I hope it left early otherwise in this heat the vegetables will be ruined," said Mavis. "I just don't know what will happen."

None of this chatter was giving Janet much encouragement as she dwelt upon Mrs Stirling driving into Wallabra in this heat for a part that might not even be here. Her only hope was that Kevin would emerge from the store room with good news or Mr Kelly would return to do the explaining to Mrs Stirling.

# CHAPTER 15
# THE COOLAGY COMMUNITY.
# FEBRUARY 1965.

With the mirages being formed on the road ahead becoming more fluid, Marg could feel the sweat off her body now flowing freely. She was not yet near half way into Wallabra and already she was wishing the journey to end. The heat in the car was now becoming unbearable with no end to it. She found it always best on these seemingly endless drives through never changing country to focus on the next anomaly in the landscape.

With the turn off to the Gilmore's place well behind her now, she knew the cross roads would soon loom. It was the meeting of Coolagy and Wymere roads. This intersection was the north eastern corner of old Coolagy station and the beginning of Wymere. Turn left for the Wymere homestead, go straight ahead for other stations situated amongst the wilderness and turn right to Wallabra. There were no signs, no traffic signals, nothing to prepare someone who didn't know the road that there was an intersection approaching. Although, as not many cars were ever on this road at any one time, the chances of meeting another car at the intersection was very rare, it always paid to be aware. The best way to search for oncoming cars was to see if there was the obligatory cloud of red dust which followed each vehicle. This system usually worked better than any signals and the like that they have in the cities, as it gave a much greater warning. On these open plains a cloud of red dust was easy to see.

There were no trails of the red dust on this day she was safe to turn right onto the Wymere road, now heading more directly towards Wallabra. Of course the change of direction brought about a readjustment of the air flow. No longer was the wind coming from over her left shoulder, but rather from over her right shoulder. The reaction was immediate, the dust poured in. She leant over to put the passenger window up and the back window on the left down. Similarly hers down and the one behind up, soon the dust was pouring out of the car again.

With the sun now projecting the heat from higher in the sky the mirages filled each horizon. The blue fluid that the mirages created seemed as though it would flood over into the car, drowned by the heat. At the horizons the only distinction between the sky and the blue terrain the mirages created was that the sky was still.

She looked for and found to her right, separating the two blues, two structures which defied the illusionary flood of heat. Two cylindrical, concrete towers, a little stained by the red dust, reached through the liquidity of the mirage and stood rigid into the sky. The tall silos stood for most of the year devoid of human activity, standing like the awaited prize, tempting the farmers, medals that could only be attained at harvest time. Out of routine she now had to check for the trail of red dust coming down Settler's road. This was a relatively new road that was constructed when the farms that made up Coolagy were established. It served as an access road to some of the properties and the buildings that made up the Coolagy community centre, a mile down Settler's road.

This collection of four buildings may not have been the geographical centre of Coolagy, but was certainly the place of most of the social activities. The angularity of their shapes drew direct contrast to the flat and uninterrupted savannah they had been placed in. By their radical uniqueness they stood almost in defiance against their unruly, flat host.

The one teacher school made of timber and a corrugated iron roof comprised of two rooms, the class room and the teacher's office come storeroom and anything else that it needed to be, was a symbol of hope. It may have been only a small school, but it was a school and the community was very proud of it. In these conditions even though the white paint would often peel off quickly, it would be caringly renewed by a working bee. The working bee also built a shelter in the playground and a shelter for Buff, who stayed in a small paddock behind the school yard. The gum trees around the perimeter and the oleanders near the entrance, only planted a few years back, were struggling against this current drought. The bright summer flowers, produced by the oleanders, glowed in protest against the starkness of the summer, had lost this year's battle. The teacher's cottage stood just beyond the school yard to the east. Made of the same materials as the school and about the same size it represented a humble and lonely existence for the occupant.

On the other side of the school was the community hall. Since television was only something that they could have in the cities and one could only take so much of pop music on the radio, this hall represented the only social diversity available. Made totally of steel and corrugated iron, two sets of large doors and not many windows. The large doors served as air conditioning, closed in winter and open in summer. There were two rooms, one large room with an assortment of chairs and tables which could be arranged for whatever the purpose, a picture of the Queen and a piano. The room off the side was the same length as the bigger room, but much smaller in breadth. It had a crude, but functional kitchen at one end and a makeshift bar at the other. There were refrigerators at both ends and it was the job of whoever arrived first to turn them on. Outside there were some swings for the children, a set of toilets and plenty of red dust.

The loneliness of their district was warded off by visits to the community hall. As such it was used regularly. There were the Country Woman's Association meetings which were held on the first Tuesday of each month. Starting at One o'clock and coincided to finish at three thirty when school finished. Each month there was a cooking competition where everyone would have to make, say, a batch of scones and then the next month a batch of pikelets and so on. Marg usually won with her sponge cakes. Sue Cave set it all up originally because she knew the most about the CWA and so she became the president for many years. Now she rotated between secretary, treasurer and vice president. Needless to say, she still ran most of it. Her other advantage in this role was that she always kept well abreast of what was going on. When a resolution was being voted upon her opinion usually prevailed because she knew the most about the issue.

To the men they were known as the Cranky Women's Association. This remark was dealt with distain by the women, they considered their role as much more than a chat fest, the CWA were in charge of the hall and everything that went on in it. They also ran the school fete and the end of year Christmas party for the children as well as helping people who needed a hand. All of which were very important functions that needed to be carried out in the community.

One of the ladies, Polly Campbell, could play the piano very well. Therefore they could have song nights and dance nights with the Barn Dance when they could all have a thirty second chat to half of those there. What was even luckier was that she enjoyed playing the piano for sometimes hours on end. It was Tim's job, because he seemed to like music, to turn the pages for Polly. Marg wanted him to learn the piano and this was a good place for him to start.

They also had card nights. Five hundred was usually played. The biggest night of the year was the Christmas party, usually held on the day school breaks up. All the women did the catering and making of the tea whilst the men talked about farming. In early spring the men would gather for their annual Bushfire Brigade Meeting.

On the other side of the road were the concrete towers, the little corrugated shed next to the weigh bridge that made up the silo complex. Shut up for most of the year, but a place of great satisfaction in late spring during the harvest.

These buildings, basic as they may have been and seemingly out of place, standing in direct contrast to the open, flat plains around them, represented the warmth of human camaraderie the community felt for each other. Since the men had come from the services and given what they had been through, the mateship acquired flowed through the community. They all got on very well and felt fortunate to have each other.

There was one time, however, when they were split in disagreement. It was this incident where Marg was given the nickname of *The Blue Healer*.

# CHAPTER 16
## LORRY'S TOIL. FEBRUARY 1965.

The shed, south of the house, faced the east. The morning sun, gaining intensity lighted the space where Lorry was toiling. The sweat was streaming off his brow as he cut his way into an old forty four gallon drum. The wind, coming from the northwest, couldn't dry off the sweat nor could it temper the sun's heat. Only the occasional puff of the red dust, when a gust of the wind found its way into the enclosure, impeded the flow of fluid escaping from his body.

By this time he hoped that Marg would be well on her way to Wallabra. Possibly even passing the turn off to the Coolagy School. Even if she did have an uneventful trip it would still be many hours before she returned with the part which would solve the day's dilemma. In the meantime he had five hundred ewes with a thirst that was life threatening. For many of them the wait for Marg's return would be too late. He had to get water to them during this scorching day somehow. The bore at the house was still giving water, so this was the source. The forty fours cut in half were going to be the container and the tractor with the carry all which had the fire equipment on it, more especially, the water tank was to be the vehicle.

Flight and Sargent, both panting in response to the day's

heat, lay on the powdery red dust which was the floor of the shed, patiently waiting for Lorry to finish this task. Only then, they knew, would they have something exciting to do.

Chisel in his left hand and hammer in his right. He had made the initial incision wide enough to fit the rough edge of the chisel into the gap created and now with care was forcing the blade onto the metal frame of the drum. The freshly cut metal, with its gagged edges, presented a type of booby trap where upon any slight touch of the skin onto this subtle weapon resulted in blood being spilt. Lorry was conscious of this threat, but in his haste it became a secondary thought. The blood now seeping from numerous little nicks along the fingers on his left hand kept reminding him of the need for care. The sweat that fell off his head and onto these little cuts as he leant over the action, created a sting which he ignored, but rather would shake his head to rid it of the excess fluid. The flies, looking for shelter from the chaotic wind outside, had found the space inside the shed most congenial. Now they even had a meal waiting for them on Lorry's hands.

When the final blow was made which separated the two sections, the top section crashed to the ground startling the dogs who had both drifted off to sleep, bored of waiting. With the disturbance they eagerly looked to Lorry for direction. None came instead, he turned his back on them and proceeded to the bench. They looked outside at the dust being kicked up by the ever increasing wind and resigned themselves to further waiting.

After a period of frustratingly pushing different items around he eventually found what he was looking for, an old, rusted pair of trusted tin snips. Happy with his fruitful search he proceeded back to the drums. The sharp edges that the cutting had created were a danger not only to himself, but to the sheep who, in their desperation for water, would not be aware of the potential knife to their necks. After freeing up the mechanics of the tin snips which hadn't been used for a while, he made a series of small incisions, each about four inches apart, across the newly formed edges. Then, with the hammer, he bashed the flaps of metal against the wall of the drums leaving a blunt and safer edge.

That job done, Lorry headed out of the shed with the tractor in mind. When he became exposed to the wind he realised that he had under estimated its increased intensity as his walk became unbalanced. The dogs had seemingly been oblivious to the previous banging of the hammer, definitely heard or felt Lorry's exit from the scene. Their excitement was instantly stimulated as they hurried about, not in the least bit concerned by the day's extremes, wondering where the next adventure would be leading them. As Lorry reversed the tractor onto the linkages of the carry all, the dogs watched carefully as if they were the overseers of the operation. With the tractor placed successfully, to the dog's satisfaction, Lorry was about to place a pin into the left hand linkage when the blood and sweat on his hands caused it slipped out. Sargent, who had positioned himself very close to Lorry, watching Lorry very carefully, pounced upon the wayward pin even before it had hit the ground. Pleased with his effort, he produced it back to Lorry wetter than it was before due to the pin's excursion into Sargent's mouth. Lorry rewarded him for his efforts with a pat on his head.

With the carry all on, as Lorry was about to move off the dogs had pre-empted the direction. It usually followed that the next station on this day's travels would be the tank next to the bore on the northern side of the house yard. They were not mistaken. They watched carefully as Lorry syphoned water out of the tanks next to the windmill and into the fire tank. Lorry watched the intensity of the dog's stare and devised a little treat for them. He took the opportunity, with the running water, to splash some over his hands and face. The instant relief from the piercing heat was most welcomed. Further to the joy of the cooling he took the hose out of the fire tank and poured it onto his head. Then watched the dog's strange expression upon his actions, when he had them perplexed he suddenly pointed the hose onto the dogs. The sudden change of stimulus frightened them and they both ran off to escape the threat. But, after a good shake, ventured back as if wanting more. When the tank was full, Lorry did point the water towards the dogs. This time they were aware of his movements and took a little time to enjoy the cooling water on their backs.

After revisiting the shed the carry all was now fully loaded with all that he would need. The cooling effect of the water had totally worn off and the heat perpetuated once more. At least the cuts on his hands had stopped bleeding. The dogs could sense Lorry's motives for another move. There was some room on the tank for the dogs to sit out the journey. He tapped the side of the tank in a signal for them to jump onto the space, but they rejected the offer. They soon realised that the direction of this day's journey was south. They knew the way. Like sentinels through the wilderness the two dogs occupied a tyre track each exactly twenty yards in front of the tractor. Keeping up a regular trot they headed off into the fluid, blue mirage that was the horizon. Not bothering to notice the obscure scene in front of them, not perturbed by the heat ever increasing, not troubled by the wind blowing them to the front, the man and his two dogs, together as company, set forth unquestioningly towards the foe.

# CHAPTER 17
# COOLAGY SCHOOL. MAY 1963

It was a genetic component of her family that turned them all grey early. Marg, however, didn't much care for the look so she kept putting a bit of blue rinse through it. She was never perturbed by what people thought of her, it was a common known fact in the community. She was never too worried about what she said. She spoke what she thought and if they didn't like it that was their problem. The more passionate she was on a topic the more outspoken she became. Lorry always complained about her lack of tact, but he has never been able to say that she was wrong in what she had said. Thus if she wanted to put blue rinse through her hair, she did.

Being a teacher, education was one of those passions that she held dear. She was never too keen on her boys going to the one teacher school at Coolagy that could only take the children to the age of fifteen. For Marg, the idea of one teacher to teach all the different classes, disregarding how good the teacher may have been, never instilled much faith of a suitable education. In fact it infuriated her that her children could finish up less educated than she was. To her the next generation must always be better educated than their parents because that is the only way society can progress.

It was *a fait accomph* that the boys would be going on

further than fifteen. Although it was such a distance that was going to separate them when they reached high school age both the boys went to boarding school. There they could do their higher school certificate. Then they would have a broader horizon in which to travel through life.

Her views contradicted many of the community at Coolagy. They didn't really see the need for higher education. They had gotten by without much education therefore their children would do the same. It was often the culture that the boys would either take over the farm they were on or get their own place and the girls would marry a farmer. The only education they needed was how to run a farm.

Besides, together with the community hall, the school was the bedrock of their companionships. How else was there going to be such constant social interaction except through the school. The afternoon chat whilst waiting for school to finish was an integral part of the daily routine. The friendships that the children gained at the school would continue the culture of the community. The children were not supposed to discover if there was a hill beyond the eastern horizon. Everything they would need was here. There was no need to leave.

When Marg would hear this commentary she would do her best to bite her tongue, but that never lasted for long. Hence the *Blue Healer* tag.

The year Tim first went to boarding school happened to be a very wet year. It was a positive confirmation of what Lorry would always be telling her in the bad times.

"It will change. This land will provide, you'll see. Just have to be patient. It all runs in circles."

This remark would be heard by Marg only when Lorry could sense that the isolation, the hardships, the fight was getting her down. She would take it on board out of a sense of duty and to keep in character with the role she had to perform. The truth was that at the time of hearing she would be too depressed by the current situation to pay it much heed.

However this was one time when he was proved correct. The harvests had been good. There was a little bit of spare money to spend. Marg even suggested new windows in the house to rid her of the accursed louvre windows. She was in competition though with the prospect of a new plough that was destined to do a better job and thus better yields, providing it rained, of course.

It was proving to be a difficult year for Marg. With both the boys now away at boarding school, she was missing them dreadfully. There was now a gap in her life. No beds to make, no lunches to provide, no developing personalities to study and enjoy. There was now a void that had to be filled.

The sun filtered in through their bedroom window and a little seeped into the kitchen as Marg was enjoying her first cup of tea for the day. It was a moment of relief that it still did exist. There had been three days of steady rain, then there was three days of clouds. The sun's appearance was welcome.

It was early May and the perfect time to be planting the crops. Lorry was up at first light, and was now on the tractor, going around and around in ever diminishing circles, sowing the seed.

Since the fire Marg and Shirley had built up a strong relationship. The previous evening Marg had received a phone call from Shirley inviting her across for morning tea, knowing that the road between them would now have dried out enough to get there. There was nothing unusual about this, it was a common occurrence, excepting that this time Marg noticed a certain formality in Shirley's voice. It was as if she had something on her mind that was troubling her. Marg was curious to find out what it was all about.

In the seemingly short time, compared to the others at Coolagy, that they had been on their farm, Eddie and Shirley had turned it around. It was now producing very good crops. Joe Harrison, who owned it before them, was never cut out to be a farmer. Before the war he was a carpenter. When the opportunity came to own his own block of dirt, how could he resist? This turned out to be a common problem with some of the soldier settler farms, the men that got them didn't necessarily have the knowledge or experience to run a farm. In the end they would suffer because they were always struggling to make ends meet. The farms would suffer because of the mistakes made. The Stirlings were sorry to see Joe go because he was very likeable and handy when they needed some wood work done.

It was only after Eddie and Shirley moved in that they found out just how badly that farm had been run, and the number of empty wine flagons that had to be picked up.

Shirley and Marg's optimism upon the state of the road between them was grossly mistaken. After seemingly slipping and sliding all the way across to Shirley's place Marg was ever so pleased to see the casuarinas in front of their house. Marg had avoided getting stuck and didn't have to get out of the car till she had arrived at her destination. Therefore she was still clean.

Fortunately their front gate was open for if she had to stop and open it she may have walked through, but the car would have to stay there, bogged. The yellow fibro house soon came into view. Marg parked as close to the cement footpath leading to the house as she could, so as not to get too much mud on her shoes. Fifty yards from the house stood the shed. The same as the other sheds on the Coolagy farms except this one had a new plough parked inside, resting now after its inaugural test.

Upon hearing the noise of the approaching car, Shirley was there to greet Marg as she alighted from the car.

"Nice drop of rain Shirley," Marg said.

"I know," said Shirley. "Eddie's been out since first light this morning. I'm to take lunch down to him and I expect I won't see him till dark after that."

"Well then let's hope we get some good follow up rain, after they get the crops in."

"Come in, I'm just boiling the kettle now for morning tea," Shirley said.

If the exterior of the house suggested small, the interior confirmed it. Three bedrooms, a living room and a very small kitchen were squeezed into a restricted space to house themselves and their now three boys aging from one to nearly five.

Shirley was fifteen years younger than Marg. She was part of a new generation that were a bit more cosmopolitan than those who had been brought up to a rural existence as though there was no other. They had come from Victoria where there was greater rainfall. They were also both from well to do farming stock who lived much closer to the city and thus were a bit broader in their expectations. Eddie had been educated at a school that taught agriculture. Shirley had been to a ladies college in the city and knew all the fineries. Marg would listen to her talk about her upbringing and would often feel a twinge of envy that she had experienced more of life. They moved up to this district because it was much cheaper to buy up here.

When they first arrived, Marg thought that this place must've been a bit of a shock to them after where they had come from, as it had been for a lot of them. But to their credit, they stuck it out, joined the local community and had made a go of the place. They had become very popular in the community. A little shy at first, Shirley was not the life of the party type, but rather a more of a one on one person which is possibly why she and Marg had formed such a close friendship.

They were part of a generation that hadn't experienced two world wars and a depression. The original settlers of Coolagy were happy with what they had, Eddie and Shirley's generation wanted more.

The kitchen was the first room on the right. There was no door or walls into the kitchen, it formed a part of the hallway that proceeded to the living room and the bedrooms. A table, with wooden legs and a plastic top which seated six, filled most of the area of the kitchen. So much, that to get by meant a squeeze by the seated. Cupboards on all the walls added to the congestion. The fuel stove however made this the warmest room in the house.

The teapot and its contents, as well as an assortment of cupcakes, already prepared, adorned the brightly coloured table cloth on the kitchen table. The hot tea and the warmth from the fuel stove took the edge of the chilling May air.

Marg could sense that Shirley had something on her mind. It was as if her thoughts were different to the conversation and it could be seen that she had difficulty concentrating on the current, to her, unnecessary small talk. Marg figured it would come out when she was ready to.

"Marg, you're two boys have gone to the Coolagy school, what do you think of it? I mean you were a teacher so you would know more about the school than I would," asked Shirley.

Her inquiry did not at all surprise Marg. Given their upbringing she realised they would be very disappointed with the education that was available.

"Shirley," she replied, "to tell you the truth, it is far from ideal. You've met Mr Plummer, the current teacher?"

"Yes."

"He's not too bad. I mean there have been a lot worse there and he is genuinely trying his best, but think of it, you have thirty or so children in a class ranging from five to fifteen, all the children are at different levels. He can't attend to all of them at once. I suppose we should be grateful that there is a school here, but between you and me it is far from the best situation." Marg said.

"Is that why Ken and Tim are at boarding school?"

"Lorry and I want them to have a better education than what they would get here, so boarding school was the only option."

"Do you miss them? How often do you see them?"

"Of course we miss them. We only get them during the school holidays now, but what else can we do? We must give them the best education that we can. You see, being a teacher I know the importance a good schooling will be in the future. It opens the door to so many other things than farming."

"I guess I was lucky. I went to boarding school, but we could go home on the weekends," Shirley said.

There was a momentary pause in the conversation. Marg could sense that Shirley had something, an idea, brewing in her mind, but was trying to find the right words to convey the thought. She allowed Shirley the space to figure it out besides she was interested by what might be revealed.

"James will be ready for school next year. Eddie and I are quite worried about sending him and the other boys to that school. It is nothing about Mr Plummer, he seems to be doing his best. We both like the idea of a community school and that we can have them every day, but it is not what they need."

"Unfortunately Shirley, living out here, we don't have much choice."

"Well no, I think there is a choice."

Marg pricked her ears with interest.

"The school at Wallabra can have the children till they can attain their higher school certificate, that's right isn't it?" Shirley said knowing the answer.

"Yes," Marg said. "But it struggles to get enough children and there is not much money spent on it."

"Just as I thought," said Shirley.

Shirley paused again and Marg waited patiently for the substance of this conversation.

"If there was a bus to take the children into Wallabra, we could close the school, send them all into Wallabra and

Wallabra might get better funding and more teachers."

Marg had opened herself to any idea and would give heed to anything suggested. However this idea took her completely by surprise. The thought of a better education for the children was a great concept, but its implementation led Marg to consider the concept quite naive. On the surface it was an excellent idea, but trying to get it into practice was another thing entirely.

Now it was Marg's turn for the dramatic pause as she sorted through the words for a reply.

"Shirley, I think your idea is excellent, but have you actually thought about the practicalities of getting this to happen?"

"Surely everyone else in the community will want this?" Shirley asked naively.

"Possibly not my dear, you see, they are all very proud of their little school. It is the founding rock of the community and a lot of these people don't comprehend the idea of a decent education. Most of them have gotten along quite fine without one and they expect their children to do the same."

Shirley looked at Marg aghast.

"The other thing is the roads. We have enough trouble getting into Wallabra as it is let alone a bus going along it twice a day," Marg said.

"Then the council must then fix them up. Roads used for school buses have priority, they will have to fix them up. As for the other parents, we will just have to educate them the importance of this," Shirley said with authority.

Marg was instantly impressed with the determination Shirley had for her plan. It was what Marg liked about Shirley, her strength and will. In that regard they were peas in a pod. Marg felt inspired by Shirley and even though the chances of success were small, she decided to at least give it a go. Shirley had obviously done her homework and wouldn't it be great to have the roads seen to more regularly. Her idea excited Marg.

"I can't fault your idea in principle, in fact I think it is a great idea."

"I had an idea you'd like it," Shirley said with a knowing smile.

"I'm secretary of the Parents and Citizens association for our school this year and we will be having another meeting in about three weeks, let's get our heads together and try and sort something out for then. We'll need to start sending letters off to get information upon how to do it ..."

As Marg was talking she could sense Shirley feeling very relieved that she had *The Blue Healer* on her side. Now they had to hope the others in the community would agree.

# CHAPTER 18
## ALONE. FEBRUARY 1965.

The right turn off Wymere road towards the school was well behind Marg now as she motored towards Wallabra on this furnace of a day. On her left, the vast open plains of Beeholme station and on her right the vast open plains of the soldier settler farms of Coolagy. The only difference being that there were more fences and buildings on the right. Otherwise the cruel drought had rendered both sides of the road uselessly barren.

The road was still flat and straight as it headed south. That did not necessarily mean that the car stayed in a straight line. Dodging potholes, suffering corrugations and reacting to the wind coming in from her right shoulder ensured the steering wheel was constantly moving. At least this road was a little bit better than Coolagy road which meant she could pick up a little time. So far on this drive she had not seen another car. She felt as if she was the only one silly enough to be driving on such a hot day as this.

Now being on Wymere road the added bonus was that she was heading in the right direction towards Wallabra, south. Once on Wymere road, with more than a quarter of the journey completed, a thought of getting there could be entertained. She glanced at her wrist watch out of habit, but quickly realised it was not there. She looked at where the sun was positioned as this was her only indication of time. All that she could ascertain was that it was still morning. Hopefully she could be in Wallabra a little before noon. Ideally she would be able to pick up the part at Jack Kelly's place, get a few groceries, exchange the library books and be on her way back by one to be home after three. With that thought a little smile stole onto her face. Lorry, who always says that she took too long when she went into Wallabra, would be surprised. He always suspected that she spend her time talking to the people she met in there. If she could get back by three it would give Lorry plenty of time to repair the windmill, get the water flowing again and have the sheep back there before dusk. Their plight motivated her to persevere on this dreadful day.

There was still a lot of driving to be done. The day's heat had now reached unbearable proportions. What was worse it was here to stay for hours. No comfort in sight. On days like this day, when the north westerlies are screaming down, the temperature climbs to frightening heights.

Marg could never handle the heat of this place, somewhere in the middle of nowhere which is the outback. She missed the Hunter where often a slight sea breeze would filter in during the afternoon to temper the extremes. She missed her family and the connections from her childhood. She now found herself totally isolated from what she had hoped for as a child. She would often ask herself Why? The answer was obvious, children, husband, sense of duty, sense of purpose, sense of future, hope, this was her lot. But was this always going to be her life? A life of fighting an enemy, the outback, with its extremes, its landscape of sameness, its unpredictability, its red dust, its mud, its lack of water, its roughness, its starkness, its defiance of her attempt to bring civility to a base environment. The question forever lingered.

It lingered still on this very hot day with the miles floating past, like wasted hours, through a never ending landscape. This was another test of perseverance, of resistance, of struggle, of fight to overcome the most persistent of foe, merely to survive. Why?

It was consolation to know that she was, but one of many in the battle. Communities all over this great land were doing the same, all with a contented disposition for their lot as though they were meant for it. How could they find solace in this place when the world offers so much more? She wondered about the Aboriginals who had mastered surviving in this place of nothingness for thousands of years and wanted nothing more than to be a part of it. She often felt, if she really wanted to understand this strange abnormal land that she should understand the Aborigines since they would have the knowledge to deal with this environment. This, however, could not eventuate since there was such a cultural divide between the two societies that one could not, through social decree, associate with the other.

The wind was now gusting with increasing velocity. With each gust came an immediate readjustment of the steering wheel. It would also bring a sudden burst of air onto her body which tendered to give a moment of cool relief. If she could time it that when the gust came and she could lean forward it might help to dry her back of the sweat that she knew would be staining her dress. She didn't want to arrive at Wallabra with too many stains on what was a clean dress.

Another milestone approached. On her right Coolagy and the soldier settler farms ended and another station, Benembar, began. Not that there was much difference except that both sides of the road now only had a fence lining the road and, of course, the poles and wires. The scenery was just three hundred and sixty degrees of a flat lined horizon. Now to look for the next differential to prove that progress was being made.

Even though she knew where it would be and the time taken before it emerged, she still strained her sight through the mirage ahead for the first glimpse. This made normal time longer, which she knew, but she was impatient to get this day's task completed, have a shower and feel more comfortable.

Her impatience led her thoughts to despair. What if the mirage, which had totally surrounded her, had swallowed her up and transported her to another place where the boredom didn't end. Fortunately, in time to keep her sanity, spasmodic blotches of dark emerged through the shimmering fluid that lay before her. Then the unmistakable thin black line burst into visibility breaking the shimmering mirage.

At this part of the journey into Wallabra the road came upon a series of gullies. Sometimes, out here, they did get what is known as a rain event. It is the land of extremes. Most of the time it is very dry and the landscape shows it, but then a freak change in the weather pattern will see inches of rainfall in a very short period. Of course on this ultimately flat terrain, there is nowhere for the water to run off to. Hence, over the centuries of these freak downpours, these gullies have evolved to cater for such an event. Since these gullies have had much more water in them, as compared to the surrounds, gum trees manage to survive. Hence the thin black line which was now appearing on the horizon.

She always felt a slight relief to see these trees approaching on the way to Wallabra. It was like the beginning of the countdown to arrival. There was still a way to go, but certainly half way had been reached.

As she approached the gully the mirage lifted to reveal the trees, now grey and green, standing resolutely. In the depression of the gully, she knew the road was a bit rougher so she began to slow down to manage the bumps that were a permanent fixture.

Suddenly the car's engine started to make a thumping noise, as though something was hitting something that it was not meant to. It was always such a worry that something might go wrong with the car somewhere in the middle of nowhere. She could feel her heart start pumping much harder. What was she going to do out here with no one in sight? Something was drastically wrong and she knew that she was not going to make it into Wallabra with the car as it was.

The trees loomed closer and she didn't want to have to stop in the middle of the gully where the road narrows. That could be dangerous if anyone else should come along they wouldn't see her till the last moment. As she descended in to the gully she could now see steam coming out from underneath the bonnet.

The journey must now stop quickly. Lorry had warned her never to let the engine boil and with this steam now gusting out, she was looking for a place to land. Ascended out of the gully and onto flat land again she pulled over to the left, on the side of the road and came to a halt. Steam was now the only item moving. Fortunately the trees that she had just passed served as a crude wind break and where she finished up was quite safe.

She knew that, at this part of the drive, there were no houses close by. There would be no farmers going past in their paddocks, on a day like this no likelihood of any boundary riders. There was only this empty road in a vast, flat, empty wilderness devoid of any humans.

The sudden inertia was of complete contrast to the previous many miles. She found the stillness difficult to accept. No engine noise, not the same airflow through the car. There was only the violent rustling of the leaves on the gum trees and the increasing annoying buzz of the flies who were delighted to have a new food source in Marg.

What to do now? Mechanically minded, she was not. There was not much point in opening the bonnet at the moment as it would be much too hot to do anything with. All she could do was to wait and hope for someone to come along and help. Out here that could be quite some time. During her drive so far on this day she had not passed anyone. Meanwhile the temperature was still rising and the wind gusts were increasing in their regularity and the sheep, at home, becoming parched waiting for her return.

The sun now had a stationary metallic object as a target. It beamed its ammunition of heat onto the car. Together with the heat from the engine and stunted airflow the temperature in the car quickly rose. Marg's position on the seat was becoming increasingly more uncomfortable.

She was alone in this vast wilderness with only the wind and the flies to break the silence. She was not going anywhere and had to endure being stuck in an environment that she could never feel comfortable with. Her anxiety grew, not only for the poor sheep and Lorry waiting for her at home, but on such a day as this, for her own safety. At least she did have some water. But how to ration it? Leaving enough for the car, with an indefinite wait ahead of her. Her anxious thoughts crowded her mind. In this state five minutes seems like half an hour with the same negative thoughts prevailing.

Do something. There was no point is sitting in this seat worrying and getting hotter. It was not in her nature to just give up and hope. The steam had stopped escaping from underneath the bonnet. Curiosity led her to wonder what was wrong. She pulled the lever that opened the bonnet and alighted from the car. Instantly she felt the full force of the wind as it propelled the door open with force and she had to exert extra pressure to close it. She could feel the wind acting on the sweat that had collected on her dress and on her face and felt the instant cooling effect enforced upon her. Indeed it was probably more comfortable outside the car. She opened up the bonnet and could feel the greater heat from the engine inflict itself upon her. The previous thought of coolness was instantly dismissed. There was still a bit of steam coming out, but as she looked closer, just behind the radiator, she could see a loose piece of rubbery cord which appeared to be not where it was supposed to be. From her limited knowledge of how cars work she figured out that this was the fan belt and it was broken. Lorry once explained to her the importance of the fan belt and that it was essential for keeping the engine cool.

She remembered that this had happened to them once before and Lorry managed to fix it up with a spare fan belt which he said he always carried. She was grateful for his fore thought at the time and naturally assumed that there would be another, spare fanbelt, in the car. If Lorry could fix it up, then it was about time she did it herself. She knew what a spanner was and had used them before this. Knowing that Lorry had been a Flight Sergeant and in charge of the maintenance for the aircraft, she felt assured that everything that she would need would be in the boot. It shouldn't be too difficult, after all, she did have plenty of time and just how proud would she be in telling Lorry what she had done. The worry was how to keep herself clean enough to be presentable in Wallabra. Car engines are such dirty things.

She moved around to the boot and opened it. The result was the freeing of much dust by the wind which now had ready access to the enclosure of the boot. The dust covered her for a moment and she had to cough it out of her lungs and brush it off her dress, quickly so as it would not stain her sweaty apparel. There was the spare wheel and the jack sitting next to it. She almost wished that if there was to be a breakdown it would've been a flat tyre. She could change a tyre, she had done that before. There was a metal box which contained the tools. She opened it up to see a lot of spanners and other metal objects that she was not quite sure what they did. At least she was assured, by the number of items in there that she would not want for the right tool. There was a large container of water, enough to top up the radiator. A can of what she suspected would be oil of some description. Then another can of what she suspected would be another type of oil, a pair of pliers and different gauges of wire. Always an essential commodity, if nothing else can fix a problem wire is the last resort. These items were easily seen, after this, in her search for a fan belt she would have to start moving items to see what was underneath them. She could feel the dust on her fingers and hoped it would not invade the rest of her body as she moved things about.

She reached and searched amongst the red dust which had found permanent residence in the boot, but she was not finding a spare fan belt. Her disappointment was turning to anger. Lorry was usually very efficient at checking the car before a trip yet there was still no fan belt. If she couldn't find one he was certainly going to find out about it when she got home. She continued the search through the back seat, but still no fan belt.

Defeated, stranded, isolated, in a hopeless situation, there was nothing to do, but wait. What was worse, the excursion into the boot and the dust there in had left stains all over her dress. She used a little bit of the water to wash her hands and face, but the rest of her looked most untidy.

It was too hot and uncomfortable to sit in the car. The shade created by the gum trees was close at hand with a fallen log conveniently place in the shaded area. She walked across to this log, checked that there was no snakes of anything else that might harm her, sat down and waited. The only other living things at this place were the flies. Sitting with her back to the wind they saw in her a suitable shelter and a ready nutrition. She soon became very popular with the local residents. They were ever so annoyed when she changed positions to face the wind. They discovered that her back did not have eyes, ears and mouths to crawl into.

Occasionally the flies would receive a respite when Marg, in her constant search for a trail of red dust to signify an approaching car, would turn her head to search the other direction. What to do? Nothing, there was nothing she could do, but wait and hope. She had learned that hoping in this environment never amounted to much. They had been hoping for this drought to end for quite some time and it was still raging. The only hope was in waiting. To lay down thoughts and accept that this will change, when it's ready to. Hoping will not change that. There was no resolution in hope.

She felt defenceless, vulnerable and annoyed. She was annoyed that she was not given the opportunity to exercise her own will, by attempting to fix the car. She had no power over her current predicament. For one who prided herself on always being in control, this current situation infuriated her. There was the added worry of the sheep back home. Also, would she make Kelly's before it closed? She had not seen another car all day, it was a distinct possibility. She knew that at this point of the journey there were no houses close by, beside the golden rule was to always stay with the car. All these concerns made waiting ever more difficult.

She realised that the trouble with worry is that it would fill her mind with thoughts that could not be stopped. She had to change her thoughts, besides worrying was not going to bring a car along any quicker. Power over her mind and her attitude to the situation was one useful rite that she could exercise. Someone would eventually come along and in the mean time to make the best of this place.

She was stuck with only pre viewed scenery to purvey. She had seen it all before and felt it didn't need re-examining. But it was all that there was. Realising that her negative mind set was on the agenda to be changed, she began to study the branches of the trees she waited under. Before they had only been trees on the road to Wallabra, a mere milestone. Now she had the chance to actually study them. The dead leaves lay to waste around her, the decaying log she was sitting on. All had been here for much longer than she had. She saw the crows seeking shelter amongst the branches, waiting patiently for a respite from the wind. The ants crawled over themselves to keep performing their mindless tasks. The flies who persisted with their annoying movements in their effort to survive. They were all undaunted by the day's heat and wind. It came naturally to them. They understood what this country was doing and they accepted it. It was what they were used to. It had been going on for much longer than she had been sitting on this log, waiting.

Sometimes, at home, mostly at night, but sometimes during the day, she would listen to the silence and would find great peace in the nothingness of the Australian outback. It is a peace that can only be experienced by being consumed by it. She could sometimes feel, when there was obviously no noise to be heard, a great contentment from the silence as though she was really a part of what had been going on for thousands and thousands of years.

Eventually, whilst sitting on this log, she could feel a similar calmness coming over her, as though she was opening herself to what fate had in store for her. Of course, when she would have these thoughts on the farm it was in conjunction with, an interlude from a task, she was already performing. This was different, there was not that directive. There was nothing to do. This situation had a sense of possible permanency about it.

The minutes now rolled past in an unnoticed procession. The variations of the wind gusts through the trees were the only stimulus that ever changed. Marg and the place she now found herself immersed, waited and endured as though time had no more relevance.

The wind and the flies kept a constant and regular noise which had quickly became monotonous. Suddenly she could sense or hear another type of noise. It sounded like something moving and it came from within the gully. She looked to her right into the gully, but could see nothing out of place. Perhaps it was a branch coming off, a kangaroo resting in the shade or some sheep doing the same.

She began to feel vulnerable again. The effort she had put into feeling less anxious about her situation had turned around. Although she could see nothing in the gully she still had this feeling of a presence there and it worried her. Even though there might be no logic to it, she usually believed in her gut feelings and at this time they completely occupied her thoughts. If it was someone there surely they would approach therefore it must have been an animal.

She was not one to sit and wonder, she had to find out for herself to put her mind at ease. Besides she did have plenty of time to investigate. She walked over to the road to see if there were any cars coming. It would be almost tragic if she missed one. There wasn't, only the mirages that melted into the blue sky. Besides if a car was to come along the mere sight of a stationary car out here, especially with its bonnet open, would cause the driver to stop. She walked slowly trying to convince herself that it was possibly only an animal of some description.

As she descended into the gully it now took on a rather ominous aspect. There was a little bit of vegetation left and she was careful where she placed her feet least she might tread on a snake. Looking further along, where the gully went into Beeholme there was less vegetation. After crossing the fence she did not have to be so careful with her foot placements.

The fallen logs now became more distinct. They appeared as angled structures, coloured differently by their state of decay and the changing shadows from the trees, portraying ominous shapes. Dead material, laying, waiting to be decomposed by the elements so it can be used to make living material again. Until another wind storm comes and blows it down again. The tree itself keeps surviving though. The ferocity of this wind on this day created more anxiety for Marg contemplating a branch that might fall on her. Then she would become a part of this material in the gully, laying, waiting to be decomposed.

At one of these angles she could see a patch of blue. Against the red soil it was quite distinct. It could not therefore be a sheep or a kangaroo. Maybe a piece of blue cloth, except this blue was containing an object otherwise it would be laying on the ground and thus unseeable.

She stopped for a moment to observe this strange anomaly. It did not move. It needed further investigation.

Curiosity overcame fear beside she knew that she was

strong enough to look after herself. As she got closer she could see that it was a human figure. What was this person doing here? Was it alive, dead, in trouble, why was this person hiding?

She arrived at the log and peered over to see an Aboriginal man obviously trying to hide. Realising he had been discovered, he got up. Besides that fact that his clothes, which consisted of a very dirty shirt with a torn collar and a rip over his shoulder as though done by a barbed wire fence. Blue trousers that had no material covering his knees and a hat that was saturated with sweat, he appeared to be in no trouble.

Their eyes met briefly and she instantly recognised him as from the mob living just outside Wallabra. She had seen him sitting with members of the Aboriginal community outside the store or in other parts of the town. He seemed to be held in high esteem by the mob and by his age he could well have been an elder. Of course, in this district and in many other such districts, there was not much conversation between the white people and the black people. The Aboriginals were not popular amongst the white people. They often got the blame if anything went missing and were always frowned upon because they did nothing all day except sit around. Many of the white women would spread unsavoury tales about the Aboriginal men as though they were to be feared.

Marg always kept quiet when the conversations would turn to the Aborigines. She suspected the truth was often exaggerated. To her eyes they were basically a passive race. Did it matter that they had different ideals? They want for little and survive quite comfortably. The white people wanted for a lot and battle constantly. She had wanted to find out for herself, one day, if they were as bad as they were made out to be.

It looked like that day was going to be today. He looked at her very shyly for a moment then turned away, almost as if he had been a naughty boy and was ready to be scolded. Although she well knew that she was totally alone with this man somewhere out the back of nowhere, she did not feel alarmed. Physically, she was not possibly as strong as this man, but mentally she knew she had it all over him. His shyness which almost bordered on embarrassment and his avoidance of eye contact gave her greater strength. The relationship with this man reminded her of her days as a teacher. This man now appeared to her as like one of her students. She never had trouble enforcing her views with her students, this situation caused for the same tact. Excepting that this student was a little shy and therefore had to be treated gently.

"Hello," she said calmly, as if not to alarm him and if anything try and place him at ease. "I'm Mrs Stirling."

She held out her hand for him to shake. Realising that his attempt to hide from her had failed, he hesitated, and then returned the gesture.

"Are you all right?" she asked.

"Yes Missus," he replied, not wanting to divulge too much.

She began to feel a little more relaxed. Neither now felt threatened, but she started to realise this was all a bit strange. Another human being seemingly just stuck out here with no transport just bidding his time. Nothing to be done, just being here. Why, she wondered?

"What are you doing here?" she asked.

He paused for a moment before replying as if trying to ascertain if she was now a threat to him. Marg observed a procession of different expression come over his face as he searched for the best reply.

"I've been Walkabout. Had to connect with country again," he replied with a definite air of truth.

She knew that it was to be believed. They did that from time to time. They would turn up at the most unlikely of places. It was natural to them, but a constant source of suspicion for the farmers. She noticed that he had nothing on him except what he was wearing. He must have been thirsty on a day like this.

"I have some water in the car. Would you like a drink?" she asked.

Again he was hesitant in his reply. Perhaps he was surprised that a white person would show him kindness or suspicious that there might have been a catch to it. She was white and he knew that the black people usually finish worse off after any dealings with the white people.

"Come on," she insisted, "You look like you could do with a drink."

She could see that he was distrustful. The cultural barrier was impeding their communication. She needed to gain his trust.

"It is over in my car. There's plenty there for you."

Again he looked concerned.

"Look, there's no one else here, I'm by myself. I'm not going to do anything to you. If you want some water I'm quite happy to give you some."

The plain talking honest approach together with an air of confidence seemed to work. They walked back to the car in silence, but with reassurance. When they got back to the car she took out the container of water from the boot and passed it to him. It was now obvious that he was very thirsty as he had a good and long drink.

"Thank you Missus," he said handing the container back to her. He looked at the bonnet which was still open.

"What's wrong with the car?" he asked.

"I've done a fan belt," she replied.

Marg could see that he was quite interested in having a look for himself.

"You can have a look for yourself if you like."

He accepted the invitation with glee and moved without hesitation proceeding immediately to the front of the car and peered in. Marg was a little taken back at his enthusiasm, but consoled herself that he could do no harm surely. He peered into the engine and took a little time in deliberating and then proclaimed profoundly.

"The fan belt's buggered," whereby his head became more submerged into the engine.

She had heard that the Aboriginals had a knack of fixing things. On this occasion she hoped, but didn't count on it. Besides, there was no spare fan belt, what could he do? She looked up and down the road again hoping for further help.

He seemed to be pocking around under the bonnet for now quite longer than was necessary, she thought. She was worried that he might do something that Lorry wouldn't have approved of. She moved around to the front of the car to see what he was doing.

"You need another fan belt Missus," he proclaimed with profundity.

"Yes, I know," she replied, as though she didn't need to be reminded and disappointed that in all the time he had deliberated upon the situation this was his best advice.

"Do you have one? I can fix it up for you," he asked, as though he was hoping that she would have one and give him the opportunity to work on this car.

"No," she replied which brought about an instant disappointment in his expressions. He looked down and appeared to be looking at Marg's legs. At first she thought it was out of disappointment, but it went on for too long. She wondered if she should have been concerned by this.

"Missus," he finally said. "You've got stockings on."

"Yes," Marg replied a little concerned.

"Could you take them off, Missus?" he asked.

This request brought about great alarms in Marg. Perhaps all those tales the ladies had been saying were true. At this point she did feel a little threatened. He must've sensed this.

"For the car Missus," he explained. "Might be able to use them to get it going again and get you into town."

She took a little while to deliberate. How were her stockings going to help? She could not see the logic in this and this created greater concern in her.

"It's all right Missus, I know what I'm doing," he said.

Marg picked up on the genuineness of his concern. What did she have to lose? Besides, there was no other help on offer. Perhaps he did have a method that she was unaware of.

"You wait here," she said and went around to the back of the car where the boot, still open, would hide her from view.

Stockings off, she passed them to him as well as the box of tools and then retreated, sat in the car and hoped that he would be able to fix it up. How he was going to do it was beyond her. She felt the car jerking as he seemed to be tugging and pulling at this and that. Then he went around to the boot and brought back the container of water.

He filled the radiator, closed the bonnet and looked at her with satisfaction.

"Should get you to town Missus, just drive slow," he said.

To Marg this seemed too good to be true. She pulled the lever to open the bonnet. She wanted to see for herself. He anticipated her intention and had the bonnet up by the time she was there.

"See there, Missus. I use your stockings as a fan belt. It works, I've seen it work. It get you to town and you get another one there."

Now it was her turn for her face to go through a range of different expressions, from amazement, to relief, to speechlessness. The thought of this episode being completed certainly led her to giving it a try. What did she have to lose?

"Start her up Missus," he suggested.

She started it up and listened carefully for a couple of minutes. It seemed to be running alright, without the previous knocking noise.

"Turn her off Missus," he then said which led her to think the worst. He signalled to her to open the bonnet again which she did and again his head disappeared into the engine. She felt series of knocks and pulls here and there. Through the gap between the top of the dashboard and the bottom of the bonnet she could see him checking the radiator. A bit more water added, he closed the bonnet and took the tools and water back to the boot, closing it when completed.

"It is all good, Missus."

To which she gave a sigh of relief. He stepped out of the way so she could drive off.

Marg was having none of that. She started the car, left the hand brake on and stepped out of the car, walked around to the passenger's side near to where he was standing, opened the passenger door and said to him.

"Hop in I'm going to take you into town."

He appeared to be quite shocked by her invitation. His eye contact was lost as he looked towards the ground, uncertain and embarrassed.

"No, it's alright Missus."

She was not going to leave this man out in this heat after what he had done for her. It was the least that she felt that she could do. Yes, it might look rather unconventional to arrive in Wallabra with an Aboriginal as a passenger. It would certainly get the town people talking. She might lose a certain amount of credibility with the white folk, but in her usual fashion she didn't much care. This man had saved her day and such kindness deserved reward no matter who this person was.

"Come on, come on," she insisted. "It's too hot to be outdoors today."

He stood there, seemingly in a confused trance. This was not supposed to happen, that a white woman would offer something to an Aboriginal. It was not normal. But it was still a long walk back to his mob and perhaps it was time to get back, he had been heading that way anyway.

"Thank you Missus," he said with relief and climbed in.

# CHAPTER 19
# COOLAGY SCHOOL. 1963.

For Marg the journey back along the slippery road from Shirley's place didn't seem quite as treacherous as the way over. She was filled with optimism about Shirley's idea for a school bus. It had ticked a lot of Marg's boxes. Being obsessed with education for the children this idea captured her.

All other chores and obligations of the day were quickly put off as she started making phone calls, typing letters and sourcing information that she would need.

Lorry could tell something was going on by the typewriter still on the kitchen table and tea was a little bit late. His questions were answered during the meal.

"You've got a few hurdles to overcome before that's going to happen," he said.

"But do you like the idea?"

"Well yes, but I think we might be in the minority."

"Then we will just have to convince them of its worth."

He didn't verbally reply to her conviction, he knew it would've been useless to do so. Rather he gave a subtle look to signify *Good luck*, sarcastically.

"We are going to put it to them at the next P and C meeting. You're going to back us?"

"Sure."

The rain continued. Three days rain, three days fine. The

crops had struck and a vibrant green emanated from the leaves. It could be another good year. The road between their two properties became even more chopped up with the numerous cups of tea shared by Shirley and Marg over the next few weeks. As each reply to their investigations arrived, more tea was drunk. Lorry and Eddie now spent some of their time pulling their cars out of a bog.

They were both so enthusiastic about the idea that the thought of it not happening had been silenced. It was such a sensible idea how could they, the community, not follow.

In the end it was always going to come down to numbers. Fifteen pupils were needed to start the bus and twenty were needed to keep the school going. There were currently twenty eight pupils at the school. This was going to be a "winner, take all" confrontation.

They were aware that the original settlers, on the whole won't approve, but just like the Bakers, there were a growing few that had not been here so long. They were all much younger than the original settlers. They were the ones Shirley and Marg were pinning their hopes on. In the end, though, it was always going to come down to numbers.

As it happened the day of the meeting was the first time the sun had shined for three days. One day's sunshine was not going to improve the roads much though.

June nights could be very cold on this open plain and so it was on the night of the P and C meeting. Marg took with them some extra blankets both for the trip there and for during the meeting.

It was customary in winter to enter by the kitchenette

door, so as not to have to open the big doors in the main room. This helped in keeping the cold air out and keep whatever warmth there was, in. A number of radiators were kept under the bar. Armed with double adapters these were quickly utilised. They were never very effective due to the fact that corrugated iron tendered to be rather conductive when it came to temperature. However the occupants liked to think that they were.

There was always a vibrant collection of women in the kitchenette at the start of each evening, sorting out and checking out what everyone had brought for supper. The men congregated at the other end of the room to the side, organising the beer. On this night all were rather up beat due to the rain and the promise of a good season. Tales flowed freely about their adventurous drive to the hall that evening because of the roads.

Tom Patton was the president at the time, he usually was, and Sue Cave the Treasurer. Together with Marg and Mr Plummer they sat at the main table, situated in the middle of the hall. In front of them were chairs in no apparent order except on this night, they were arranged closer to the radiators. Ursula Dunn usually sat closest to the kitchenette as she saw it as her duty and responsibility to guard the urn for the tea afterwards.

Mr Plummer, the teacher was always a little on edge on these nights. His Christian name was Doug and at his first P and C meeting he requested that they call him Doug in an effort to casualise his position. However, since the parents mainly all went to similar type schools, it was almost in grained into them that they call all teachers, "Mr". Added to the fact that when the children come home from school, they all referred to him as Mr

Plummer, thus he was always, Mr Plummer.

The Coolagy School was his first appointment after graduating from teacher's college. When this was discovered the community were a little disappointed that the education department would send such an inexperienced person to this school. However he had proved them wrong. They had not taken into account the enthusiasm of a graduate set on building his career. They quickly appreciated his worth and he usually felt very comfortable in their company, socially, excepting that he didn't know much about farming and rural life.

When Tom moved from the bar into the main hall area it was the signal for all to assemble. Due to the state of the roads there weren't as many people present. Unfortunately the Burtons and Williams, two of the newer families to the district, couldn't make it. Shirley had made special phone calls to the newer members of the community. Not to tell them of the plan, but that there were a few urgent matters to discuss.

The chairs closest to the radiators filled up quickly. There was no plan of where the members sat. The segregation of the genders which was created in the other room carried over into the main hall. The men sat at the back of the hall and the women closer to the main table. Marg, as secretary, sorted out all of her paperwork. Sue, satisfied that all in the kitchen was prepared moved to her space on the head table and Tom stood trying to gauge the readiness of the members. When he moved to behind his chair, standing, was usually the signal for the meeting to start and the conversations, disappointingly, to be put on hold.

When Tom was satisfied that all was in readiness he

would clear his throat loudly which brought about the silence he was after.

"If I could just get your attention, we will get this meeting underway," he suggested in a voice filled with authority, very different to the voice he was using at the bar.

In character with his military training the meetings always had to follow a certain formality. It was now well known and the members settled their minds into a state of patience.

"It's a cold night so we'll get this meeting underway so we can all get home. Let's hope we don't get another shower or else we will all be staying here for the night."

This attempt at humour brought about a polite giggle. Tom, although trying not to laugh at his own jokes, always seemed to gain satisfaction from his mirth. It didn't last long and he quickly regained his composure to move on.

"Apologies," he said and sat down. This was Marg's cue to arise.

"The Burtons and the Williams couldn't make it..."

"That's no wonder, you should see the road down their way," interjected Sandy Geppert, a large framed man with a jolly disposition who had difficulty in following meeting etiquette and was always too eager to interrupt.

"Were the Gilmore's told?" Marg asked.

"I sent a notice home with Kevin last week," answered Mr Plummer.

"You wouldn't expect them on a night like this, that old car of theirs wouldn't get through this mud tonight," said Sue.

"We passed the Judds near their gate. They were bogged down to the chassis. Terry was going back to the house to get the tractor. I don't reckon they'll make it," added Brian White a wry man who usually didn't say too much at these meetings. He usually let his wife, Joyce, do the talking.

"Poor Vicky got in the road of some mud which flew up from the wheels and it landed all over her new dress. She wasn't happy," said Joyce.

Paul Jones arose to speak which was quite unusual not only for the fact that he rarely spoke at these meetings, but for his sticking to formalities by rising to talk. Most of the members spoke seated unless they had something really important to convey.

"Sam Harvey asked me to convey to you his apologies," where upon he sat down quickly.

"Sandra hasn't been too well," added his wife, Megan.

"What's wrong? Sue asked.

"Same old thing," answered Ursula.

"Are there any more?" Tom asked trying to bring the meeting into order.

"That's all that we've heard from, the rest are more than likely stuck like the Judds," said Sandy, which brought about a round of laughter.

When the laughter died and in an effort to progress the meeting Tom rose,

"If that's all, could we have the minutes of the last meeting please Marg."

The minutes were read in silence as the members entered back into the patience zone. In this state it was even difficult to find seconders for the motion to accept the minutes and matters arising. On this occasion, Tom and Sue fulfilled the procedure.

When this was processed, Tom arose again.

"Thank you Marg. Now we come to general business. Are there any matters to be discussed?"

This often signalled the beginning of the end of the meeting, as often there wasn't too much to be discussed. If there was it was often put off in preference to the social chat that would follow the meeting and the supper and beers which would be even colder now. Ursula saw it as her cue to go and check the urn and disappeared into the kitchenette.

As meetings go there wasn't much on the agenda. Shirley and Marg had decided that their motion would be put last. Heather Smith brought up the fact that her daughter, Elsa, had been bitten by meat ants and some of the other children were getting them in their lunch boxes. Mr Plummer commented that there was an ant nest growing near the shelter shed. George Dunn, Ursula's husband, volunteered, to bring down a bit of diesel and pour it down the ant holes. Since they lived closest to the school they felt themselves as sort of guardians of the community buildings. It was agreed that that should fix them up.

It was also agreed, at this meeting, that they could plant some trees in the paddock where Buff, the horse that brought the Gilmore children to school, stayed during the day. Since there had been plenty of rain it would give the trees a better chance of establishing themselves. Tom agreed to ring up Kelly's place in Wallabra and get some ordered in from Worthton.

Pat Thompson wanted to know when the council was going to fix up the pothole outside the silos. It was decided that the P and C meeting was not the right forum for such a discussion. By this stage everyone was thinking that the meeting was coming to an end. Ursula, feeling that her duty to the urn was more important, again adjourned to the kitchenette. With her departure the rest of the people started to get a taste for supper. There was a pause in the proceedings before Tom rose.

"Well if there is nothing else..."

At this moment Shirley's and Marg's eyes met as a signal for their moment. It had been discussed that Shirley would bring the motion. It was her idea to do this, despite the fact that she basically didn't like talking in public, but with heartfelt determination she rose to her feet.

"There is one other matter," she said.

This brought about a sense of disappointment from the members present as they were already moving for supper.

Tom was surprised to see Shirley speaking at a meeting as she very rarely did.

"Yes Shirley," he invited, then sat down.

"As you would realise, Eddie and I don't yet have any children attending the school. Next year our oldest boy will be ready to go to school. I do appreciate the good work Mr Plummer is doing with the school and what I am about to say is no reflection on him. Fortunately I never went to a one teacher school as I know many of you did. I think if I was a teacher at a one teacher school I would consider it a very difficult task indeed. Therefore I compliment Mr Plummer on the job he is doing."

For a woman who did not like talking in public, with steely resolve she pushed through with her assault. Obviously she had rehearsed what she was to say, but it was the determination to overcome her fear for the sake of a greater advantage for her children that surprise Marg. The rest of the members present, although surprised to listen to her talk, were just not certain where this was leading. Supper was beckoning and they were waiting for her to get to the point. They didn't have to wait very long, with a slight pause to gather strength she stated.

"It is my belief that we should be looking for something a bit better for our children's education. The world is changing. In the future people will need more than just school in order to obtain better employment. Most children in the cities now go to tertiary education like universities, colleges, technical colleges and the like. To do this they must do well in the higher school certificate. They can't get that here at this school."

She paused for a moment to collect. The members were in shock. It was like the worst of enemies had just entered the room and they needed time to sort out a response. It was obvious that supper was now put on hold as it was evident that this meeting had a long way to go. Treachery was afoot and the details needed to be sourced.

"I wish to put a motion to the meeting that we have this school closed and we start a bus service to take the children into Wallabra and back each day where they can at least get a higher school certificate."

Her motion delivered she sat back down and waited for the barrage. In keeping with her shy demeanour she could have placed herself on the seat hoping it might devour her and she would be hidden, but then she sat upright as if in defiance. The attack, at first did not come in verbal abuse or in diplomatic protocol, they were still too stunned by the motion. A deathly silence invaded the space like an unwelcomed guest.

The prolonged pause continued which concluded in a sense of amazement that a relatively new person to their community would come up with an idea, which would be so detrimental to the very fabric of their society. If treachery was afoot, who else were the traitors? Suspicion and anger abounded.

Sue Cave was the first to re-emerge.

"But the Wallabra school only has limited facilities, it's run down and I've never heard a good report about the teachers there," she stated, as though stating the obvious and putting paid, quickly, to this idea. She had not taken into account that this conspiracy had been planned.

Their suspicions were heightened when Marg, anxious to support Shirley and show her true colours, arose to speak.

"But if the school at Wallabra suddenly got an influx of our children they would have to expand and upgrade it. I have it here in writing from the Department of Education. They would've had a bigger school before if they could've gotten the Aboriginal children to attend the school more often," she said.

An *Et Tu Brute* moment had presented itself. The shock that one of their own, a genuine original in the community, was a part of the conspiracy was scandalous. There was a momentary pause as many of them now realised that this was now a major threat to their beloved school. With an early supper now out of the question, even Ursula returned to investigate the sudden change of atmosphere.

Tom, being the president, was the first to compose himself and in an effort to bring the discussion to an organised debate rose to speak, but Barry Lucas, one of the original settlers, beat him to the voice. He was a burly man, who never stood on the convention to stand whilst speaking and pulled no punches when he spoke. The type you would want on your team.

"Have you thought about the roads? How's a bus going to get through in the wet when we barely can?" he commented.

Shirley was quick to the fore as she had anticipated this question.

She arose to speak, "A road that has a school bus running on it has to gets priority treatment from any council."

Marg, who had written clarification on the situation, knew that she could back Shirley up on this one.

"That's right Barry," she said producing the correct letter. "It is written here."

"That might be all well and good, but are they actually going to do it," he said.

"They have to," Shirley replied.

"With a school bus on the road Barry, it gives us more leverage with the council" Marg added.

"But we will still have to battle away with them to get them to do anything."

"Not as hard as we have been though Barry. They know, we know, that they now really have to fix up the roads." Marg said.

"Yeah, well, good luck with that."

"Now we have a motion put forward, do we..." started Tom in an effort to bring order into the discussion, but he was interrupted by Bethany Davis, another of the originals to the district, who stood up. She was the discerning type who would always listen very carefully and commanded enough respect that when she stood all would stop and listen to her.

She held a distinct dramatic pause to make certain that

she had their attention.

"Even if the roads were better, it is still over an hour's drive to Wallabra from here. Then back in the afternoons. It all makes it a long day for the children don't you think?" She asked with genuine concern and a touch of sarcasm in an attempt to voice the obvious and quell this ridiculous attack.

"Then they have to do their chores at home and do their homework, no I think it would be much better for them to stay at this school."

"We don't know what types they will be mixing with in Wallabra, at least here we all know each other and our children. It's much safer and better for all of us if they stay here," said Sue.

"Besides, we wouldn't be able to have these meetings anymore, or the school fete. What about the Christmas party and the awards night. It is what we've always had, what's going to happen to all of that?" said Polly.

"We can still have the Christmas party. We will still meet for our card nights, sing-a-longs and all of that," replied Marg.

Marg could feel herself becoming very annoyed. It was not as though she was surprised with this reaction from them it was what she was expecting, but the short sightedness, the failure to comprehend what was best for the children in the long run was infuriating her.

"They still have got a few Aboriginals attending that school, we don't want our children mixing with them," said Barry.

This statement tipped the tables for Marg. Her temper had built to such an extent that this show of racism tipped her over the edge. It was a given that she always did have a temper and quite a spiteful tongue to go with it. Although she had always tried to modify it as she had learnt that it got her into more trouble than it was worth, this was not such an occasion. She could never contend with the racism shown by the white people in the district. Although she usually kept it too herself, this was not such an occasion.

"Would that be such a bad thing? The children might learn to be not as bigoted as what you are," she exclaimed.

This almost person attack drew looks of disbelief from the people. They were astonished that she would say such a thing. It did not go down well. In retrospect, it was this comment which possibly led to the start of her *Blue Healer* image.

When the astonishment had settled, Eunice Long, who was always given to be asking silly questions, broke the silence.

"What would happen to our little school and to Mr Plummer. I don't know what the day would be like if I didn't have to drop them off and pick them up again?"

"Surely the question here is what is best for the children? Do we have the right to subject them to the same life as what we've had? Battling the elements, struggling from year to year, hoping for rain, never certain if we will have money next year. Putting up with the heat, the flies, the dust, the isolation and for what, so our children can keep on doing the same? Can we not give them a choice, let them decide? It is a big and changing world out there with great opportunities for the young and you want to shelter them in this wilderness of nothingness. A proper education is their key to the door which leads to the outside," said Marg.

The moment of silence which followed was Tom's chance to try and gain control of the meeting which had suddenly become quite heated.

"So we have a motion put forward by Shirley Baker that we should close our school and start up a bus service to take the children in Wallabra. Do we have a seconder?"

"I second the motion," Marg replied.

"Then..." Tom started.

"But I just don't..." interrupted Eunice again.

Outside the temperature was getting colder, but inside quite warmer. Still the questions kept coming and to each Shirley and Marg gave informed answers. Their frustration grew on their replies. Defying logic the community seemed determined to stick by what they knew and felt comfortable with.

Eventually they started to run out of criticisms and the discussion had reached a stalemate. Tom, exasperated by the aggressive mood of the meeting and his inability to keep order, saw this opportunity to bring back civility and rose to speak.

"Well now, I believe we've all had our chance to speak on the matter. Could I suggest we now put it to a vote?"

Full of good intentions and sound reasoning Shirley and Marg were a little bit hopeful before the meeting that common sense would prevail. However they had not fully taken into the account the strong bond amongst this community and the resistance to change. They didn't win.

Supper that night was rather shorter than usual and the conversations tense. This battle may have been concluded, but the war was only just starting.

# CHAPTER 20
# KELLY'S STORE. FEBRUARY 1965.

The back room at Kelly's Ag Supplies now looked totally disarrayed. Kevin had been through everything that was in the room three times and still couldn't find a part with Mr Stirling's name on it. He had even studied the back yard, kicking through mounds of dust to see if there was anything hidden, crawling amongst the machinery, old and new, looking under the tines for a small parcel. Lifting up pieces of corrugated iron to see what they revealed underneath. Under one such piece of rusted iron he found a brown snake hiding from the sun's intensity. Kevin was alarmed to see the snake, but not as surprised as the snake was to see the sun so suddenly. It quickly wriggled out of the yard, carefully observed by Kevin whose heart was still racing. He was much more careful with the other sheets of metal that he lifted up. The excursion into the backyard was all to no avail, there was still no part to be found.

Janet was working herself around all the products, replacing them onto the shelves where the wind had blown them off, and wiping away the dust, hoping that she might stumble across the missing part.

It was now past one in the afternoon. The wind was increasing and with it more of the red dust. It was now pouring into the building making Janet's task, besides being increasingly repetitious, quite futile. Mrs Stirling's arrival was imminent. It was only a two hour trip which probably started about three hours ago. What was she going to tell Mrs Stirling? She felt a great guilt towards Mrs Stirling which bordered upon wanting to blame herself. This thought drove her to consider as many nooks and crannies she could fine in this large building. She had even gone through the office several times. This part was not to be found, but she still kept looking. Kevin was now assisting in the main room, doing what Janet had been doing for hours.

She kept an ear on the road outside, although the wind impeded her hearing, she wanted to have pre warning of Mrs Stirling's car approaching. Like the dread of a death bell, she thought she could hear a car, muffled by the wind, it was definitely an engine. It stopped, but she could tell it was not outside this shop. It must be outside Spear's store. Her curiosity and dread led her to the entrance to satisfy her concern.

As she slowly placed her head outside the shop, not wanting to be seen, the wind caught her hair and flung it across her face. She could however see the car that had caused her the concern and was relieved to see that it belonged to Mrs Kelly, who was now in the store.

Relief turned to joy. Mrs Kelly was bound to drop into her husband's business. Janet now hoped that Mrs Stirling would arrive when Mrs Kelly was here and she could do the explaining, perhaps. Of course with Mrs Kelly's imminent arrival would follow the subtle, but definite inspection. It always followed. Janet's thoughts instantly went to the back door still a little bit open, not what Mr Kelly would like.

"Hey Kevin, Mrs Kelly's coming. You better go and close the back door," she called out to Kevin who instantly performed the task aware of the impending scolding if it was seen open.

"You better make sure that back room is closed too," she added knowing the condition it was in and grateful that in her searching through the office she had not created such a mess. With the drop in the draft from the closing of the back door the infinite dust pouring into the open front door, now became finite. Janet and Kevin now had renewed motivation for removing the dust out of the shop.

To Janet, Mrs Kelly was still a bit of an unknown quantity. Their relationship had remained the same as if she was still her parent's daughter. Seen, but not heard. Janet, now being a young adult, wished that their relationship might change to being less formal and more personal. Janet felt that there was a mystery behind the facade of being the wife of the richest and most important man in town. In Mrs Kelly's dealings with the other folk in the town she was always very polite and seemed to take an interest in them. Her Christian name, Christine, was rarely heard in public, she was always known as Mrs Kelly. Janet would often see a rather superficial element to her conversation, as if she was playing a role. Janet wanted to know why? Her answer was not likely to be revealed since Janet's role now was as an employee in her husband's business. Not a great difference to what it always had been.

Without actually hearing her footsteps, Janet knew Mrs Kelly was on her way. Their eyes met as soon as she entered. Janet immediately sensed concern on her face.

"Good afternoon Janet and Kevin," she greeted politely, with a smile that appeared as an afterthought.

"Good afternoon Mrs Kelly," said Janet and Kevin.

She looked about the shop and felt the atmosphere.

"It is so hot in here. Why don't you open the back door a bit and let a draft in?" she asked.

"Mr Kelly doesn't like it to be opened," Janet said.

"Well Mr Kelly isn't here to feel how hot it is in this building. Open it up a little please Kevin. Not too much, with this gale outside you'll have things flying everywhere. Talking of Mr Kelly," she began, to which Janet caught an air of sarcasm in her tone. "Where is he?"

"He left before nine," Janet said.

"By himself?"

"No, a Mr Wykes was with him."

"I've never heard of that name. A Mr was it?"

"Yes." Janet was perplexed by this line of questions. "Is there anything that I can help you with?"

"Where were they going?"

"Out to Kandar station to look at a mob of sheep, I believe."

"Kandar!" Mrs Kelly said. "That's at least four to five hour round trip."

"He said he wouldn't be back till late on."

"He's not going to be any good to me then," she let out as though verbalising her thought and immediately felt embarrassed when she realised that her thought had become audible.

"Is there anything I can do to help?"

Still a little embarrassed by what she had said, Mrs Kelly was in two minds as to how much she should confide to an employee.

"The wind has loosened some of the sheets of iron on our roof. I'm worried that they might come off. Is there anyone in town that might be able to help?" she asked.

"I don't know Mrs Kelly. I suspect all the men are out working."

"I tried to ring Jack Smith, but the lines are down apparently. No one can ring anywhere at the moment," she informed.

"Well I do know he's out on the Evan's place doing some repairs to their sheds," Janet replied.

"You could try someone out at the camp, some of them are useful," Janet suggested referring to the Aboriginal settlement. However in her effort to be helpful soon realised the folly of her suggestion.

"Oh no, I wouldn't go out there," was Mrs Kelly's curt reply.

There was a slight pause as Janet could see Mrs Kelly trying to decide what to do. She did think of perhaps explaining the Mrs Stirling situation to Mrs Kelly in the hope of some guidance. Then she dismissed the idea. Obviously Mr Kelly was in enough trouble as it was and since this situation was largely down to his making all Janet would be doing was to give Mrs Kelly bullets to fire at him later on.

The only hope was that Mrs Kelly would still be here when Mrs Stirling arrived. It could happen, Janet hoped. She strained her ears in hope of hearing an approaching car. But it wasn't going to happen. In the same huff as when she arrived, Mrs Kelly was gone. With her departure Janet didn't now want to hear that approaching car.

There was nothing for it, but to keep fighting the

invading red dust. At least there was now a legitimate reason for keeping the back door open even if it did prolong their sweeping. The time was passing slowly for Janet. It does that when the mind is set on one reoccurring thought. With an ear constantly centred outside to hear for that approaching car and the impending embarrassment it would create. Janet knew Mrs Stirling to be a fair minded lady, perhaps she would understand. However their relationship had not developed enough to be certain. After all Janet was still her parent's child.

Suddenly a figure of a woman burst through the entrance. No car noise, no premonition, just there. For a moment Janet was in panic till she saw that it was Mavis Anderson.

"Have you heard anything?" Mavis asked.

Janet wasn't quite sure which anything she had in mind, but since the phone hadn't rang since she left the last time Janet felt safe in saying.

"No, I haven't."

"No, I haven't either. We are right out of green vegetables now. Mrs Kelly bought the last of the lettuce and now there's nothing. If the truck was coming it should've been here by now. Did Mrs Kelly see you?"

"Yes."

"She was looking for Mr Kelly. I said he took off somewhere hours ago. She didn't look too happy about it. I don't know what's going on there. She said that her phone was out too," Mavis said.

At this point Helen Davidson appeared, another heart stopping moment for Janet.

"There you are," Helen said.

"Have you heard anything?" said Mavis.

"No, I haven't heard anything," Helen said.

"Neither have I," said Mavis.

"You haven't heard anything have you Janet?" said Helen.

"No," said Janet.

"What about Jack Spicer, has he heard anything?" said Mavis.

"I went up and saw Jack, he's waiting for the truck too. He says he's out of engine oil. He hasn't heard anything about it though," Helen said.

"Does he know about the telephones?" said Mavis.

"Yes, he can't get through to Worthton either. He also reckons a pole must be down somewhere," said Helen.

"What are we going to do?" said Mavis.

"Jack said that if anyone stops at his place for fuel on their way to Worthton he was going to ask them to let them know in Worthton that we've got a problem with the telephones," said Helen.

"That's a good idea we'll do the same at the store."

"Trouble is there haven't been many people coming through today," Helen said.

"Monday you see, all at home working," said Mavis.

"And the heat, who would want to be driving on a day like this."

"We will just have to hope that someone will. Janet, if anyone drops in here you'll make sure that they know we haven't got the phone on. If they are heading towards ..."

"I certainly will Mrs Davidson." Janet said.

"Did Mrs Kelly catch up with you?"

"Yes, she did Mrs Davidson," said Janet.

"She didn't look too happy," Helen said.

"She wasn't, she didn't know where Mr Kelly was," said Mavis.

"Oh is that right," said Helen.

"I don't know what's going on there," said Mavis.

"Neither do I," said Helen.

"Have you been able to get anyone on the phone?" said Mavis.

"Not at all. They are all dead. John's been trying everyone and gets nothing," Helen said.

"What are we going to do?" said Mavis.

"It's the wind, John says. It must've blown down a pole somewhere. Just where, he doesn't know. There are so many poles leading off to everywhere, there's no telling where it might be."

"The way this wind's getting up there might be more poles down before we get the change," Mavis said.

"John said we just have to wait till someone finds the trouble and reports it," Helen said.

"But how are we going to let them know in Worthton to come out and fix it?" said Mavis.

"John said if he knew where the trouble was he might be able to do something to get it going again," said Helen.

"Still if we see someone going to Worthton..." said Mavis.

"We'll get them to tell them in Worthton," Helen said.

"I haven't seen anyone all day, except for Mrs Kelly," said Mavis.

Suddenly a very strong gust of wind hit the building. The ladies took fright and looked outside.

"Oh my goodness, it's getting worse," said Mavis.

"Oh dear, I think I just saw that power pole near the pub move with that gust," said Helen.

"Oh no, don't tell me we're going to get a blackout as well," Mavis said.

"If it has been strong enough to blow down telephone poles, it could blow down power poles as well, perhaps" said Helen.

"What will we all do?" said Mavis. "Just as well the red dust doesn't burn otherwise we would have a bad fire on our hands if a pole was to go down on one of the properties."

"There's nothing to burn out there, but there is here. If that pole goes down we might lose the pub and these building too perhaps," said Helen.

"What will we do? If there's no power we won't have the pumps going to hose anything down," said Mavis.

"We better go and warn Betty at the pub," said Helen.

"We will need to keep a really good eye on that pole," said Mavis.

"Can you keep an eye on it Janet? Your shop is directly opposite it," said Helen.

"I can do that," said Janet.

"I wonder if she's got any spare ice. We haven't got much left and if there is a blackout the meat will get ruined," said Mavis.

The two ladies left and crossed the road. Janet was left to fear the noise of an approaching car.

# CHAPTER 21
# WYMERE HOMESTEAD. AUGUST 1963

The August winds had started early as they often do after a spell of good autumn rain. The crops were flourishing, the roads were drying, all that was needed for a good harvest was rain in September. The biting chill in the wind however mirrored Shirley and Marg's mood. The prospect of a good harvest paled into insignificance behind the disappointment of not getting the school bus up at the P and C meeting.

The waiting outside the school at three thirty with the southerlies blasting forth was made even cooler by the attitude of the mothers towards this idea of a school bus. Marg and Shirley had kept a socially low profile since the meeting, conscious of the discontent they now attracted.

Unperturbed Shirley and Marg kept their focus squarely upon the concept. It was too good an idea to ignore. The betterment of the children's lot was much more important than social standings. Logic should always win over sentiment. Their subjective passion for the plan was based upon objective realities. They were convinced that they were right.

Numerous morning teas served as post mortems of their defeat. From the study of their defeat a plan for the next conflict was to emerge. It was all a matter of numbers. They needed numbers to get the bus going and the school needed numbers to keep running. It was a pity the night of the meeting had been so wet. It had restricted the attendance. Doubtless social pressure would have by now swayed the absentees to be in favour of keeping the school going. They needed more children.

Like Buddhist monks they meditated upon the concept. Like Buddhist monks enough repetition of a mantra to reach a higher plain of concentration. Together with a fair bit of logic and the freakish way in which a thought will enter a mind without any precursor, a truism emerges. It just appeared, as if another party had guided it into Marg's cognitive processes. So strong was the inspiration she recognised straightaway it was absolutely correct. Instantly she knew this was the answer to their problem. It was so obvious she was surprised she hadn't thought of it earlier.

It was after nine in the morning. Breakfast had been completed and Lorry was out on the farm somewhere. The chill of the morning had not as yet worn off. The gathering strength of the southerly gave doubt that it ever would. Marg was collecting the broom to give it some exercise when the idea occurred. Instantly the broom's task was cancelled and it stayed were it was. Marg was to Shirley's place, bound.

A quick excited phone call to Shirley, a touch of makeup, just lippy, a brush of the hair and donning a very warm coat she braced the biting wind. She knew the car would provide sanctuary from the seemingly Antarctic gale and she hurried towards it.

The ruts in the road, created by the cars trying to get through the mud, were still evident. A council grader had not been seen all year. However due to the drying effect of the winds the higher edges of the ruts were drying out. As Marg headed west the force of the wind caused the car to skip out of the ruts that all the vehicles stayed in. This invariably landed the car on the higher edges of the ruts which, in a fashion, tended to level out the road although making a rougher passage.

To Marg the trip to Shirley's possibly seemed longer than usual, but in actual fact was probably shorter. At least she knew she wouldn't get bogged this time.

"Good morning Marg," Shirley, who had seen Marg coming through the gate and was waiting for her. She had sensed the excitement in Marg's voice over the phone and was anxious to find out the content.

"Good morning Shirley", Marg replied.

"Come in, I've put the kettle on."

The wind gave added impetus for their move to the protection of the house. Coats off and seated comfortably in the kitchen with a cup of tea. Comments about the weather concluded, Marg could not restrain herself any longer.

"Shirley," Marg started. "Do you remember the day we had that big fire that came in across from Wymere?"

"Yes," she replied.

"Do you remember Mr Kincaid? He runs the show at Wymere."

"Yes I do remember him," she said.

"That night we were all sitting around keeping watch. I had a conversation with him about his staff. He told me that he had great trouble keeping married staff because there was no school, only the school of the air," Marg recounted.

"Yes," Shirley replied as if almost anticipating where

Marg was going with this.

"If they had a bus..." Marg continues.

"But how far would those children have to travel each day?" She asked now knowing where Marg was coming from.

"I reckon about two, two and a half hours each way," said Marg.

"That's a very long day."

"It's their choice Shirley. All we can do is offer it to them. What I do know is that Mr Kincaid will jump at the idea of some education as opposed to none. The other thing is, the Gilmores weren't there at that meeting. I know they very rarely come, but I do know Mrs Gilmore is very keen to have her children properly educated. That is why they live up this part of Wymere, because it is close to the school," said Marg.

"It is all to do with numbers," said Shirley now realising that all was not lost. "Do you know how many children there are at Wymere?"

"No, but I will find out. I'll ring them and ask if we can come and see them. Mr Kincaid will remember me I'm sure and we'll see what he thinks of the idea. Would you like to come along as well?"

Marg wasted no time in contacting the Wymere homestead. Mrs Kincaid answered the phone. Marg explained to her who she was and that Shirley and her would like to see them about the education of the children. They were invited instantly.

Lunch that day was a little later than usual, Lorry noticed and the broom was still standing in the same position it was left in, waiting for instruction. Lorry could tell that Marg was excited about something, but left it to her to relate in her own time. He didn't have to wait long, even before the soup had a chance to cool, she was explaining to him her plans.

"Worth a try," he commented after a considerable pause.

"What's the road down that way like?" Marg asked.

"I don't think it ever sees a grader," Lorry replied which didn't inspire much confidence.

The fact of the matter was neither of them had ever been down that road. There was never any need to. When they would get to the crossroads of Wymere and Coolagy road they would always turn right to either, the school, the silo or Wallabra. To turn left and head north was never contemplated. There was nothing down that end of the road except for the Wymere homestead. The road ended at the homestead. The Woods River, flowing east to west, blocked any plan of continuing the road north. Across the river the stations access roads headed to Mularbra. Another little settlement much like Wallabra, many miles to the north. To the east, the next station, also with a northern boundary of the river was accessed from Worthton. To the west there wasn't very much at all. Soon after the Wymere boundary the river becomes a series of waterholes connected only during times of excess rain. Not very often. The Wymere community were on the outer limb of a branch that only had themselves as visitors.

The date of Shirley and Marg's journey into this unknown place arrived. Shirley had arrived at the appointed time, about ten in the morning, leaving Eddie to mind the children for the day. Subtly Lorry gave special attention to the car to ensure all the necessaries were present. Subtly because he had no idea what this road might have in store and didn't want Marg to see his special attention in case she might become alarmed. They wasted no time in embarking.

With excited expectations, rugged up and with a thermos of tea the ladies set forth. There had been a little shower the previous evening. Not enough for the road to be a concern, but enough to be sticky. Marg drove with caution. The change that had gone through had sparked up the southerly wind to the extent that it tended to blow the car around a bit. The sun in full view was trying hard to dry the terrain. However with a few wispy clouds forming in the south, heading their way like sails pushing the car, the sun's help was going to be short lived.

The crossroads loomed. No need for a hand signal, they were turning left. The mystery of this road was soon to be realised. The twenty miles to the homestead was soon to be experienced. So used to the constant and continuous landscape of treeless flat plains stretching on to eternity, only broken by the occasional man-made structure, the ladies yearned for something different. Perhaps it would be along this road which stretched beyond the horizon. A tree perhaps, even a hill would be a major spectacle.

They turned the corner just as the first of the invading clouds from the south covered the sun. Now heading north the shadow, made by the cloud, guided their path. The sunlight was disappearing towards the horizon as if to hurry them along to catch up with it. This was never going to happen. Soon after straightening the northerly direction was changed to avoid a pot hole which had spread to have covered two thirds of the road. Too deep to go into it had to be avoided by going around it. The lush and structured green of the wheat crops had now given way to a paler green of the natural pastures interrupted by the left over dry Spinifex. The only sign of human interference were the fences, the road or more precisely the track, the telegraph and electricity poles. Keeping their parallel structures to the horizon where they formed into a singularity, seemingly continuing to an endless destination.

Due to years of neglect the road was certainly different. Instead of being at the same level as the terrain it traversed this road was sunken. No grader and years of dust trails made from the vehicles had seen the road sink below the flat plain it crossed. This meant that during a wet spell there was nowhere for the water to run off to, only into the centre of the road where it stayed. Marg had her choice of tyre paths. Years of differing ruts had cut into the track. They crisscrossed each other like train tracks near a terminal, punctuated with numerous holes, some like dams, which still had water in them so deep that the bottom could not be seen. The steering wheel was rarely still.

Marg's concentration was centred on the road. Occasionally she would glance at the terrain and see nothing different. Shirley's gazing around, in search of something different, started to lose its frequency. There was the odd mob of sheep, lazing in a never ending haven of plenty, a few kangaroos watched the car trailing pass as if to them the car was really something different. There were no hills. There were no trees, so far.

Shirley's body had sunk into the seat. The bumps in the road were more tolerable that way, beside there was no more need to be turning about for a view. It was all the same. Her eyes became transfixed upon the singularity where the parallels met at the horizon. Suddenly her body jolted a little. Not from the bumps in the road, but rather from within, as though she had suddenly been delivered out of a trance.

Marg noticed the positional change and chanced a look at the horizon ahead. The straight lined horizon had indeed changed. There was now an ever increasing dark line spreading from east to west, filling more of the scene as they progressed. The singularity of the parallels had been broken. Now the lines were being consumed by the ever increasing black mass's they ventured closer the black mass began to form angular shapes of brownish red and grey with green blobs on the end of them.

"Trees," said Shirley.

"This must be the river then," said Marg.

"We must be nearly there."

Without warning the road suddenly lifted, the ruts were gone, the sound of tyres on dirt was replaced by tyres on small stones as what composed a gravel road. Certainly machinery had been used on this section of the road and it would not have been councils. The native pastures now gave way to healthy wheat crops on either side of the road. Well established paddocks with banks of dirt through them. The river, with its ready access to water, had provided a type of insurance against drought, irrigation. Emerging from out of the wilderness, buildings now came into view. Subtly, but most definitely the scene had changed. The human touch had transformed the view.

The road ended with large mud brick walls bordering the road with a ramp where walls ended and a sign saying

Wymere. Beyond the walls large well established deciduous trees, Liquid Ambers, adorned the gravel driveway. Currently they were bare for the winter, but would be spectacular in the autumn. About two hundred yards over on the left were a series of small huts made of timber and corrugated iron. All uniformly positioned and obviously lived in, although not cared for. With no trees around them and certainly no garden they looked out of place and barren compared to the right side of the driveway. To the right was a thicket of trees, mainly imported and currently leafless. They were bordered behind them by the grandeur of the native red river gums which adorned the river bank. Through the branches they could now see the outline of what must be a most splendid house made of mud bricks, timber and, as usual, the corrugated iron roof. Beyond the trees which tendered to hide the building was a large, cultivated lawn. It was broken up with a series of garden beds planted with roses, azaleas, camellias and freshly planted annuals waiting for the spring to display their glory. Obviously this was the homestead.

To Marg and Shirley the splendour of the scene represented a fantasyland of flora not usually experienced out here. Back on their respective properties at Coolagy they were pleased just to have a few gum trees. The miracle of having water in abundance in a parched landscape was evident.

Marg parked the car near to where the concreted pathway led through the garden to the front door, made of polished wood. It was lined with healthy rose bushes and beyond the beautifully manicured lawns were vegetable patches and fruit trees. Mr and Mrs Kincaid had heard them arrive and were quickly onto the pathway to greet their visitors.

"We try and be as self-sufficient as we can," said Mr Kincaid as he showed them into the drawing room which was filled with furniture that made Marg melt with envy.

The interior of the house was made of timber sourced from the abundance of river gums which lined the river. The style was very colonial with large rooms, high ceilings, fire places and a verandah which stretched around the whole house.

Mr Kincaid made them feel comfortable before Mrs Kincaid entered with the tea and a freshly made batch of scones. He had obviously changed out of his working clothes and into more suitable clothes as befitting the landed gentry. Mrs Kincaid similarly had donned a pretty dress and jewellery either as an excuse to wear something to show her status or as a chance to dress up a little.

It was obvious that they had been looking forward to their arrival. Being fellow landowners the Kincaids relished a conversation with people similar to their standing. The type of people they didn't meet very often. There was however a bit of difference between owning a soldier settler farm at Coolagy and managing five hundred square miles with river frontage. Although the Kincaids tried not to make it felt that this was not the situation, it was an undercurrent to their relationship. Marg and Shirley couldn't help feeling a little out of their depth, social standing wise. They continued to address them as Mr Kincaid and Mrs Kincaid.

By their posh surrounds and by the way they easily fitted into it, as though it had always been this way, the Kincaids were a part of the aristocratic squatters that opened up this wilderness, made a fortune and now their descendants live in complete contrast to their pioneer ancestors.

"How old is this house?" asked Shirley whilst reaching for a scone.

"It was built about a hundred years ago now by Mr Murdock who claimed the property, as the squatters did in those times, for himself. I always reckoned it must've been really tough to arrive here with nothing, but a flock of sheep and a tent. He had married a woman who had come out from Sussex in England and apparently it was she who designed a garden similar to what she had been used to in England," stated Mr Kincaid.

"This was the first of many such properties. He was obviously a very shrewd man. Now his descendants live in the city and get others to run their properties," said Mrs Kincaid.

"We both came from large properties like this, you see," said Mr Kincaid.

"It is almost like we own it except that we get a regular income," said Mr Kincaid with humour.

Marg and Shirley were learning about a lifestyle, that of the squatters, the 'old world' charm, that they had only ever heard about. The Kincaids relished in having their company. A rapport had been established. It did come time, however, for Marg to explain the reason for their visit. She suggested their plan to them and told them about the meeting that ensued. The Kincaids were quite surprised at their concept. They would've been quite happy for the visit to have been social instead it had turned out to be a god send for their troubles.

"You may remember, Mr Kincaid, when we had that fire

that time, you said to me that you had a real problem with regards to education for the children, so I naturally thought you might be interested," Marg concluded.

"Marg," replied Mrs Kincaid, "I think we would be very interested."

"It is a matter of numbers. We need at least fifteen children to get the bus started," Shirley stated.

"Schooling has always been a problem out here. We've sent our children, Elizabeth and Caroline, to ladies colleges in Sydney, but as for the rest of them there is very little except the school of the air. We have some couples with children on the place, but we'd like more. More reliable, you know, some of the single men we get here. Well you know, they just aren't our types," said Mrs Kincaid.

"Leave it with me," said Mr Kincaid. "I will ask around all of our staff who have children and see who would be interested."

"I don't believe they will take much convincing."

"Shirley and I thought we might go out and see Mrs Gilmore next week," said Marg.

"I know she will be keen. Dear lady, I often wonder about her. Stuck out there and she is basically very shy, it is not as if she seeks out company. She does it so their children can go to your school, you know?" added Mrs Kincaid.

"Do you see her very often?" Marg asked knowing very well that Mrs Kincaid would never set a foot inside the place.

"Oh no, I've never been out there. Stan sees them occasionally and he says that they are all right," said Mrs Kincaid.

"When do you need to know by?" said Mr Kincaid.

"There is another meeting on Tuesday fortnight at the hall," said Marg.

"We should know by then, would you like us to attend the meeting?"

"If you wouldn't mind, yes that would be very helpful, thank you," said Marg.

# CHAPTER 22
# MARG'S JOURNEY CONTINUES.
# FEBRUARY 1965.

Marg was on the road again. The gum trees that lined the gully, where she had just spent all that time in the heat, faded into the mirage on the horizon like an event that didn't want to be remembered.

The timelessness she experienced at that place had disappeared and now real time had urgent relevance. The mission needed to come back into focus. She had no way of knowing what the time was or how long she had spent there. Meanwhile the sheep at home were becoming thirstier. The sun was now shining on her right shoulder, unleashing its full fury. Since she was travelling south the sun was now in the western sphere of its daily travels. It was obviously well after midday. The time of day when one wonders just how hot is this day going to be? Knowing it would continue to grow until it peaks usually between two and three in the afternoon. Such was it on this day, excepting, with this wind still growing in intensity, there would be no respite until the change came through. It appeared that, at this stage, the change had gotten lost. There was no sign of it.

At least now she had company however unlikely the company turned out to be. He was obviously a little shy at first and the atmosphere was a little tense.

"What will I call you?" Marg asked trying to break the

silence and add a bit of familiarity.

"Charlie, Missus," he said.

"You can call me Marg."

"Sure Missus," he said politely, but by the reply Marg assumed that to him she was going to be 'Missus'.

The silence resumed.

"Any idea what the time might be Charlie?"

He deliberated before replying, "After lunch."

Marg was none the wiser. Without words and with Charlie's help the windows were re arranged. Now all of them were open as much as they could go. Marg had realised that although it was very civil of her to insist that she gave Charlie a lift back into Wallabra, she had not taken into account the smell of a man who had obviously been in the outback for a number of days. The extra circulation did alleviate the situation a little, she just hoped the smell would not invade her dress or be a permanent odour in the car.

That was it as far as communicating went for a number of miles. She was curious though about just what he was doing out here alone in the heat. She knew a little about their connection to country and thought this was possibly her chance to learn more.

"What were you doing out there Charlie?"

He paused for a while before he replied. Marg didn't know whether he didn't want to make conversation or whether he had something to hide and saw her as a threat. Eventually his thoughts reached a conclusion.

"Go walkabout Missus."

"Bit hot for that Charlie. How long have you been out there?"

"Five days, Missus."

"How did you get on for water?"

"I know where to look, Missus."

"Where have you been in these five days?"

"All over, Missus," he said, which didn't say very much at all to Marg, but to him possibly meant a lot.

"Why?" She asked to which there was a bit of a pause before he replied.

"Had to go Missus, I had to connect with country again. Needed to get away from the mob for a bit and spent time with m'self."

"I see."

That could've ended the conversation although Marg was wishing it to go further. She could see that he was a little troubled. As though he wanted to say something, but was reluctant to do so. She hoped that what was troubling him would reveal itself in words and so she might be able to be of assistance, even if it was only through listening.

"Big trouble with the mob at Wallabra," he said.

"Is there?"

"They not do anything back there, just sit around all day. That's not good Missus."

"Not much work around with this drought."

"No work even in the good times Missus. No one employ us."

Marg didn't respond, as she was beginning to understand the hopelessness of his and their situation.

"Used to be different Missus. Once we used to hunt, collect bush tucker, tell tales of the dreaming at night next to the fire. We were happy then. Then we had all of country to roam around in. We have special stories about each place. We learn about country by being a part of it. Being in country is very important to us Missus. Now we have no more country to roam around in. White fella got it all now. I try to tell them now the stories of the dreaming and they not interested. I try to tell them things about country during the day and they walk away. They don't look at the crows like we used to, they don't look on the ground for tracks no more. All they want to do is just sit around and get cranky. We got nowhere to go, we just stay in the one place. Not good Missus," Charlie said.

"I see."

"Got to get them interested in something Missus. It's the young ones that I worry about. They see their father and their mother and the rest of the mob doing nothing and they think that is the way it is. I get old wrecks that no one wants anymore and I bring them down to the camp. Maybe they get interested in that. See how it works. Give them something to do."

"Does it help?"

"Sort of does Missus, for a while. It white fella stuff. Seems like we always have to be like the white fella. Eat what he eats, talk like he talk, use money, fight over who's got more. It never used to be like that Missus, once we shared everything. Then white fella teach us about owning and it's not the same. We see white fella running around buying stuff, fighting country, and still not happy. We had nothing except our bond with country and were very happy."

The miles ticked by unnoticed by Marg as she had become quite absorbed in what she was hearing.

"I needed to get away for a bit Missus, you know. Too much agro back at the camp," he said.

"What did you find?"

She noticed from out of the corner of her eye and by his

manner a sudden happy expression began to overtake him.

"I visit big gully out that way, sat there for a bit. Then up to river, catch a fish there, listen to the river floating past. Very peaceful there Missus."

"I imagine it would be."

"Need that time Missus, by yourself to listen to the crow fly past, watch the goanna going up the tree, feel the dust underneath your feet. We are all apart of mother earth Missus. Just need that time to feel connected to it all again, time with just me as a part of country. It might be hot, it might be cold, that's just the way that it is. No point fighting it, better to be a part of it and go with country, it's not going to change. It is really peaceful like that Missus. It makes me feel happy again."

Marg could relate to what Charlie had been saying. Their cultures might have been different and thus the perspective altered, but an affinity to the peace of the outback they did share. A timeless peace that can never be attained anywhere else. She hated the hardships that this country held, but she was beginning to appreciate the connection with its soul.

"So what now, Charlie?" Marg asked.

"I have big think over last few days. Think we need to get them to school more often Missus. Get the young ones out of the habits of their parents. Get them doing something. Learn white man ways, we've lost country. Maybe one day they teach them about country in school. That might get them interested."

Marg could see sense in his plan, but did feel sympathy for a vanishing culture. A culture that had survived much better in this land than her culture had.

To her surprised the landscape ahead was different. She could now see other telegraph poles spreading from east to west. She had been so caught up in listening to Charlie that she had lost concept of where she was. Fortunately the car had not missed a beat. She was grateful to Charlie for that as well. She recognised what was approaching as the Worthton road. She felt a sense of relief not only that the car was still going, but if there was a further mishap she would soon be on a road that was used more. Turn left to Worthton heading east, right to Wallabra heading west. There was only fifteen miles to Wallabra from this intersection. She could hardly wait.

# CHAPTER 23
# OUTSIDE KELLY'S STORE. FEBRUARY 1965.

Since Helen had seen the pole outside the pub move there had been quite in depth discussions upon what to do. It was now after two pm, the wind hadn't eased nor had the temperature. The dust was swirling through the main street of Wallabra as if to give warning of an impending event.

Janet and Kevin kept up their vigil of trying to keep the dust out of the shop. Keeping an eager eye on the pole outside the pub and listening for an approaching car. Janet was becoming increasingly worried. Mrs Stirling would have been on the road for over four hours and she still hadn't arrived. What could've happened? In a way she sort of hoped Mrs Stirling would arrive to alleviate her of this new concern. Of course with no telephones there was no way of knowing if anything had happened. Perhaps Mr Kelly would get home earlier and before Mrs Stirling, or Mrs Kelly would reappear. There was the hope.

The road between Mr Kelly's and the pub was serving as the meeting place to discuss the situation. The group would vary in size, with sometimes Harry and John coming across to add their take. Some of the mob from the camp had ventured up to the main street, as they often did, and parked themselves on the wooden bench seats outside the post office. They sat and watched the collaboration of the whites in silence. They would often do this, as if wandering what these people were doing. They had plenty of time to observe. Of course by placing themselves outside the post office a meeting on the main road of both, John and Helen, Mavis and Harry together could not be contemplated since one of each pair had to guard their shops. The Aboriginals were never to be trusted. As a result communication was a little impaired. They didn't have to consider traffic on this day, there was none.

Curiosity got the better of Janet, she had to venture across to the meeting place and see what was happening. She braved the blustering wind to join Mavis, John and Betty from the pub. John was a small man and rather thin. His back was slightly hunched as though he had spent his life bending over things and had never straightened it up properly. Dressed in his old PMG uniform that had long past its use by date, it tended to give him some importance, as though he did have expertise. He didn't need to promote himself in such a way, everyone knew he was quite clever, but his insecurities would never let him believe it.

Betty was small and carried an increasing middle aged spread. She had bright blue eyes which were very warm. The type of warmth that instantly made one feel very comfortable in her presence. She preferred to listen rather than talk and would keep her thoughts to herself. Possibly it was a behaviour adopted from years serving in a pub.

"Janet, have you seen any of the poles moving since Helen saw this one move?" said Mavis.

"No I haven't and I've been keeping a pretty good eye," Janet said.

*The Red Dust 188*

"It only needs one sudden gust. What will we do? Do you think we should support it somehow?" said Mavis.

"What with?" said John.

"Get a bit of rope and tie it to something," said Mavis.

"There's nowhere to tie it too," John said. "Besides they are pretty heavy them power poles and rope wouldn't hold it. If it did snap it is still going to fall somewhere. I reckon that it is just that the ground is so dry at the moment that it has just moved in the earth somehow."

"Then it could just pop out," Mavis said.

"No it won't they are down too deep in the ground for that," said John.

"Well I still think we should support it somehow. What if we got one of Mr Kelly's tractors out and a steel cable? That should keep it steady," said Mavis.

"I don't think Mr Kelly would approve of it," said Janet.

"But this is an emergency," Mavis said. "The whole thing might fall down and start a fire..."

"It won't start a fire. The circuit will shut off, besides there's nothing to burn..." said John.

"Well how will we know? It's a live wire and it might fall on the pub and..." said Mavis

"Because it will land on the road and there's nothing to burn on the road," said John.

"What if it landed on the pub? That could burn down," said Mavis.

"The wind will blow it away from the pub, onto the road," said John.

"Well I still don't like it. I still reckon we should get a tractor and... Kevin would be able to drive one of them tractors wouldn't he Janet?" said Mavis.

"He probably could, but we don't have the keys to them," said Janet.

"What? Where are they?" said Mavis.

"Locked in the safe," said Janet.

"Haven't you got the keys to the safe?" said Mavis.

"No, Mr Kelly keeps them," said Janet.

"Well what will we do?" said Mavis.

"When will Mr Kelly be back, Janet?" asked Betty who had been listening intently.

"I don't know. He went out towards Kandar with a Mr Wykes to look at a mob of sheep," said Janet.

"When was that?" said Betty.

"About nineish?"

"He won't be back for a while then," said Betty.

"What about Mrs Kelly, does she have any keys?" said Mavis.

"I don't think so, he keeps them with his car keys," said Janet.

"We couldn't get in touch with her anyway, no phones," said John.

"And the mood she was in this morning," said Mavis.

"In that mood again was she?" said Betty.

"Is that the Wykes fellow car parked outside there?" said John.

"Yes," said Janet.

"You don't suppose the pole might hit his car if it falls," said Mavis.

"Wouldn't reach over to it from where it is. Your car would be safe too Janet," said John.

"What will we do?" Mavis said again.

"Might be an idea not to have people parking their cars anywhere near the pole," said Betty.

"That's a good idea," said Mavis.

"We haven't seen anyone all day..." Janet said.

"But just in case," said Mavis. "And better make sure the children stay well away from it when they get out of school."

"We'll go and put the chairs out onto the footpath and on the road," said Betty.

"Do you need a hand?" Mavis said.

"We should be right. Pretty quiet today," said Betty.

"What about hoses?" said Mavis.

"Hoses?" John said.

"In case there's a fire," said Mavis.

"But..." began John, before he was interrupted.

"Best to be careful," said Mavis.

"We've got a little hose that I think will fit onto the water tank, trouble is we don't have much water left," said Betty.

"Mr Kelly must have a bit of water in his tank there, Janet? said Mavis.

"I suppose so," said Janet.

"Surely he must have some hoses there that aren't locked up?" said Mavis.

"I guess so," said Janet.

"Good we might have to use them," Mavis said. "Just in case, it's better to be prepared."

The wind kept up its threatening force, swirling the dust around them as they kept up their discussions of contingency plans. With each sudden gust their eyes would turn to the pole in question to see if they could notice any movement. There wasn't, but the threat was kept alive by Mavis' hysteria which spread through the group like an infection.

Janet also kept a vigil upon the road to the east to see if she could see the approaching car that might be Mrs Stirling.

The section of the mob who had parked themselves on the wooden bench outside the post office, kept up their pondering what these people were doing. Why were they standing in the middle of the road talking most emphatically? Yes it was hot and yes there was a big wind, but it had been like this before, it was going to happen again. This was the way of this country. Better to ride with it than fight against it.

"Oh, by the way Betty, do you have much spare ice? If there is going to be a blackout, we'll need plenty to keep the meat from going off in the shop," said Mavis.

"I'll see what I can find for you," said Betty.

"I'll see if we have any hoses, if we have enough we might be able to hitch them up to our tanks. I'll get Harry to look into it," said Mavis.

With this they all dispersed to perform their different tasks and the Aboriginals, on the bench, who had viewed all of this, were left to wonder, what was happening?

# CHAPTER 24
# THIRSTY SHEEP. FEBRUARY 1965.

The sun was still beating down upon the earth with full fury, aided by the ever increasing wind as if to blast them with the inferno. The mirages covered the entire horizon as though to give the impression they were moving in a fluidic mass of blue flame. But they pressed on, there was a task to be done and the conditions were not going to stop them.

Sergeant was on the right and Flight on the left, twenty yards in front of the tractor, with only the noise of the tractor to break their trotting trance. The wind coming in from their right, picking up tiny particles of the red dust and landing them with force on their bodies, was not going to deter them either. Nor was the oven hot ground on which their tiny paws would land going to delay them. Nor was the mirage horizon which obscured their destination going to keep them from their purpose. They were transfixed upon the noise of the tractor, when it changed would be the signal of something different.

The fire tank on the back was as full as it could be. With each bump the tractor passed over Lorry could hear and feel the water swirling around inside it. Each bump brought about a look behind from Lorry to make sure everything was still on board. There was a lot of stuff that could fall off.

He was in a hurry to get to the sheep, but was careful not to travel too fast lest to damage or lose his cargo. They had been crossing the barren plain long enough that he hoped that he might be able to see them through this totally surreal landscape hidden by the mirage, the dust and the starkness.

About on cue he could make out an object fighting to gain its visibility through the elements. Soon it revealed itself as the windmill. Now, where were the sheep? The windmill was close to a fence which divided two paddocks. There was also the gate which could unite the two paddocks. It was situated about a hundred yards east of the windmill. Lorry and the dogs were in the paddock where the sheep were, where he had previously placed them so they wouldn't get bogged in the dam in the paddock, which also had the windmill/bore.

He strained his eyes to each horizon waiting for the mirage and dust to unveil its occupants. He didn't have to search for very long. They were in the obvious place. Not far from the gate. Laying down, resting, dying a thirsty death. Lorry feared for what he might find.

From his advantage of height on the tractor the sheep now were well in view. This meant that the sheep would soon become in the dog's view. He knew that once that happened they would no longer gain their instructions by the noise or the tractor, but rather from Lorry. To go and round up the sheep was their primary task and greatest joy. Lorry kept a constant eye on them and when their bodies reacted to the sight of the sheep they jumped with excitement. With expectation they looked at Lorry for further instructions. He had been waiting for this and his response planned.

"Come back behind here," he commanded sternly, pointing to the rear of the tractor. Their disappointment was obvious. With heads bowed and tails lowered they retreated. Lorry knew the sight of the dogs would scare the sheep, whereas the object of the exercise was to bring the sheep to him.

He had no reason to be worried. When the sheep did observe their approach some stood up slowly, but the rest stayed down. They were in no condition to take fright. He reversed the tractor towards them and stopped it about twenty yards from where they lay and he started setting up his wares. The sheep, the ones that were awake and conscious, watched carefully. They were concerned about the dogs that could not help themselves, but be seen, although they kept stationary for the moment. Also just what was this man doing, was it a threat?

Placing the drums on the ground and keeping the floor of the carry all higher Lorry soon had a syphoning system in operation. Lorry looked at the sheep and wondered if they knew what he was doing. He lifted the hose out of the drum so that they could see that it was water that was coming out of it. Some did look curious, but possibly fear was keeping them at bay.

Calling the dogs with him Lorry retreated to the right of the mob, hoping curiosity and thirst would overcome their fear. The dogs, eager to set off on a run around the mob, were jumping out of themselves with expectant excitement. Only to be constantly disappointed by Lorry's harsh words.

Keeping very still and keeping the dogs as still as possible, with the threat now gone some of the ewes became increasingly curious. One started to advance towards the tractor and the drums standing on the ground. As they do, when one starts to move others follow, led blindly by a course of habit.

The courage continued until the smell of water quickened their progress. The closer they got the more obvious the smell of water. Some of them started to bleat their realisation which stirred the rest of the mob. Suddenly lots of heads lifted and as they saw many of them now advancing toward the drums, the rest, or those that could, soon followed.

Their desire for the water dispensed with the smelling before tasting ritual. Once the word was out, many of the others suddenly found energy which had seemingly abandoned them, to move towards these drums which promised salvation.

The drums now became very popular with the sheep, so much so that they had attracted quite a gathering. All trying to gain a taste of what they had been dying for. The stronger ones were pushing themselves past the others to dip their heads into the drums.

With the commotion now being created around the drums and the vulnerability of the hoses pouring into them Lorry thought it prudent to quietly wander back to the tractor to protect the hoses. The dogs, who had now been forced to heal beside Lorry, now saw their opportunity to do something. They were sadly disappointed when Lorry commanded them to stay where they were. They watched Lorry's every step as he pushed his way through the mob onto the carry all. Still attentive they waited patiently for the signal from Lorry for assistance.

Upon climbing aboard the carry-all, he realised, what the

sheep had already realised, that there was not enough room for them under the carry all to drink from that side of the drums. The hoses were relatively safe. The first ones that reached the water had now had their fill. They would lift their heads out of the drums and stand for a moment with great contentment and relief. They were quickly interrupted by others whose demand was greater and were pushing themselves towards the drums. All around the tractor was a moving mass of red stained wool, each animal trying to gain access to the drums. Lorry looked into the fire tank and could see it was emptying and still a lot of the sheep hadn't had their fill. It was obvious that more trips like this one was going to be necessary. He knew this was going to be the case, but the amount of water each ewe was consuming did surprise him.

Soon the unmistakable sound of air entering the hoses became audible, a sure sign that the water had run out. He quickly loaded up the hoses onto the carry all as before ready for the return journey with as much urgency as before. He started up the tractor hoping that the sound of it might spread the woolly masses enough for him to set off back for a refill. However, the demand for water out-weighted the threat of the tractor's noise.

The dogs, who had been keeping a very keen eye on the situation, then realised this was their chance to do something. Without instruction and knowing what Lorry wanted to do they ran across to the front of the tractor. With speed of attack, loud barks and little bites on the legs, they created a path for Lorry to move. He seized the opportunity and soon after the drums could fit more heads into them.

"That will do," commanded Lorry towards the dogs to which they assumed their positions at the front of the tractor about twenty yards in front of it for the return journey. The headwind that they now trotted into could throw the red dust into their eyes. Undaunted they kept up their steady pace into the obscured heat filled horizon.

By mid-afternoon the days heat, which should have reached its peak, was still rising. The wind, coming from even hotter places, gave reinforcements to the sun. As Lorry was filling the tank for the fourth time he welcomed the cool water which he liberally splashed over his body. The cycle of trips to the sheep with more water was well entrenched. The dogs were used to the routine. The highlights of which were, parting the sheep to make way for the tractor and the cool water Lorry would pour onto them when they would fill up again.

To Lorry's reckoning, with the time now having to be near three pm, Marg would nearly be home by the next trip. She left before ten, five hours driving, an hour in Wallabra, she could be home by the next return. The next returned would be a little delayed. The sheep that could move now knew about the liquid medicine the tractor held. Some had not moved. This time it was going to take longer, Lorry was either going to bring the water to them or carry them to the water. A bucket would be handy.

The dogs happy to be wet again, the tractor heading back south, the usual positions were assumed. Wordlessly and subconsciously, ignoring the elements, they continued their duty. The wind was gusting with greater force and after one such blast Lorry noticed the dogs sniffing the air. Two signs of the approaching change. Maybe it will bring rain? Maybe it will at least bring a cooler air? All

Lorry could do was to always be positive. He tried to ignore what he had always known, in that hope was not feasible in this land where the future is indefinable.

# CHAPTER 25
# THE TRUCK GOING NOWHERE.
# FEBRUARY 1965.

With the intersection onto the Worthton road looming Marg released her foot from the accelerator and depressed the clutch. She hoped the sudden change in tempo would not upset the flimsy fan belt which so far had lasted. Second gear, the change in speed was quite noticeable as if to awaken her from a trance to see that the landscape had not really changed much. At this intersection another parallel joined the fray. The railway line from Worthton was the first obstacle to be navigated. This one was a first gear job and carefully so as not to disturb her stockings. Although she knew that it was not necessary she glanced on either side for trains.

Railway line crossed she chanced a look into the rear vision mirror and was not surprised to see only red dust coming from her car. Straining to see if there was another car behind her, she consoled herself to be assured that there wasn't. Realising that there was not likely to be a policeman out here, she decided not to place her arm outside the car to indicate that she was turning right. There were no trails of dust coming from the east or the west, thus she felt quite safe in turning.

Upon turning right the road changed a little. It was still dirt with potholes and corrugations, but it was wider, wide enough to fit two cars on it. From here she didn't have to worry about heading into the scrub when another car came along, they could pass each other with ease.

The change of direction had also given the sun a different angle. Instead of attacking her right shoulder it now shone directly into the car. Her visibility was restricted by the unrelenting hot light from the sun until she lowered the sun visor. That helped. She would be in Wallabra before the sun crept below the visor. The other adjustment to be considered was the wind which now presented itself more as a head wind with a slight angle so as to push the car to the left. She soon realised how to adjust. Thankfully the wind blew past her before circulating through the car and exiting on the left. This meant that the smell emulating from Charlie, could be kept at bay, a little. She knew she looked dirty enough as it was without another objectionable smell lingering on her.

Still, however, the scenery had not changed. Open plains that disappeared into the mirage. The parallels of phone lines, power lines, fences, railway lines and now this two tracked road, all melted into one at the horizon.

Marg and Charlie sat in silence. Not in a manner uncomfortable, quite the opposite in fact, very comfortable in the fact that they had come to an understanding. A connection had been established, a mutual trust formed. Both were in the many miles to travel mode of being patient as they traversed this wilderness.

The continuing emptiness leads to an expectation of sameness. The inertia was broken when Marg noticed Charlie starting to shuffle a little in his seat. At first she wondered if he had heard something from the engine and she worried that it might break down again. She listened carefully, but could not hear anything extraordinary. His twitching continued and his eyes fixed firmly to the front as if concentrating.

Marg wondered if she may have needed to stop.

"Are you all right Charlie?" she asked politely.

"Something up there Missus?" he replied with his eyes still fixed to the front.

Marg looked further forward, past the immediate pot holes and digressions of the road, towards the horizon. To her surprise she could see a dark angular shape emerging from the mirage. It was a little to the left of them, but seemingly still on the road. Something different, the trance broken, an angled, mysterious shape was now well in view.

Just what it was, still an uncertainty. They both strained through the sunlight to gain greater clarification. Certainly it was not another vehicle travelling as there was no red dust behind it. A new structure perhaps, but being so close to the road, that was not likely.

The black blob soon took greater shape until it obviously revealed itself to be a truck parked on the side of the road, unusual, but perhaps not unexpected. The sight of another human structure drew direct contrast to the natural landscape it habited. Just what it was doing here was still a mystery.

"He broken down, Missus." Charlie proclaimed profoundly, anxious to answer the same questions circulating in his head.

As they approached Marg started to slow down. Help may have been required if there was someone about. It was a single tray truck, like many that the farmers use to transport the grain to the silos, except unlike the farmers with a bin on the back, this truck was covered in as though to protect the goods inside. Originally the metallic sides of the truck would have been silver, however years of neglect and the red dust had tainted the colour to be similar to the terrain it transverse.

She parked the car behind the truck and turned the motor off. The only noise left was the wind still howling through the car and the first of the local flies who quickly realised the car as a shelter from the wind, with food inside of it.

There was not much sign of movement. The back of the truck gave no indication upon its nature. Just two large doors that opened it and by the wear and tear they displayed, had been opening and closing for quite a number of years. It appeared that the only attention the truck received was to just keep it going, any attempt to make it look cared for had long since dissipated.

It was not normal for a truck to be just here somewhere in the middle of nowhere. It stood like an abandoned ship in a sea of red dust. There had been no sign of life since they had parked. Marg could see Charlie anxious to see what this was all about. The situation needed investigating.

They alighted and were hit by the full force of the wind. Although it felt uncomfortable, the wind did bring a different air to that which permeated inside the car. Charlie's aroma was kept at bay for the time being. Charlie led the way to the left hand side of the truck, looking anxiously for whatever he was to find. When Marg came into his view he was quick to point out to her what he had found.

"Flat tyre, Missus," said Charlie pointing at the rear axle.

Charlie kept pointing at it whilst Marg caught up. He was right, in fact he had understated the situation. The outside tyre of the two that held up the left hand rear axle of the truck was not just flat, it was in tatters, with strips of rubber broken away, flapping in the wind. Obviously an effort had been made to get to Wallabra with the flat, but it had failed. Upon inspecting the other tyre it was not surprising to see it was also bad condition. No thread left, as bald as the steel sides of the truck with wire starting to be exposed.

There was still no sign of life. Charlie, like an inquisitive kelpie, turned away from the tyre in search of other evidence. With almost ghost like steps Charlie continued along the side of the truck. Not knowing what they would find, maybe nothing, Marg followed cautiously.

Charlie suddenly stopped and pointed at something to Marg. Like a dog, with a wagging tail, beckoning the farmer to investigate.

"Here, Missus," he said.

Not knowing what she might find, Marg obeyed.

Her concern and curiosity was solved with the appearance of a couple of legs emerging from underneath the truck. The body of a man displayed itself, crawling urgently as if a little startled.

A small middle aged man appeared with dirt and dust all over him, a three day growth on his face and clothes that had seen better days. The wrinkles on his face gave him a greater age than he really was. His clothes hung off him either because there were too big for him when they were new or had been stretched and pulled so much they gave him more size than he really was. His very thin body that looked in need of a good feed, was revealed by the wind that blew at his loose clothes to expose an outline of just bones.

He stood in absolute amazement and at first speechless, surprised to be seeing what he had least expected.

"Where did youse come from?" he blurted out when words finally reached his voice.

Charlie pointed towards the car and the man not really wanting to gain direction from an Aboriginal, eventually looked beyond to see the car behind his truck.

"Couldn't hear us for the wind," Charlie said to Marg. The man now realised why their appearance had been unnoticed.

"Can we help?" asked Marg.

The man looked blankly, possibly wondering what an Aboriginal or a woman could do to help and further what an Aboriginal was doing with this woman who, despite her current untidy appearance, was certainly a cockies wife. Marg could sense the misapprehension from the man and quickly wanted to explain the situation.

"I'm Marg Stirling. I'm on my way to Wallabra. This is Charlie. I'm just giving him a lift."

She thought about shaking his hand, but given his extremely dirty appearance decided not to. Charlie, however, who was much closer to the man, extended his hand as a friendly gesture.

"Charlie."

The man looked suspiciously at Charlie, but decided to reciprocate the gesture.

"Toby," he said without much enthusiasm.

"You've got a flat tyre, I notice," Marg said in an effort to get the situation more productive.

"Not only is it bloody well flat, but the spare is too I

think. I don't know if it's got a hole in it, or just hasn't been pumped up for a while. I could find out if I could get the bloody thing out. I've been battling away here for hours and this nut just won't budge. Hot day I guess, but it isn't helping me much. What's more I don't know if this jack they've given me will hold this truck, it's pretty full and I've never worked with this jack before. The old one they had finally buggered up and I reckon they've put the wrong jack in here. What's more I've got perishables in there, in this heat, even in the ice box I've got in there, they won't last long," Toby said.

"Where are you heading?" said Marg.

"Just to Wallabra, I'm bringing in all the supplies from Worthton."

"You haven't got far to go then," Marg said trying to be positive.

"I bloody well know, but I'm not bloody well going anywhere at the moment," he said as if to express all the day's frustration and anger.

Marg got the impression that his language was being kept under restrain due to the fact that he recognised that he was talking to a lady. Marg realised that the best tactic was to be objective.

"So why can't you get the spare out?"

"Because the bloody well nuts are frozen. It won't budge," he said as if stating the obvious. To Toby, this pair represented no help at all.

Charlie, who had been listening inconspicuously, suddenly had a suggestion.

"Missus, you got oil in your car. Alright if I get some, might fix this bloke up."

"Sure Charlie," Marg said hoping Charlie would again

find a solution, as she knew she certainly didn't have one.

Charlie set out on his errand and Toby looked after him.

"What would he know?"

"Well I was broken down along Wymere road, fan belt, and he fixed it up enough to get us here," Marg answered and was pleased to see the surprised look on Toby's face.

"How long have you been here?"

"Too bloody well long. Left Worthton about seven this morning. I should've been there before lunch. It must be bloody well after two by now and there's all this stuff. Some of it will go off in this heat. What do you expect? Do you see the bloody truck they've given me today? The new ones off the road and struck me in this one. No coppers on this road you see, they reckon they can get away with it."

"Hasn't someone come along in that time?" said Marg.

"No one, wouldn't expect anyone on a day like this," Toby said.

"Have you got water?" said Marg.

"Got a bit left," Toby said.

Charlie reappeared with the container of oil, a piece of wire and a hammer. Without saying anything he climbed under the truck with such enthusiasm as to suggest that he was grateful for the opportunity.

Toby and Marg looked at each other quite bemused and curious about what Charlie had in mind. Nothing much seemed to happen for a while. Inertia set in except for the wind and the flies which kept up their intensity. Only Charlie's legs, dangling out the side of the truck, were the only indication that something might happen and they were still.

"Don't burr the bloody well nut up mate and use that big

spanner, lest you can't stuff that up," said Toby, as a tension release created by the waiting.

A series of shuffling noise began to be created. Marg and Toby could sense something was about to happen. Then they heard a series of little taps. Toby was looking quite alarmed.

They ceased and another period of inertia descended.

"I hope he doesn't bloody well bugger it up," Toby said.

Marg also hoped that he wouldn't either. She had pinned her recommendations upon Charlie. Then they felt and heard the truck give a little jolt. The shock of it caused Toby to panic about what this bloke had done, expecting the worst. Soon after, Charlie emerged.

"She good now, give us a hand, we get her out."

Toby looked at Marg with speechless, disbelieving surprise before climbing under the truck. Charlie followed. There were now two sets of legs dangling from the side of the truck. This time, however, they were moving. Although there were no accompanying voices, Marg assumed that something positive was happening. The increase in leg movement also resulted in more dust being stirred up. Realising that there would be even more dust created when they did got the spare out, she moved towards the front of the truck, that way the wind would blow the dust away from her. No point is getting more dust on herself she was dirty enough as it was.

The legs grew longer, dust ridden bodies were emerging and miraculously so too did the spare tyre, coloured very red. Standing the tyre up the inevitable bounce was about to occur. It happened to which Marg was very pleased she had moved herself up wind. There was plenty of red dust which caused the tyre to change colour, but no bounce.

Not even a bit of a bounce. The men let the tyre go in disgust and it fell to the ground.

"Not enough air in her mate," said Charlie.

"Yeah" said Toby with no expression.

Eyes fixed onto the tyre a silence ensued.

"Do you have a tyre pump?" asked Marg.

"No," Toby said.

"I think there's one in our car," said Marg.

"Wrong value size Missus," said Charlie.

"Oh," said Marg not quite sure what that meant.

Silence again dominated. Toby was occasionally kicking the ground and Charlie deep in thought.

It was Marg who broke the spell.

"Would Joe Clements in Wallabra have one?" Marg said.

"Probably," said Toby.

"Charlie, do you reckon that tyre would fit in the boot of my car?" said Marg.

"Might Missus," said Charlie.

"If it will, why don't I take it into town? Get Joe Clements to pump it up and he'll probably bring it back out to you, or if he can't I'll bring it back when I'm returning," Marg said.

"That might work," said Toby.

"He might have to check if he got spare tyre too," said Charlie.

"Might be a good idea," said Toby.

After a little deliberation Toby said, "Would you mind?"

"Of course not," Marg said.

With that the two men wheeled the spare tyre around to the boot of the car, disturbing more of the red dust as they went. Marg stood well up wind. She opened the boot and stood back. It sort of fitted, but not without a deal of shuffling and a length of wire to tie the boot door down.

Toby was beginning to feel a little more at ease. Marg's thoughts now turned to the sheep at home and her original errand. Preparing to get a move on she realised that Toby and this truck would still be stuck here, in this heat, for a while yet. It would be uncomfortable for Toby, but perhaps disastrous for the perishables in the truck.

"I've got some room in the back seat, could I take some of the things into Wallabra?" she asked.

"That would be bloody well great. You wouldn't mind?"

"Of course not," Marg said.

The mystery of what was behind the battered doors soon became realised. Not before a burst of even hotter air was expelled from within the truck as he opened the doors. Marg and Charlie waited near the opened doors as Toby fossicked about inside.

Soon after, the back seat was being filled up with boxes of vegetables and cans of food. It didn't take long before it was completely full such that now Marg would have to use the rear vision windows on the side of the car since the back window was completely covered.

"Is there anything for Kelly's? I'm going there as well," Marg asked.

"Yeah there is, but you don't have enough room," Toby replied.

"Put them on the front seat, I stay here and help get that flat tyre off," suggested Charlie.

Marg looked across at the Toby knowing from the attitude he had already expressed towards the Aboriginal he might not have been too keen on the idea, but he said, "I don't mind and I'll give him a lift into town afterwards," grateful for the help.

He ventured back to where all the stuff was in the truck and after more fossicking around eventually came out with boxes of varying sizes. It was just as well as Charlie decided to stay and help otherwise they would not have all fitted.

They piled up on the seat next to Marg as she started the car for the final leg into Wallabra. The smaller parcel, which was most visible to her being on top of the pile, took her attention as from a glance she thought she saw the name Stirling written upon it. Upon closer inspection her suspicions were correct. The name of Lorry Stirling was written on it for all to see.

She wondered.

# CHAPTER 26
# JOE'S GOT SOMETHING TO DO.
# FEBRUARY 1965.

Car started, fortunately as the stocking fan belt still seemed to be holding, Marg chanced a look behind her to see if there was any oncoming traffic. It did not surprise her that there wasn't. The journey continued. She left the two men to the heat, the flies, the wind and themselves. They looked longingly after her as if all their desperate hopes went with her until the dust from the car covered them and they retreated to simply waiting.

She had forgotten to ask Toby the time, but then he probably didn't know anyway. She noticed that the sun had not yet sunk below the visor so she could still see the road without competing with the sun in her eyes.

As the car gathered speed and the wind began to circulate the dust that had gathered whilst they were stopped took flight and swirled around Marg like the taunting of an adversary before it exited. At least Charlie's smell was disappearing noticeably. She shook her hair, realising it was probably more red than blue and brushed down her dress trying to appear as presentable as possible before she reached Wallabra.

Soon the truck was swallowed from view by the horizon. Not far now to Wallabra, she was impatient for the first landmark to be visible. She was tempted to go a bit faster as the wind, now head on, seemed to be impeding her progress. Afraid of the improvised fan belt and the fact that she could feel the car straining under the newly acquired load, she kept at a steady pace and tried to be patient.

The sameness of the open plains, straight road, parallels of different wires and no buildings soon set in. The trance was entrenched waiting for the first Wallabra landmark or something different to dispel the illusion.

Surprisingly it was the latter. The loop of the telegraph lines between each pole suddenly became irregular. This was indeed something different, something that was not normal. Its inconformity caught Marg's attention. She kept glancing over to the left to understand this occurrence and slowed down when she saw the cause.

From one of the poles the wires had fallen to the ground. There was no more loop. Further along, she could see that the next pole had fallen over. She decided that this needed investigating. Pulling over to the side of the road and bracing herself for the full force of the wind again, she wandered over to the pole.

The pole had been snapped by the wind, and with the fall had broken the wires. This could only mean that there were no phones working in Wallabra. There wasn't much that she could do, but report it when she got to town. Back in the car again she noted the odometer so she could give a definite placement of the break. Arriving now had greater importance. Wallabra would be cut off from the world.

The wind had not abated at all nor had the heat decreased. The two still worked together as a blockade against the car. No sign of a cool change, just time passing on a seemingly endless journey.

At last the first glimpse of the town was now visible. The silos, standing out like worshipped monuments to a good season, were the first objects to come into view. They rose from just a dot on the horizon to become beacons of accomplishment. She started to feel easier because at least if something went wrong here, she could walk into town and find help. Then the driveway into Mr Kelly's place on the left, together with the mob of sheep in the front paddock waiting for fate to give them a purpose, was passed. Soon after, the bitumen road was reached. Her body could relax a little.

On cue, Joe Clement's joint appeared on the left. She started to slow down. The patched up car had made it. Cynically she reminded herself to note the expression on Joe's face when he sees the fan belt. She parked it near to the door where he did his repairs and felt most relieved to have made it.

Joe emerged from his office, as though pleased that he had something to do. Attired in his usual overalls, this week the blue ones, he cast his curious eye over the car.

"Looks like you've got a bit of a load on there, Marg," he said as Marg was getting out of the car.

"Hi Joe," she said, "There's a bloke in a truck broken down about ten miles on the Worthton road."

"Is that the truck from Worthton, is it?"

"Yes," said Marg.

"Did he have that oil that I ordered on it?" Joe said.

"Don't know Joe, he did have a bit of stuff on there. I brought in the perishables for the store," she replied.

"What's wrong with the truck?"

"He's got a flat tyre and the spare's pretty flat too. That's the spare in my boot."

"It hasn't got a puncture in it as well has it?"

"He doesn't think so," Marg said. "He's hoping you will pump it up for him."

"Who is it?"

"Toby he said his name was."

"He's all right. It's his offsider, Cyril, that I don't have much time for. Still owes me fifty quid from years back."

He thought for a moment.

"Well we better have a look at it then," he said on his way to the boot. He glanced at the inside of the car.

"You have got a bit of a load in there, haven't you?"

"Just a few things for the store, in this heat they would go off, so I've brought them in," said Marg.

When the wire was undone the boots roof flung open as with a lot of dust. Joe struggled to get the tyre out. When it did get out and didn't bounce Joe proclaimed, "Not much air in it."

He rolled it around and punched at the side of the tyre.

"Not much thread on it either. This is the spare?"

"Yes."

"What's the one that's flat like?" said Joe.

"In pieces," said Marg.

"So he won't have a spare for the trip back?" said Joe.

"No."

"I might have an old tyre around here somewhere we can fix him up with. I'll get the compressor onto this one first if we've got any power."

"Is there a blackout?"

"Not the last time I looked, but with this wind you never know. The phones are down, I know that much," said Joe.

"Doesn't surprise me, there's a pole snapped out along the Worthton road."

"Is that it, thought it might have been something like that. Oh well better get this tyre looked at," he started to role it, with difficulty, towards the shed.

"There's something else too Joe."

"What's that?"

"I had a bit of trouble with our car on the way in, would you mind having a quick look at it, please."

Dropping the tyre he started to walk towards the bonnet of Marg's car. She pulled the lever so it would open and then moved to a suitable position to observe his reaction.

"I think it is something to do with the fan belt."

She watched his face carefully, as he peered into the engine. The reaction was instant and expressive. His mouth dropped, his eyes opened as wide as she had ever seen them and for a moment he was speechless. Marg tried very hard not to laugh.

"Is that a pair of stockings, or what was a pair of stockings?" Joe said.

"I expect I won't be wearing them again," said Marg.

He looked at her quizzically and in amazement.

"Did you do this?" said Joe, not really believing that she could.

"No it wasn't me, Joe."

"I've never seen that before. How far have you come like this?"

"About thirty miles, I suppose, I took it pretty steady," Marg said proudly.

"And it's still holding together. Who did this?" Joe said.

"Bloke called Charlie. Lives down at the camp, part of the mob," Marg said.

"What was he doing out there?" said Joe

"He said he was out going walkabout and happened to

be where I broke down," Marg said.

"You were lucky he was there," Joe said.

"I sure was," said Marg.

Marg saw the opportunity to maybe return Charlie's help and throw a spanner into, what she knew, was Joe's rather negative view on the mob. She wasn't going to let it slip pass

."He seems to be pretty handy with vehicles, Joe. The truck driver, what was his name?"

"Toby," Joe said.

"He was having trouble getting the spare out. It looked like he'd been trying for hours. Charlie had a go and in no time, out it came."

Joe went a little quiet for a moment as though he was trying to figure out a way in which he had done it. He couldn't so a change of tact was required.

"What was he doing there anyway" Joe said.

"I was giving him a lift into town."

Joe looked at her awkwardly as if it was taboo for white people to give the Aboriginals a lift. Especially a cockie's wife as what Marg really was. It didn't worry Marg, she was proud of what she had done and she really didn't mind stating her case for the Aboriginals. She pressed the point and gave further information to set Joe's mind at ease.

"It was the least that I could do for him. If it wasn't for Charlie I would be still out there, there's no one on the road today. Besides I don't feel threatened by him. He seems pretty useful with vehicles Joe. You might be able to use him sometime," she said, tongue in cheek.

She didn't really fancy her chances of success in getting Joe to maybe employ Charlie sometime. There was still that silly racial divide. Maybe, though, one day Joe might be stuck and need a hand and he will remember her suggestion. She often thought that if the white people would only give the Aboriginals a go, instead of condemning them constantly, the attitude toward each other might improve. By the stern look that invaded his face she knew that she had not succeeded.

Joe knew Marg to be a woman who spoke her mind no matter what the circumstances. He decided a change of topic was necessary, besides his day had totally changed. No more sitting in his room, waiting for a customer that was not likely to arrive, watching the time pass, now he had more than he ever thought was possible fifteen minutes ago. There were a lot of things that needed to be done.

"You'll need a new fan belt," he said changing the topic.

"Might be handy," Marg said.

"Think we've got one for this model in there somewhere," he said as though he knew that there was.

"Look, if the car got me this far, it will get me down the street. I really should deliver all these boxes to the store before they are ruined." she said.

"June! "He called out with an enormous voice that startled Marg.

June eventually appeared from the door of the shed. This surprised Marg as she expected June to appear from the office where Joe had come from. She appeared flustered as though she had been dragged away from something she was intensely involved with. By her attire it certainly wasn't house work. She was wearing overalls, which might have fitted her many years ago, but middle age, not only brought her grey hair, it had accumulated extra size such that now they pressed tightly onto her body. The tee shirt underneath wore the result of a close fit with sweat marks clearly evident. Her hair, which usually was a creation made by curlers, lay flat from sweat. Marg assumed it must have been even hotter in the shed she'd come out of.

"What do you want?" she commanded, but upon seeing Marg changed her attitude and inquired.

"How are you Marg?"

"Well thanks June. Hot day isn't it?"

"Too bloody hot," said June.

"Can you see if we've got a fan belt for this car? I've got to pump up this tyre and take it out to Toby. He's stuck out on the Worthton road somewhere. Marg's going to drop off a few things at the store. If she gets back before I do, you might start working on it, will you?"

# CHAPTER 27
# RESOLVING WALLABRA. FEBRUARY 1965.

With the school children now out of school, the traffic had suddenly picked up. Four cars had passed down the main street within five minutes of each other, peak hour in Wallabra. Mavis was worried. She was standing in the middle of the road warning the drivers of the pole that might come down. She was suggesting to them that they keep well over close to Kelly's shop, closing one side of the road. She figured it was pretty safe to do so as there wasn't a lot of traffic. The red dust being picked up by the neighbouring bare paddocks found a tunnel between the buildings and made it difficult for the drivers to see her. However she was determined to keep up her vigil.

The mob from the Aboriginal settlement kept their positions on the bench outside the Post Office. Occasionally others members would venture up from the camp. They would be greeted by the usual hail fellow, well met procedure before assuming their positions, usually in silence, on the bench. Occasionally some of them would retire back to the camp. It was to be expected. It was a daily occurrence. Not regimented, more ad lib, but regular. This day they did have something to occupy their watch. The whites were doing irregular things, like all these hoses, someone in the middle of the road, lots of coming and going by the shop owners. All this activity enthralled them. The answers however were not forthwith as there was no conversing between the blacks and the whites.

Janet felt worried for Mavis and instructed Kevin to go out there with her. He didn't complain as he was sick of trying to keep the red dust out of the shop. With each car that appeared Janet anxiety would increase. Would this car be Mrs Stirling? Where could she be? There was no sign of Mr Kelly even though the afternoon was getting on. There was always that hope. She resigned herself to trying to keep the dust off the products. That way she could keep herself out of the wind and maybe get her mind off worrying.

Betty had arranged a barrier of tables, chairs and old furniture along the footpath before the pub on both sides to warn the children of the danger. She saw it her duty to stay outside, being swept by the wind, to clarify the situation to those who wouldn't understand.

Between them, John and Harry had collected enough hoses and a pump ready and had set up a bit of a water system, just in case. It was Janet who commented that if the pole was to go down, it would cause a blackout which meant the pump wouldn't go. Her statement was accepted. Luckily Harry's old diesel powered generator still went so they hooked up the pump to it. John and Helen took it in turns to man the system whilst the other was in the Post office. Harry took care of the store.

Although the main street of Wallabra was sealed with bitumen, Marg couldn't help noticing the amount of dust already being kicked up by this ferocious wind as she drove towards the store. Hopefully the store will have some new library books, or even have her wristwatch back from the repairers. Perhaps there might be a pleasant surprise in store for her. She fantasised for something to have made this journey, this day of toil, worthwhile. She glanced down at her dress and wish she hadn't. It had changed colour to red, but not consistently and with sweat marks on it. She looked a proper mess, but what could she do about it? Try as she might this land forbids gentility.

A surprise did present itself even before she arrived at the store. Through the gust of red dust she could make out the unmistakable figure of Mavis and with her Kevin standing in the middle of the road. This was most unusual. By the sternness of Mavis' expression directed solely upon her, Marg realised that something was amiss.

It was apparent to Marg that Mavis was gesturing her to keep well to the left. This suited her as she was now looking for a park. There was never too much of a problem finding a park in Wallabra and as such there was a vacant spot right outside the store. Whilst pulling into the spot she then noticed John standing on the footpath next to a coil of hoses. They exchanged hand waves of recognition, but no indication upon what he was doing. Something different was happening in this town and she wasn't quite sure what it was.

She wasted no time in getting into the shop. Harry was sitting at the cash register and was surprised by her sudden entrance. It was as though she had awoken him from a long thought process that was leading nowhere. He stood his tall and thin body up either out of surprise or from good manners. A smile lit up his face and caused his grey moustache to point upwards to emphasise his pleasant demeanour.

"I thought I heard a door close. Looks like you've had a busy day Marg," was his dry comment upon her appearance.

She couldn't help a wry smile from invading her face as she appreciated his humour.

"You could say that Harry, yes. The truck from Worthton has broken down about ten miles down the road. Joe's seeing to it now. I've got a stack of boxes for you from the truck in my car with the perishables in them."

"Good on you Marg," he said.

As they were preparing to go out to Marg's car their thoughts were suddenly changed by a fresh stimulus. Mavis entered the shop with as much anxiety as she was showing in the middle of the road.

"Hullo Marg," she said. "I saw you arriving and thought you might know something. Do you know what's happening?"

"I'm not sure what you mean Mavis?" Marg replied, a little perplexed about her question.

"We don't have any phones. We haven't had them all day. It is the wind you see. I thought you might know something," said Mavis.

"Well, come to think of it, I did see a pole down on the Worthton road. That might have something to do with it," Marg replied dryly.

"Did you? Well that explains it doesn't it. Where abouts did you say?"

"About seven miles out," said Marg.

"No wonder we haven't got any phones," said Mavis.

"Marg's brought in some of the stuff from the Worthton truck," said Harry, who had waited patiently for Mavis to obtain the necessary information.

"The Worthton truck! Where was it?" asked an excited Mavis, who was getting many of her questions answered by Marg's arrival.

Harry realised he had opened up another box of information to be transferred to an eager Mavis thirsting for news. He would have to wait longer before he could get the produce into the store.

"Broken down about ten or so miles out on the Worthton road," said Marg.

"Broke down was he? What was wrong?" she asked.

"Flat tyre."

"See, I told you his tyres were buggered," said Mavis.

"Couldn't he fix it?" said Harry.

"He was having trouble getting the spare out," said Marg.

"It must have been that old truck he's been using. Why they keep it going is beyond me," said Mavis.

"So what's happened?" said Harry.

"We got the spare one out eventually and we put it into my boot. Joe Clements is looking at it now."

"So when does he expect to be here? We got all those vegetables coming. They'll be ruined sitting in that truck in this heat," said Mavis.

"Well that's what..." Marg started, but was interrupted by Helen entering the shop.

"What's happened? Hullo Marg," said Helen anxious for news.

"The Worthton truck's on its way, but it's got a flat tyre. I told you that tyre was no good. Why they don't do something about it I don't know," said Mavis.

"Where is it?" said Helen.

"Where did you say it was Marg?" said Mavis.

"About ten miles out," said Marg.

"That's right about ten miles out. Joe Clements is looking into it," said Mavis.

"That's right," said Marg.

"Oh and there's a pole down on the Worthton road. That's why we don't have any phones," said Mavis.

"That would explain it all. Must have been the wind, I suppose," said Helen.

"I think it must have been too," said Mavis.

"Were the wires cut?" said Helen.

"I don't know. Were the wires cut Marg?" said Mavis.

"Yes," Marg said.

"John might be able to do something about it, perhaps. Where about was it Marg?" said Helen.

"About seven miles out didn't you say Marg?"

"Yes that's right," said Marg.

"But we'll need John here in case this pole falls down," said Mavis.

Marg saw the opportunity to get some of her questions answered. Namely, why Mavis was standing in the middle of the road and why John was standing outside in the heat and wind next to a hose.

"What pole?" said Marg.

"The pole next to the pub. Haven't you heard? Helen saw it move with a big gust this morning. We're worried it might fall over," said Mavis.

"That's why we've got all the hoses out and the pump ready to go..." started Helen.

"And we were worried when the children came out of school in case they might be under it when it did go. We're taking it in turns to stand out on the road warning everyone," said Mavis.

"I see," said Marg. "Has anyone seen it move since?"

There was a slight pause as they all looked at each other.

"I haven't heard anyone say that it has, but it still might, that's it," said Mavis.

"Which reminds me, I must ask Betty if they have any spare ice just in case there is a black out. That is of course if we have anything that needs to be cold," said Mavis.

"When will the truck get here then?" asked Helen.

"Goodness knows, at least we know it is on its way. By the time it gets here everything will be ruined in this heat," said Mavis.

"It's all right Mavis, I've brought a lot of the stuff in, it's in the back of the car now," said Marg.

"Oh good on you Marg. You should've said so before," said Mavis.

"We tried," piped Harry, which brought about a critical look from Mavis.

"Harry, you better go and stand with Kevin on the road, he's out there by himself at the moment. We'll get all the stuff out of Marg's car," said Mavis.

As they all progressed to their respective duties, Marg chanced a look at the questionable pole. It seemed steady to her. Even as a sudden gust of wind placed her off balance as she walked to the car, the pole held.

The street had gone quiet again. The school rush had finished. Kevin and Harry still kept their positions though, in the wind and the heat, just in case.

John and Helen gave a hand with the supplies and soon they were all in the shop. Mavis now was busy placing them all ready for the customers. Hoping the vegetables would cool down before anyone came to buy them. Needing a few groceries herself, Marg had first choice of what was available. After placing them in the esky and carrying the esky back to the car Marg had one final errand at the store.

"I don't suppose there are any new library books in are there Mavis?" she asked.

"No, they haven't sent any new ones out for ages. They might be in the truck perhaps if you want to wait around," said Mavis.

"I'm in a bit of a rush to get home. What about my wristwatch, any sign of it?" Marg asked.

"Not this time I'm sorry Marg. I have been asking about it though. Perhaps it might be on the truck as well."

Within moments Marg's fantasies had been dashed.

Sensing her disappointment and having observed her less than tidy appearance, Mavis asked.

"Would you like a cup of tea, or a bit of a wash up?"

"Thank you Mavis, but I'm in a bit of a hurry to get back home. Lorry's waiting for the part I'm to pick up from Kelly's next door. I'd like to be home before dark. Thank you for asking though."

"Thank you Marg for bringing all this in. It would've been ruined in this heat," replied Mavis.

"Oh and, you won't find Mr Kelly there. He's gone off with that bloke that owns that car down there, somewhere. Won't be back till later on, Janet's there though," added Mavis.

Next for Marg was the object of the day's exercise, the building next door, Mr Kelly's place. Get this part and be on her way, once the fan belt was fixed. She had forgotten to ask anyone the time, but by the level of the sun in the western sky, she had no time to lose.

Janet had been biding her time attending to the products that kept falling down and sweeping the dust. She had not been paying attention to what was going on outside. Kevin was out there and there wasn't much she could do. Her job, in this instant, was to man the shop. Her preoccupation presently was however, worry. As she perused the store on her errand of dust, she kept looking in the most unusual places for the part Mrs Stirling was to pick up, to no avail.

She was feeling very guilty that Mrs Stirling's trip was going to be in vain, and on such a terribly hot day as this had turned out to be. She had decided that all she could do, when she arrived, was to tell her the truth and hope she wouldn't get too annoyed at her. She knew Mrs Stirling to be a very fair minded person, but she also knew that she had a way of saying what she thought no matter the cost, with a bit of a temper thrown in. She hoped that she would not have to witness that.

"Bugger Mr Kelly for putting me in this position," she thought.

Kevin, in his capacity of traffic controller's assistant, had seen Marg's car pull up. He instantly recognised it. His parents and the Stirlings didn't mix much so he knew who she was, rather than knew her to talk to. At this instant he was happy to keep it that way. His strategy was not to be engaged by her. Keep in the middle of the road, looking for a car that might just come along. Now that Mavis had retreated to the shop with Mrs Stirling, it was all up to him. With the school children now all picked up, he didn't have very much to do. He kept looking into Kelly's building to catch sight of Janet, to try and give her warning, but their eyes never met. He was pleased that when Mrs Stirling did go to Kelly's, he would be out here.

Although it was only forty yards to the front of Kelly's

building, with the heavy items to be delivered to Kelly's, Marg thought it better to drive the small distance. The stockings had held up so far and there wasn't much further.

With Harry now back to help Kevin, Kevin made certain that he was staring west for traffic whilst Mrs Stirling was in eye sight. For him, ignorance was going to be bliss.

Marg had always been quite fond of Janet, although she had always been her parent's daughter. Marg knew that Janet was quite smart. She was dux of the school. Realising that it was totally up to Janet, Marg secretly hoped that Janet would do something with her intelligence and that did not include spending her life in Wallabra. She was curious to discover the Janet as an individual, instead of being her parent's daughter.

As if in a trance, Janet kept sweeping and worrying. The day's heat and toil had taken its toll and she was starting to wish this shift would end. Her spell was broken by a figure at the entrance. Any figure would've startled her, but when she recognised it as Mrs Stirling her surprise turned to panic.

Marg was pleased to see Janet when she entered, but was dismayed at Janet's attempt to keep the red dust out.

"Hullo Janet. You've got your work cut out for you there on a day like this," said Marg.

"Hullo Mrs Stirling. I've been worried about you. I thought you would've been in before this," Janet said.

"You might say I've had a couple of hold ups. You will have to excuse my appearance. Bad hair day, I'm afraid," said Marg.

Janet stood mute. Any moment Mrs Stirling was going to ask about the part and she still wasn't sure what she was going to say. She was at a loss as to where to go next. The decision was made for her.

"I've got some boxes of stuff in the car for you. Could you give me a hand please," said Marg.

This was not what Janet was expecting. What boxes of what stuff and how come they were with Mrs Stirling? At least it was delaying the inevitable. She moved apprehensively towards the car. Marg could sense that Janet seemed a little on edge. She was usually quite cheerful, but not today. Perhaps it was the weather.

"I came across the Worthton truck, broken down about ten miles out. So I've brought some of the stuff in. Some of it for Kelly's," said Marg.

As Marg was opening the front door where the stuff for Kelly's was stacked, she noticed that Janet seemed more than usually curious about the items.

"Some of them might need the two of us to lift them in," said Marg.

"I'd get Kevin to take them in, Mrs Stirling, but he's out on the road warning any cars that come along about the pole," said Janet.

Marg looked onto the road to see the back of who she knew to be Kevin.

"Janet, between you and me, that pole is not going to fall down," said Marg.

"Do you think so?" said Janet.

"I think it will be safe for Kevin to give us a hand with the bigger ones."

With that Janet walked to the front of the car and called out, towards the road, "Kevin!"

At first Kevin, with his back to them tried not to hear. However Janet's second call was certainly much louder and more insistent, he had to take notice whatever the consequences.

"Could you give us a hand with some of these please," said Janet.

Kevin glanced at Harry as a last hope of staying where he was, but chivalrous Harry could see ladies in need of assistance and beckoned him to help them. With raised shoulders expecting the worst and with eyes lowered he wandered across. Marg leaned into the car and started to put things out to Janet who was waiting.

"Janet, how many things am I supposed to be picking up from here today?" said Marg.

"Oh no," thought Janet. She could sense the dreaded facts soon to be uncovered. They can't even find one let alone that there might've been more.

"It's just that there is a parcel here with Lorry's name on it. I thought I was only getting one part. He didn't mention anything about two?" said Marg.

Janet and Kevin stood mute with amazement, drop jawed and speechless, they couldn't react, but only to wonder what was the parcel in Mrs Stirling's car. Marg pulled out the parcel in question. Janet and Kevin looked at it. An uneasy quiet ensued, Marg felt, by their reactions, that there was something going on that she was missing out on.

"Do you mind if we have a look at it please Mrs Stirling, just to see if it's the right one," said Janet.

"Sure," said Marg.

"Kevin, you'd know parts better than us, could you open this parcel up and tell us what it is please?" said Janet.

Marg was becoming quite bemused by this procedure. She noted that Janet had not answered her original question. Yet she could feel the anxiety emanating from them both about this particular parcel.

Kevin reached into the small cardboard container and pulled out a piece of metal and other smaller associated parts. These meant nothing to Marg, but by the reaction of Kevin it certainly did to him. His shoulders sank, he became looser and he was happy to look up.

"This is it," Kevin said.

Marg observed Janet suddenly became so much more relaxed. The stress in her that she had observed when she arrived had left. A smile began to creep onto her face and it appeared that her old self was returning.

Janet, realising that her reaction, however spontaneous that it was, had to change so as not to let on too much of the day's events to Mrs Stirling, a client. Marg observed this and was curious as to the reason.

"There was only one part that you had to pick up today, Mrs Stirling," said Janet answering the original question.

Kevin could sense Mrs Stirling still had a few questions to which the replies might be a little awkward. He seized his opportunity to escape.

"I'll start taking these other ones in for you, Mrs Stirling."

"Thank you Kevin," said Marg who stood out of the way.

Like a child waiting to be chastised, Janet felt an impulse to help Kevin and thus avoid any tight questions. She realised however that that would be rude. Mrs Stirling was a client and had to be respected as such, by being polite. Perhaps Mrs Stirling would just accept that she had the right part and that was all that mattered. Wishful thinking, Marg was too smart for that.

"It was just as well as I stopped and gave a hand to the truck driver, wasn't it Janet?" Marg said it with evident tongue in cheek, as though she was privy to what had just happened.

"Yes it was Mrs Stirling," said Janet, feeling guilty that the truth was now evident.

"Have you been looking for this part?" asked Marg in a way that was very sympathetic.

Initially Janet wanted to respond in a manner that Mr Kelly would've approved of. However she picked up on Marg's sensitivity and knowing her, as she did, decided to be open about it. Mrs Stirling would have realised the folly in her trying to be diplomatic.

"We've spent all day looking for this part. I was there when Mr Kelly was talking to Mr Stirling and he told him that the part was here. I didn't think so at the time, but Mr Kelly said that it was, so we've spent the whole day looking for something that was never here."

"That's men for you Janet. They create a mess, then rush off to do something else and leave us women to tidy up after them," Marg said trying to console her, since she now realised the full extent of Janet's anxiety.

"Can I get you a cup of tea perhaps Mrs Stirling? You look like you could do with one," asked Janet, composing herself to be good mannered.

Marg knew that she really didn't have the time to stop, the part was now in the car, there was a fan belt to be fixed up and the sun was lowering. Marg could also sense Janet needed some comfort after what had been possibly a worrying day for her.

"That's very kind of you Janet, thank you."

As they entered the office they were both pleased to be

out of the wind. After showing Marg a seat, Janet proceeded to prepare the tea. She looked about for something to eat and could only find a jar with, as she knew, stale Milk Arrowroot biscuits.

"I'm afraid these are all we have to eat. The biscuits run out pretty quickly next door," said Janet.

"They will be fine, thanks Janet."

"Must have been hot driving today Mrs Stirling?"

"Janet, please call me Marg. You can now you know," said Marg, an acknowledgement of Janet's maturity.

"Thank you Marg," said Janet.

"I've had better trips. What's with the pole that's causing so much concern outside, Janet?"

"Apparently Helen saw it move this morning and they are worried it might come down."

"If it hasn't blown down by this it probably will last the distance. Mavis likes to have something to be a drama. Fills up her life I suppose. You've settled in well here Janet?"

"I don't mind it."

Now that the atmosphere between them was much warmer, there was a lot about Marg that Janet was keen to inquire. Being her parent's daughter for so long, thus seen, but not heard, she could only discover what was being said through others. She knew Mrs Stirling had been a teacher and she wanted to find out more about it, as she too had ambitions in that field. Marg had come from somewhere else, seen the city and had seen a lot more than Janet was likely to see living in Wallabra.

Janet passed Marg the cup of tea and placed some biscuits on a plate.

"You used to be a teacher, weren't you Mrs Stirling?"

"Yes."

"Is it hard to be a teacher?"

"You will need to go to teacher's college, but it is not that difficult. It helps if you really want to do it. You must have done well in the Higher School Certificate. You were dux of this school. You shouldn't have any trouble getting into teacher's college."

"Oh yes. I could've gone to teacher's college."

For Marg the obvious question beckoned.

"Then why didn't you Janet?"

"Dad and Mr Kelly are really good mates and so this job was sort of waiting for me. It is the best job in town, you know, Marg."

Janet's reply struck an annoying chord within Marg. She had heard this so often and it distressed her. She could never understand why people, especially women, would simply assume a boring routine existence, at the men's request, for security's sake, when there was so much to see and do. She was determined to sow a seed of thought into this young lady's mind. Marg could see the enthusiasm for life in Janet, which would become a stale existence living in Wallabra.

"My dear Janet," Marg began. "There's a whole world down the Worthton road. You are too young not to want to go and see it all. If you want to be a teacher then do it. See life, meet new people, be a part of what there is beyond Wallabra. You only live once you know. What's stopping you?"

"It's just that I'm going all right in this job, I might be letting Mr Kelly down and I know Dad wouldn't want me to go."

"Much that I do respect your father, but you must do what you want to do Janet. That is what is important. It is the trouble with our gender out here, we are too subservient to how the men want to run their lives and we are expected to just tag along. The times are changing Janet, We women must stand up for what we want out of life. Dear Janet, don't just hide away your life out here because you are expected too. Give the outside world a try at least, you can always come back and if you do you will be so much the better for the experience of being away for that time."

Meanwhile in the store, with Harry out on the road, Mavis was busy organising the produce Marg had brought in. Members of the mob now filed in at irregular intervals, curious about what all the stuff being brought in from that car really was. With Harry not currently available, Mavis had to keep a suspicious eye on what they were up to in their wander around the store. Eventually they departed only purchasing a packet of biscuits.

Mavis was worried. She had hoped that by now Helen would've talked to John about the lines being down and if he could fix it. If he could then they could ring up Worthton and get someone out here to look at the pole. But then again John would be needed here in case the pole did fall down, and he'd probably need someone to go out with him and help. There were just not enough people. She was still figuring out what to do. One thing though there didn't need to be two people out on the road anymore. The school hour had passed. She made an executive decision that it should be Kevin out there which would leave Harry free to look after the store whilst she saw Betty about some ice. Perhaps she might be able to get Peter to go out with John. Betty could run the pub while he was away, she didn't need to be on the footpath now that school was out. That depended, of course, on if he wasn't in one of his moods.

She ventured outside the shop to see if anything was happening. With the mob still parked on the bench, she knew she couldn't leave the shop for too long.

She noticed only Harry manning the road.

"Harry! Where's Kevin?" she yelled out in her loudest voice in an effort to combat the wind.

"In Kelly's helping Marg," Harry called back with not as much effort as Mavis had to exert as he had the wind assisting his voice.

"Can you come back here please?" she yelled again.

Harry gestured his concern about having the road unmanned, but by the insistence of her hand gesture in reply he consoled himself that the road would be unmanned for a bit. With Harry now on guard, Mavis set out with determination towards Kelly's.

Passing John, outside the post office, she asked, "Has Helen told you about the pole down on the Worthton road?"

"Apparently Marg saw it on her way in."

"Yes. Do you think you can patch it up so that it will work?" said Mavis.

"Might be able to. I'll need to have a word with Marg though to see how bad it is and what I'll need."

The mob, parked on the bench, watched with interest.

Cup of tea drunk and a pleasant break for Marg she now realised that she would be further behind in her day.

"Any idea what the time might be Janet? My watch is still not back from the repairers."

"After four, Marg," Janet said after looking at her watch and also realising Marg's dilemma.

They both stood up and Marg collected her bag.

"Thank you for the cup of tea, I think I really needed it and the break."

"My pleasure, Marg. I am just pleased your trip wasn't in vain," said Janet with a little smile, which was shared by Marg.

"I am pleased we've had this little chat. You do what you want to do and all the best with that," said Marg.

"Thank you Marg," said Janet, as she opened the door of the office to let her out.

From the wind sheltered office they proceeded into the shop proper to be reminded, by the wind's force, of the day's offensive. Suddenly the wind was interrupted by the large frame of Mavis entering is a hurry.

"What's Kevin doing Janet?"

Janet, a little taken back by the sudden and forceful presence of Mavis, looked about the shop to see Kevin busy fighting the ever intruding red dust.

"Cleaning the products Mavis, see, down there." Janet pointed to him across the shop.

"We need him to look after the road. I've got to get Harry to mind the shop whilst I get some ice and see if Peter, at the pub, can help John with the broken telephone lines," said Mavis.

Janet was perplexed. She knew Mr Kelly would be back soon and possibly would not appreciate his employee wasting time out on the road. Yet Mavis was being so insistent. As it transpired the decision was not left to her.

"Kevin," called Mavis. "We need you to guard the road."

Kevin, respecting the elders of his community, returned to the road.

Mavis, pleased with the result, said, "Right now I have to

go over to the pub. Nice to see you Marg. I bet you're looking forward to getting home and a shower, eh? Could you have a chat to John about the pole that is down before you go, he might be able to fix it up. See ya."

Soon Janet was left in the shop by herself, as before, but without the worry. As Mrs Stirling left she felt that the day's worrying had come to a successful conclusion. She was also still annoyed with Mr Kelly for putting her in this predicament. There was a lot to be said from what Mrs Stirling had told her. She had always felt that Mrs Stirling would be a help to her one day. Perhaps this was the day.

John was ready to pounce upon Marg as she entered the street.

"Marg" he called politely as he walked down to see her.

"Hullo John," replied Marg, happy to have a conversation with John with whom she had only previously gestured.

"Apparently there's a pole down on the Worthton road."

"Yes that's right John."

"Whereabouts?" he asked.

"About seven miles out," Marg replied.

"Were the wires broken?" he asked pointedly.

"Still attached to the pole on the Worthton side, but broken off the pole on the Wallabra side."

"Well done Marg," John said, impressed by Marg's useful observation.

"You have to watch out for these things John when you live in the bush. If you are able to fix them, would you mind giving Lorry a ring? I was expecting to be back home by this and he will be worried about me," she asked.

"Certainly will Marg," he replied.

Their conversation was broken by the loud voice of Kevin calling out, "Janet," with urgency.

Marg and John turned west to see what had caused Kevin's outcry. Beyond the town limits they could see a cloud of dust emerging from out of the wilderness. Kevin's keen eyesight could see that it was a familiar car.

Janet appeared at the entrance of Kelly's shop, looking at Kevin.

"Mr Kelly's on his way."

Janet's worries started all over again. The shop looked a mess with red dust painted all over the floor and shelves. The back door was still open. Kevin was out in the middle of the road. Because of their vain attempt to keep out the red dust, a lot of the office work that was supposed to have been done this day, hadn't been. The only customer all day was Mrs Stirling. Mr Kelly may not be too impressed.

Mavis, who had been talking to Betty on the footpath outside the pub, suddenly became attentive to what Kevin was saying. She could also now see a car coming in from the west. As more dust was being created along the road between the car and Kevin, she felt it her duty to aid Kevin, just in case they didn't see him. She proceeded out onto the road to assist. In Mr Kelly's absence all day she was pleased to impress upon him how capably she had assumed command. Standing in the middle of the road, to her, seemed a good way to do it. With the wind and the heat focused against her she stood her ground.

Marg, who was about to leave, thought it would be polite to stay a bit longer and pay her respects to Mr Kelly. John stayed with her, he was interested to know if the plan to fix up the wires for the telephones would meet with Mr Kelly's approval.

The dust from his car subsided as his car hit the bitumen on the western edge of town. All waited for his arrival except Janet who had decided that a cleaner shop, minus as much of the red dust as she could get out, would be the path of least criticism. She had forgotten about the open door at the back.

As Mr Kelly does, when he is coming in from the west and because he is Mr Kelly he parked behind Mr Wykes' car facing east, the wrong way. Since Wallabra rarely saw any police, in actual fact if there was a dispute it was Mr Kelly who sorted it out, he felt safe in doing so.

The two men alighted shaking the dust of their attire before they realised the wind was doing it for them. A walk to Mr Wykes' car, a cordial handshake and Mr Wykes got into his car and prepared to depart. He wanted to do his u turn to head east, but was confused by the two people standing in the middle of the road. After a few hand gestures from Mavis he realised not to go near the pub for whatever reason that he did not understand, but did oblige the direction. Mr Kelly saw this and a frown entered his face. He too was obviously perplexed by this scene.

Mr Wykes, on his way, a friendly wave from Mr Kelly changed to a sort of snarl when the car was out of eyesight. Upon seeing Marg though, his expression changed as she was a client.

"Hullo Marg, did you get the part?" he asked.

"Yes thanks Mr Kelly," replied Marg.

"Looks like you've had a bit of trouble on the way in," he said, looking at her crumpled dust stained dress.

"Just a broken fan belt. One of the things that happen out here on a hot day, isn't it?"

"Are you right to get home?"

"Yes thank you."

"You better get going then the day's getting on," he said, as a parting gesture, before entering his shop to find Janet. He didn't have to search she was in full view, broom in hand. Janet had known Mr Kelly long enough to instantly know that his mood was not good.

"What's all this carry on out here Janet?" he asked.

Janet was a little taken back and in her anxiety was uncertain what Mr Kelly was alluding to. Mr Kelly sensed her hesitation and explained further.

"We've got two people out on the road seemingly directing traffic, there are hoses everywhere, the pubs barricaded..."

Janet now knew what he was alluding to.

"They're worried about the electricity pole near the pub," Janet started to explain.

"What's wrong with it?" Mr Kelly asked.

"They think it might fall down and start a fire."

Meanwhile, outside, the locals including Marg had been so absorbed by Mr Kelly's arrival they had forgotten to look to the east. Marg was preparing to return to Joe Clement's place to get the fan belt fixed when a car had pulled up behind her. All were quite surprised by the new arrival and instantly recognised Mrs Kelly alighting from the car. Marg, although happy to see Mrs Kelly now realised that she wasn't leaving just yet.

"Good afternoon Marg, Looks like you've had a rather trying day."

"You could say that, yes," Marg said, embarrassed by her appearance.

"Dreadful day to be out driving."

"Homeward bound now though."

"Hope you have a good drive," Mrs Kelly said.

Fortunately for Marg it was obvious that Mrs Kelly had urgency to her purpose, which did not include a chat with Marg. Marg realised that this holdup was concluding.

"We must have a cup of tea sometime," Mrs Kelly invited as a parting comment.

Hoping the car would go as she turned on the ignition. The stockings had lasted very well, now they only had the short drive to Clement's to go. She was grateful for the cup of tea with Janet, she needed it, and now felt ready for the trip home. She hoped that what she had said would help Janet as she seemed very grateful for the advice and company. Certainly they had established a connection.

Inside of Kelly's shop, Janet had been doing some explaining.

"And what's the back doing open?" he asked, just as Mrs Kelly was making her entrance.

"I told them that they could leave it open," said Mrs Kelly.

"Hullo dear," Mr Kelly said, as if by custom.

"It has been too hot a day to expect these people to swelter in here and not let a draft in," she explained with force as to not receive any complaint from him.

"How did you go?" she said changing the topic.

"Got all the way out to Kandar and old Paul Louden wanted too much money for them. He's got no feed, his water is running out, I've found him a buyer and he wants to hang out for more money. Silly old bugger, he's done this to me before. I think he just likes to get me out there for company. Now I get back in here, no phones because there's a pole down on the Worthton road somewhere, they've got Kevin out on the road giving traffic directions to no one all because they reckon that poles going to go," he said.

Mrs Kelly picked up on his annoyance, but still had to convey her dilemma. She decided to do it with tact. A different approach to what Janet had witnessed earlier in the day.

"Just to add to your day, my dear, we've got roofing flapping in the wind. Has been like it for most of the day."

"Couldn't you find someone to fix it?" he asked.

"Everyone was out working."

"Should've taken Kevin out with you," he said, stating the obvious.

He stood there for a moment as if deciphering all that he had heard and figuring out all that had to be done.

"Right," he started with reassured confidence. "Janet, I want you to close the front door. You won't get too hot now it's not long till knock off time. That will stop the dust from getting in and sweep as much of it as you can out the back door. Might be easier if you leave this front door open a bit and the wind will help you. Lois, I will get Kevin to go out with you and he can fix up the roof, all right."

Mrs Kelly nodded in agreement.

"Now you say John might be able to fix up the lines?" he said looking at Janet.

"Apparently."

"Well we better get him doing it," he said moving out of the shop onto the road to meet with Mavis. Kevin looked a little sheepish as Mr Kelly advanced, like a little boy who was caught with his hand in the cookie jar. He had a feeling, by Mr Kelly's determined and almost angry style of walking, that he was going to be chastised. To his way of thinking he had only been doing what he had been told to do.

"Mavis, what's with this pole?"

"Helen saw it moving this morning when a really heavy gust of wind came through. We are worried it might fall over, cause a blackout, but what's more might start a fire."

Mr Kelly paused for a moment as if trying to find the right words to convey what he had to say without treading on her shoes.

"Mavis, do you see the trees down there past to the hall?"

She looked west to the scraggly trees that had been there for years, struggling.

"See how they're got dead branches still on them. Some of those dead branches have been hanging there for years. With this drought there would be no moisture in them to keep them on those trees. Yet on a day like this, with the wind blowing as hard as it is, they are still there. They have not blown over. If anything was to blow off it would be them. Now with that in mind I think we are pretty safe that this pole is not going to blow over."

He stated his facts with such learned authority and with such persuasion, Mavis could hardly disagree with him. As the centre of the road had now become the town meeting place, Mr Kelly's attention was now focused on John.

"John could you come over for a bit please."

John quickly made his way across.

"John,' Mr Kelly began. "Apparently the telephone lines are down somewhere along the Worthton road."

"That's right," John replied.

"Do you reckon you could have a look at it?"

"I want to, but we were a bit worried about this pole."

"You won't have to worry about the pole, the lines are more important. You'll need some help, won't you?"

"Might be handy."

"What's Peter up to? He might be able to help."

"He's in one of his moods again Betty said. It happens to him sometimes, especially on hot days like this," said Mavis.

"Then I'll need to have a word with him," said Mr Kelly. "So John you better go and get everything that you might need. Is there anything from my shop that you might need?"

"A bit of wire, a few steel posts..."

"All right. Kevin, will you go over with John and get him what he will need. When you've finished that you can go out with Mrs Kelly, she's got a job for you out on our place, all right?"

"Yes, Mr Kelly."

"I'll go and have a talk with Peter," said Mr Kelly.

Mr Kelly and the others, except Mavis, exited for their respective purposes. Mavis stayed on the road unsure as to what she had to do and equally unsure if her decisions had been correct.

What remained of the mob, sitting on the bench outside the store, looked on still wondering what these white fellas were doing.

# CHAPTER 28
## JUNE TAKES OVER. FEBRUARY 1965.

As Marg headed east towards Clement's and home she could feel the late afternoon sun pouring through the back window onto her neck. She knew time was getting on and the day was not getting any cooler. Already she could feel the sweat collecting from her hair and starting to seep down her back.

Time now to get this fan belt fixed, hoping that they would have one that is. Knowing her luck today she would see that to be the last straw, if there wasn't one there. She hoped Joe might have been still there or have come back by now. She would feel safer if he was to do the fan belt.

Approaching their building she could see that his old Ute wasn't there and neither was the tyre that she had brought in. She had to resign herself to trusting June. As she parked the car there appeared to be no sign of life. The doors were all shut and the windows closed tight. She alighted from the car and closed the door with force to combat the wind blowing against her efforts. The noise of it closing created another noise of a door opening at the shed.

June appeared from the shed quizzically with even more grease and sweat than she had before.

"Thought I heard a door close. Get everything you needed done?"

"Yes thanks June. Joe out on the road is he?"

"Yeah, that tyre had a leaking valve. We've fixed it up. Don't know when he'll be back. Got that fan belt for you. We'll get a start on it eh. Get you on your way. I'll get what I'll need, you open up the bonnet will ya?" she asked, and disappeared again into the shed.

June had reappeared by the time Marg had the bonnet up. Obviously she had been well prepared.

"Would you like to wash up a bit Marg? You can use our bathroom. The doors are open if you want to go in, I only closed it all up to keep the red dust out."

"Thanks June. No I might be able to help you."

Methodically June placed the tools where she wanted them to be.

"I've done plenty of these Marg, but you can watch if you want."

Tools in place, June picked up the first one and her head descended into the engine.

"So that pole didn't fall over. We've still got power."

"I don't think it was ever going to June."

"Silly bloody Mavis, she always likes there to be a drama, and when there isn't one she'll create one. Lord help her if anything serious did happen. I'm just pleased there is a distance between them and us, we don't get involved too much. Just do our own thing up here." said June from within the engine.

"Get Mr Kelly to sort it out if that ever happens."

"Is he back yet? Went out to Kandar apparently today. Bloody awful drive that would be on a day like today."

"He got back as I was getting ready to go."

"I heard Mrs Kelly going past there at some stage. I know the sound of her car, always going too fast as she's coming in. It's as if she ignores the speed limit sign on purpose."

"She arrived just after him. We didn't chat long she seemed in a bit of a flap."

"Yeah, she got a flapping roof from the wind today, that's it. Come in earlier trying to get someone to go out and fix it. Joe couldn't go out, in case anyone comes here. Why she couldn't fix it up herself is beyond me. Always got to get someone else to do stuff for her. Anyway if Mr Kelly's back he'll sort something out. I suppose."

If Marg's aim was to be of assistance, it was not going to happen. So enthused was June in her task, her body, bend over and inside the engine, consumed the whole space such that Marg couldn't see what was going on. At least the job was being done and she felt more assured about her journey home.

"You want your stockings back Marg?" June asked pulling the remnants of the stockings out of the engine.

"They've done their task June. They can be retired now."

"Some bloke from down at the camp did this, Joe said."

"Yeah, seemed to do the trick, got me here."

"It did that."

Marg noted the spanner that June used and where she placed it when it came time for her to fit the fan belt. Marg watched closely anticipating the spanner would be wanted soon. If she could hand the spanner to June on cue, she would feel as though she had done something to assist. She succeeded, much to June's surprise.

A particularly strong gust of wind suddenly broke bringing the dust of the side of the road underneath the car till it found an escape through the engine. Marg could see it coming and turned away to avoid the dirt. June plugged on, head submerged into the engine, it had no effect on her.

With a final strong push of the spanner which shook the whole car June's head reappeared. Collecting the tools that would be in the road of the next operation, she suggested to Marg.

"Turn her over Marg, see if it goes."

Marg was surprised that it hadn't taken as long as she expected it would. A little disappointed though that she hadn't learnt very much, however if it was ready, that was the object of the exercise.

As she moved to the driver's seat their attention was drawn to a car heading east, in a hurry.

"Don't have to see the car. You can tell it is Mrs Kelly by the speed. Did she have someone in the front with her?" June asked.

"I think it was Kevin from the shop."

"I would've thought she would've gotten him to help her in the first place."

Marg climbed into the driver's seat, fingers on the ignition key, she gave a quick glance at June not only to see that she was clear of the engine, but also for reassurance.

"Give her a go Marg, it's all right," June said, knowing what Marg's look was about.

To Marg's great relief the car started and appeared to be running well. She noticed June looking carefully into the engine before stepping back.

"Turn it off Marg."

The engine became silent again. For a moment Marg wondered if there was anything wrong. Without a word June set off for the shed, returning not long after with a bucket of water. Marg again felt relief and had the radiator cap off before June arrived.

"Should be right now Marg," June said as she was filling the radiator. "Would you like to have a bit of a wash up now before you head off?"

"If you wouldn't mind."

"Go ahead, through the shop, second door on the left. It might be a bit dirty, but don't worry about that. I'll go a fix up the account."

Their bathroom was as June described, dirty, but the water splashing onto Marg face refreshed and cooled her to such an extent that the room's appearance did not matter. She now felt ready for the return journey.

June was in their shop when Marg emerged.

"Feel better?"

"Much, thank you June."

"Would you like a cup of tea before you go?"

"Thanks June, but I really should be heading back. Lorry's expecting me."

"I understand," said June.

Transactions completed June followed Marg out to the car. Their attention was drawn to another car heading east.

"Looks like John's car. He must be heading out to fix up the phone lines. Should've been done before this. Was that Peter in there with him?" June asked.

"I think it was."

"That won't do him any harm."

As with the trip into Wallabra, Marg still had no way of knowing what the time was.

"Do you happen to know what the time might be, June?"

"Be getting close to five by now I reckon."

"I've got no time to lose then," said Marg, as she started the car. "Thank you for your help, June."

"No worries Marg, hope you have a safe trip home."

Car started, now there was only two hours of nothingness to get to somewhere in the middle of nowhere.

# CHAPTER 29
# THE P & C MEETING. AUGUST 1963.

The August winds had set in. They usually blow harder after a wet autumn. It had the effect of drying the countryside and more especially the roads. With the little bit of extra sunlight that August presents, the crops were now flourishing, all that was needed was a good rain in September. The chances were good, it usually followed that the southerlies, as cold as they were, did bring good showers of rain.

Shirley and Marg were grateful for the drying conditions on the day they went and saw Mrs Gilmore. They had been worried that if there had been rain, the road out to the Gilmore's would have been impassable.

They had been buoyed by their meeting with the Kincaids at the Wymere homestead the previous week. Just how many children there would be from Wymere was the unknown factor. Not trusting that Marie Gilmore would have been fully informed about the situation, they decided to venture out and see her.

As a result of the first P & C meeting that was held about the bus there seemed little point in canvassing the ones that voted against the bus. They were too set in their ways. They liked the concept of the community school and they weren't going to be swayed. Besides, Shirley and Marg thought it rude to approach the people already with children going to the school. That action would've lead to more discontent within the community. The more tactful approach was to ensure greater attendance at the meeting. Like Wellington waiting for the Prussians, they hoped the reinforcements would arrive in time. What was needed, were dry roads on the day of the meeting. That factor was beyond their control.

It was to be noted that Marg and Shirley's time on the phone socially to the other people at Coolagy had been drastically reduced. As a result of the threat they represented to the community, their social interactions became much less. A little taken back by the reaction Shirley and Marg did not let that distract them from their purpose. The fate of the children was much more important to them than their personal social standings.

Shirley had never been out to where the Gilmore's lived. The track through Wymere to their house showed the results of a wet winter. Large pools of water still lay in the potholes indicating to Shirley the depth of them. By the hoof prints still deep in the soil and the sulky tracks that scared into the soil their respect for Buff grew greatly.

Marie was pleased to see them and had a cup of tea and a fresh batch of scones waiting. Marg could sense Shirley's hesitance as they entered the house. To Marg, it was not as if it was the first time she ventured out to this residence. Perhaps a little bit muddier due to the fact that the house and the paddock were only separated by a foot step, however she knew what to expect. To Shirley, this was something she had never experienced before. She had obviously never realised that people lived this kind of existence.

Onto the second cup of tea, Marg explained to Marie their plan.

"So as you see Marie, it will come down to numbers. We hope that you will come along to the meeting," Marg concluded.

As she was explaining their plan, Marie at first was a little apprehensive as reflected by her usually impassive face. Closing down the school was not something that she wanted to hear and a worried expression filled her face. However with the idea of a school bus to take the children into Wallabra, and the realisation that her children would be able to attain the higher school certificate, her demeanour completely changed. It was as if her wildest, fanciful dreams were coming to a reality. She could see that her children were going to attain an education that would separate them from the existence their parents had, had to endure. It was as if her life's ambitions were finally going to be realised. A joy that she had never experienced filled her face. She sank deeper into her chair and they could see little tears of happiness collect in the corner of her eyes. It was as if she could envisage her life's struggle coming to a satisfactory solution.

"We will be there," she replied with determination. "Even if we have to get Buff to take us."

On the drive out along the rut ridden road Shirley was rather quiet. Marg could sense that she was digesting where she had just been. Eventually she voiced her thoughts.

"Marg," she said, "Last week we went down to see Mr and Mrs Kincaid at the homestead, and as we've discussed, a superb residence. Yet today, on the very same property we saw a family living in a shed."

Shirley obviously found it hard to accept that a family could live in such isolation. She was even more aghast when she saw the house a family of four children was supposed to live in with only a generator for power. It was not what she was brought up to believe.

"That's the squatter mentality for you. There are the ones who own land, and the ones that work on it. I sometimes think it came from the fact that we started off as a convict settlement and thus a ruthless class system was entrenched from the outset," Marg replied.

"We are not like that though?" Shirley stated.

"No. The soldier settlers are different. Those men saw the worst of times and have possibly learnt the futility of elitism. The worst can sometimes bring out the best. We are lucky, Coolagy is in the twentieth century, and Wymere is still in the nineteenth. I hope one day Marie might have Christmas in a modern house, in a modern town, owned by one of her educated children who has a good job. Wouldn't that be marvellous," Marg said.

"No reason why that couldn't happen. Did you see the smile on her face when it all dawned on her what we were trying to do?" asked Shirley.

"Seeing that joy in her today makes it all worthwhile, doesn't it?"

With Eisenhower precision, Shirley and Marg had their bases covered in preparation for the conflict that was to happen at the P and C meeting. The days prior had turned out to be dry with the never ending southerlies blowing monotonously. The roads were passable. The meeting was set for seven thirty which meant the advance was carried out in the dark. As Lorry and Marg progressed along Coolagy road, Lorry could see the headlights of the Bakers behind him. On his left, through the darkened wilderness that was Wymere another set of headlights. Thin and often disappearing, vague, but real, small, but present, the Gilmore's emerging out of the captivity that was the darkness. Buff was not needed this night.

At the intersection of Wymere and Coolagy roads there was reason to look to the left. There were a couple of sets of headlights heading south. Like Prince Faisel's army coming out of the desert, the Wymere homestead was advancing. Camouflaged amongst the enemy, the headlights aimed towards the community hall.

Six forty five, the headlights from Ursula and Bevan's car illuminated the structure of the community hall that had been hidden by the moonless landscape. Being closest to the hall it was customary for them to be first there to give the building life again. Searching by headlights Ursula found the side door to the little room. Bevan parked their car to give the next people to arrive and indication where to park their cars in an orderly fashion. Lights on, heaters attached, stove ignited and fridges activated, Ursula then started collecting plates from the cupboard for the supper. She wasn't expecting too many people on this night since it was so cold. Many of the plates were left stacked where they were.

Hearing another car arriving, she knew it would have been Tom and Lizzie Patton. It always was. Lizzie usually brought too many lamingtons, so Ursula reached into the cupboard to find the biggest plate for them.

Lizzie, Tom's wife, didn't always come to the P and C meeting. Lizzie didn't like formality, but rather enjoyed the social gatherings more. A little older than the other women on Coolagy and being the wife of the commanding officer she could've asserted some superiority, but never did. Her smaller frame and petite looks didn't give her the charisma to attain this role. Rather she just liked to be the same as everyone else. She did have a cheery disposition which made her very popular. Ursula could hear her distinctive laughter as she approached which motivated her to get the large plate out.

Tom was the first to enter, supported by Lizzie and Bevan. After the usual greetings Tom surveyed the larger room to see that it was in order. Upon seeing that it was still there, he made his way to the bar end of the small room to place the beer he had brought.

"Are we expecting many tonight, Tom?" asked Ursula, still wondering how many to cater for.

"It is so cold I don't think that many will turn up," said Lizzie.

"Is there much on the agenda?" asked Ursula.

"Not that I know of," said Tom. "Just the usual things."

Most important was to get the heaters out of the steel cupboards in the small room and set them up in the bigger room to give the place a bit of warmth. This was detailed to Tom and Bevan. Their task was however interrupted by the arrival of the Kincaids. Tom was surprised to see them arrive. He could not recall any other time that they had come to a P and C meeting. However, since now two brigade commanders were in each other's company the heaters were left to Bevan. Upon seeing them, Tom resumed his position as president of the P and C. Tom felt it his duty to welcome the leaders of

Wymere personally. Stan McLean, the foreman at Wymere also made it along as well. Coming in separate cars, he now stood with the Kincaids for security amongst people he didn't know.

Soon after, many more started rolling in. The kitchenette was a hive of activity as was the fridge at the other end of the smaller room. Ursula was losing control of the kitchenette, reaching for more plates as the outside door continued to open. In the excitement of such social activity, the drama of the earlier meeting about the bus, was not relevant or purposely forgotten for the sake of congeniality.

The door opened again and another blast of cold air forced its way in together with Joe and Marie Gilmore. Upon witnessing the chaos of human bodies busily moving about inside they were a little startled. Sue Cave noticed their arrival and aware of their lack of social confidence greeted them warmly. She escorted Marie and her plate of scones to the kitchenette. Joe became a little lost, not being used to so many people being in the one place, he was uncertain where to go or what to say. His dilemma was solved when he saw Stan in the main room. He was someone that he did know. Stan was pleased to see Joe as well, he had felt out of place in the *Officer's club*.

Any thoughts Ursula had of a small gathering were now vanquished.

"I never expected there to be this many coming tonight," she said to Lizzie.

"It's good to see the community coming together."

"I just wonder if I've put enough water into the urn, I better check," said Ursula and moved off for the task.

When it was decided to use the fold away table stored

against the wall, there was enough room for all the plates that the women had all brought. Supper was ready, except for the urn which now had extra water in it. Ursula had put it on high so they could only hope that it would be boiled by the end of the meeting.

Attention now focused on the large room, as chairs were now being arranged close to the heaters.

"This must be a record attendance, I never seen so many people here. Even the Kincaids from Wymere are here," commented Sue who was arranging the front table with the help of Marg.

"It's good to see, isn't it," replied Marg, keeping her cards close to her chest.

"My word it is," agreed Mr Plummer who had come to help the ladies set up.

"I wonder why tonight? I mean it is so cold," Sue asked suspiciously.

The men, beer in hand, assembled at the back of the hall with the women towards the front where the heaters were. Even Ursula ventured into the large room, seated closest to the kitchenette, signifying all was in readiness for the meeting to commence.

Tom, however, was too busy conversing with the Kincaids to notice. Sue, who could see that the *tête-à-tête* between the leaders of the tribes was holding up the whole show, moved across and had a quiet word to Tom, which brought about an immediate reaction from him.

"If I could just get your attention, we will get this meeting underway," he suggested in a voice filled with even more authority since there were so many people present, especially the Kincaids who he wanted to impress.

He did not have to stand for very long before the audience settled and became quiet. They had been ready for the meeting to start anyway and the sooner it was over the closer they were to continuing their chats.

"Well it's great to see so many of you have been able to make it here tonight. I suppose we can only put it down to the roads now being a little dryer," he pronounced trying to be humorous. Not getting the laugh he was hoping for he progressed.

"I would like to bring the meeting to order. Are there any apologies?"

The room went silent.

"I didn't think there would be. It looks like the biggest meeting we've ever had," Tom pronounced proudly, glancing at the Kincaids. Could we have the minutes of the last meeting please, Marg?"

When Marg had completed the text and sat down, Tom rose again.

"Thank you Marg. Do we have any matters arising from the minutes?" he asked.

Shirley and Marg had already discussed when they would bring the matter forward. They could've done it after the minutes were read out as a matter arising from the minutes, but decided to leave it to last again so it would then become a new motion.

There were, as it turned out, other matters that did arise from the minutes. The gums trees, that were to be planted in Buff's field, had arrived. Tom and Bevan volunteered to plant them the next time it rained. Tom also proudly announced that he had also purchased some Oleanders which he thought might look good planted near the school gate.

"Might bring a bit of colour when they flower in summer," he said.

It was agreed that it was a good idea.

Mr Plummer commented that the ant nest problem had been resolved by Bevan's diesel. Communal appreciation followed.

Sue's treasurers report followed. There wasn't much to report. The balance, which was too low, hadn't changed.

"We might need to reach into our pockets at some stage," Sue said nonchalantly.

Strategically Sue paused for a moment to sense the reaction. The silence and stiffening of bodies that followed indicated a resistance to the idea. Tom picked up on the feel.

"Perhaps we might delay a decision of this matter and see if we get good rain in September. Bring it up again in October, say," he said.

Upon this idea the bodies freed themselves and moved in a more approving manner, emphasised by the odd nods from a few heads.

"Right, well then, that brings us onto general business?" said Tom.

Not expecting there to be much in general business, Ursula chanced a glance out to the kitchenette to see if the urn had boiled yet.

With something on his mind and wanting to be first, Barry Lucas voiced from his chair, "When's council going to do something about these roads?"

"Perhaps I can help with that one," said Tom rising to his feet. "I rang them up the other day and they said they can't do anything until it all dries up a bit."

"What, do they reckon they'll get bogged?" said Barry.

His comment brought about a genuine round of laughter. By the time Eunice started talking about her Aunty Mary's trip to Broken Hill, the gathering was assuming this would be the last item.

When she had eventually finished Tom rose quickly to close the meeting so that they all wouldn't be subjected to another rave. Shirley's and Marg's eyes met to signify that this was the moment. Ursula exited to continue her matronly maternal duties in the kitchenette.

"If there is nothing else..." Tom said.

Shirley rose to her feet quickly, "There is another matter to be discussed."

"Yes Shirley," said Tom, a little disappointed. The excitement that had been building amongst the parade, anticipating the end of the meeting, suddenly died, to fall back to patiently listening mode. Ursula sensed the change of attitude and re-entered, wondering why.

Shirley proposed her motion. Whilst she was talking the penny was dropping with Sue. She now knew why all these extra people were here tonight. A conspiracy had definitely been a foot. The counter attack would need to be quick and simple.

"Hasn't this matter already been discussed and defeated," said Sue.

"Yeah, we don't want to keep going on with this every meeting. It's been dealt with," said Barry, leaping to aid Sue in his usual forthright manner.

"But this time everyone is present. Better to have a vote that represents everyone's thoughts on the matter," Marg said.

Tom was quite concerned. He could also see now the reason for the numbers here on this night. Obviously strategies had been carried out without his knowledge. Could this threat be the end of his command? If the school closed it would. He did not want that to happen. Yet in a sense of fair play and democracy, after all that is what they had been fighting in the war for, the motion needed to be discussed.

"Do we have any discussion upon the motion?"

Discussion did follow. Not heated, trying to be civilised, but with an underlying atmosphere of anger and frustration. To Barry's insistence upon the roads, Marg had also been in touch with council.

"I have it in a letter here that if the school bus was to proceed, they promise to gravel the roads and that would give them all weather status."

"I'll see that to believe it," said Barry.

"It's here Barry, in black and white," said Marg, in a manner that exposed her temper.

Having known Marg for many years, Sue could sense Marg's growing anger. Sympathetically and softly she said, "We believe you Marg."

Ursula now realised that the urn must've boiled and went out to check it as the topic continued to be argued. The people from Wymere were noticeable by their silence, but were rather observing the situation. Sue searched for arguments and eventually came up with one that she believed couldn't fail. Mr Plummer wouldn't want the school to close, surely. She rose to speak.

"Of course none of us have heard from you Mr Plummer. You're the teacher here, what do you say?"

Mr Plummer was at first a little taken back, but realised that his word needed to be heard. He could've been a little bit resentful given that the motion stated that the children would be better educated elsewhere. However he was an objective thinker and could see both sides of the argument. He had come from the world outside Coolagy. Besides, much that he did enjoy this community, if it was to close he would surely gain a posting somewhere else. Diplomacy and tact were skills that were needed. These skills weren't covered in teacher's college.

"I am enjoying my time in this school and I hope I have been giving the children here the best education that I can. I really respect the community here and how you've welcomed me as a part of it. Unfortunately I cannot give these children the opportunity to gain a higher school certificate," Mr Plummer said.

When it was apparent that all that needed to be said on the matter had been said, Tom called for a vote on the matter. It was decided that each family would declare verbally their children for their choice. It was up to Sue and Marg to do the recording.

As was with the previous meeting on the matter the declarations were lining up strongly for the school. There were mixed movements of bodies as each vote came in and Tom was feeling a little more relaxed. By the time Mr Kincaid arose to declare the children from Wymere, there were already enough children declared to keep the school running.

"Stan here has been to all the people who work on Wymere and I have a list here of the children who would use such a bus service. Including the Gilmore children there will be twelve children that wish to use the school bus into Wallabra. I think Stan would like to say a few words."

His moment had come. There had been a reason for his

presence and this was it. First though he had to overcome his fear of public speaking. Eventually.

"I'd just like to say that we at Wymere would be really grateful that we might get our children educated. Our oldest will be ready for kindergarten next year and....." Stan was cut of midstream by Sue.

"You are not seriously considering placing a five year old on a bus for, just how many hours from Wymere to Wallabra?"

"Not sure," said Stan.

Mr Kincaid came to his aid with more certainty, "Possibly two and a half to three hours each way."

"You've got to be kidding us. The poor bloody children," Sue said.

Sensing Sue's increasing temper Marg said quietly and as soothingly as she could, "It's what they want to do, Sue."

Sue, without words, did appreciate where Marg was coming from and sat down. Bethany Davis then rose to speak, pausing for a moment before speaking.

"Have you considered just who you are going to get to do this bus run? I mean whoever it is will surely have to stay out Wymere during the week, then there's the route."

"We have someone in mind," said Marg, forearmed to quell another argument.

"Wouldn't it be much easier if the Wymere children could be bused up to our school here? It would save a lot of travelling for them" Bethany said.

"I've looked into that," Marg replied. "Even with the extra numbers there wouldn't be enough to warrant an upgrade to where they could get the higher school certificate. However with the extra children then going to Wallabra that school would be upgraded."

"What!" said Barry in disbelief.

"Departmental regulations Barry, that's the way it is."

The counting continued. When all the declarations had been counted it was obvious what the outcome was going to be. Marg announced, being the secretary, the numbers to the forum and in conclusion suggested.

"It would appear to me that we have enough numbers to start a school bus and also enough to keep the school running. Therefore we can all have our pick as to which way our children will be educated."

In retrospect it was the perfect diplomatic solution. All were pleased. The bodies relaxed themselves into social mode. The meeting was completed, the chats continued as if the brief interlude was, but a passing phase. Ursula was now busy washing up.

# CHAPTER 30
# THE JOURNEY HOME. FEBRUARY 1965.

Refreshed by the wash at the Clement's place and with everything done that was needed to be done, Marg set off for the journey home. There was no time to mess about. Lorry would be looking for her by now and wondering what had happened. With the phones down there was no way he could know. Together with the fact that she did want to make it home while there was still light in the sky so Lorry would be able to fit the bore up with some natural light, hurry was the optimum directive.

Outside the "city limits" and onto the dirt she picked up speed with urgency. She now felt safe to do so, not having to worry about a make shift fan belt. With a tail wind to the Wymere road turn off, she was already going faster than ever Lorry recommended. However, she also knew that this was the best of the roads and the best of the conditions. If she was to pick up time this was the place to do it. She would just have to chance that by going over the speed limit, she would not be caught. She fancied her chances on that one. All the windows open and the interior quite vacant, as opposed to her arrival at Wallabra. The wind was teasing her hair in any direction and producing ripples on her dress, yet it didn't bother her as she was homeward bound and no one to look respectable for. As for trying to stay cleaner, why bother?

She was as dirty as she had ever been. The red dust had invaded her space to such an extent it was useless not to accept it. She looked forward to a hot shower and clean clothes when she arrived home, only a matter of miles away.

Heading east, the wind and the ever sinking sun seemed to be pushing her along, illuminating the road with its fiery glaze. The parallels of, the sides of the road, the fences on either side, the railway line and of course the telephone and power poles, pointed the way with monotonous regularity to the horizon where they all met. It was a very familiar sight.

Suddenly, even before she drifted into the driving trance, the spell was broken. One of the parallels had broken its regimental structure. Then she remembered, returning to the current situation, further along she could see John's car parked by the side of the road with John and Peter surveying the broken lines. She beeped the horn as she passed them and they returned the greeting with a wave until the red dust from her car obscured them.

Pre-warned about exceptions, she now cast her eye for a dot on the horizon which would signify Toby's truck. She wondered how they were getting on.

She did not have to wait long, interrupted by the gust of red dust sweeping across the road a definite structure was evolving, getting bigger. In many ways her journey on this day had been successful. The part had been attained. The car now had a new fan belt, which should last for a while. She had alerted Wallabra to the phone lines being down and she had gained assistance for Toby. The disappointment of the day's drive had been no new library books and her watch still wasn't back from being repaired.

Perhaps they might be still in Toby's truck. Her wanting for something just for herself convinced her that a short stop at Toby's truck was now compulsory. The black dot on the horizon had grown enough to reveal distinctive recognisable structure. She began to slow down. As she approached there appeared to be no sign of human activity. The truck set a lonely sight stuck out in the middle of nowhere, abandoned and destitute. However upon parking behind the truck a hive of human activity was revealed. Joe's Ute with stuff scattered around it and three men, with peering eyes through the dust created by Marg's car, curious as to the nature of this anomaly of another human's presence.

Questions answered upon recognising Marg, walking across the road to greet them. The three men stood, camouflaged in dust which had virtually turned to mud with the addition of sweat, happy to see her.

"How are you going?" she asked.

"Yeah, all right Marg," replied Joe. "We've got the spare on and it's stayed pumped up. Just about to put the blown tyre into my Ute. I might have an old tyre that might fit at home and then we will be out of here. June fix you up all right?"

"Yes, thank you. The car's going well."

"You're on your way home then," said Joe. "Get there before dark, you reckon?"

"Hope so. How are you off for water?" asked Marg.

"Got plenty thanks, besides we're out of here soon," replied Joe.

"Going to be a late night for you Toby?"

There was a slight pause before Toby answered, "You get that."

Charlie listened to the white fellas chat. He didn't feel comfortable enough to join in, but rather waited like a kelpie puppy eager for instructions. Quickly bored of it, unlike a kelpie puppy, he used his initiative and started putting stuff back in to Joe's Ute whilst still attentive to the conversation. Drawn to Charlie's plight Marg asked.

"You'll be right to give Charlie here a lift into town?"

"Yeah he's coming in with me. There's too much stuff in the front of Toby's truck. He's right," answered Joe in such a manner to suggest that the two men had built a positive attitude towards Charlie. Marg was very pleased with this reaction. She felt satisfied that she had created this situation for Charlie. Perhaps the first wall of the racial divide might be weakening.

All seemed to be in order here and all seemed in a hurry not to be here, Marg had one final question.

"Toby, I don't suppose there is a watch amongst the stuff for Wallabra, is there? I've been waiting for it to be repaired by Mr Hulme in Worthton."

"You might have to wait a bit longer. His offsiders left him. He's still got stuff there to be fixed from four months back."

"What about library books, have they sent any out this time?"

"No, Worthton doesn't even get new ones very much now. Even the Missus says it is a waste of time going to the library. They can get reception for television now in Worthton," Toby replied.

Disappointed, there was nothing for Marg to do here anymore and the men, happy for the social interlude, now wanted to be away from here. Marg prepared to leave them.

"Oh well, I hope you make it back tonight Worthton all right," she said considerately.

"Thank you, and thank you for your help today," Toby replied.

"See you later Joe," and calling out to Charlie who was now involved with the flat tyre, "You right Charlie?"

"Yeah, thanks Missus," he called out.

Marg's journey home resumed. The parallels on the side of the road once again took up visual residence. The country around her stayed the same. The afternoon's heat continued unabated. It would now be after five in the afternoon, the time of the afternoon when the day's heat should've noticeably tempered. It hadn't. The wind, far from abating during the day, had increased. Bringing in air from the centre of Australia where it had been stewing in heat for the whole summer. Now, with force, it was still unleashing itself onto this district and community. Only the southerly, that had been promised, would change the situation and cool the air. From Marg's position, travelling east with the wind still pushing the car to the wrong side of the road, the cool change was still a fantasy. Only when she arrived home, still well over an hour away, would she attain relief from the heat.

The sameness of the landscape continued and the hypnotic effect started to invade Marg's space once again. Thoughts now focused on the next variation, the next difference in the scenario, to indicate to her that she had progressed in her journey. Shorter in time than she thought it would be the crossroad where Wymere road started loomed. She was grateful, a distance from Wallabra had been travelled. A section of the journey accomplished.

No cars in sight, certainly no trains, she was safe to turn left. Even slower over the railway tracks, she was now heading north. Building speed, although not as quickly, the wind coming in from the northwest was no longer a help.

Narrower road, more potholes and deeper corrugations, smaller telegraph posts with less lines on them, the sameness of the landscape, devoid of life, the mindset established for the next hour of the same. Nothing to do, but head towards an ever elusive horizon.

To save her body from becoming totally inert, Marg chanced a look over her left shoulder, towards the western horizon. Having no way of knowing what the time was, still, she might gain some indication from where the sun was. Squinting her eyes from its glaze she could see that it was getting lower. To her surprise, however, below the sun she could see an invasion commencing that was capturing the sky. High Cirrus clouds were advancing from the south west, it could only mean the cool change was in progress, getting closer.

Reacting to both of these objects, Marg turned back with more focus. The drive would now become a race to be home before the sun set and also before this change arrived. Although the coolness that it would bring would be appreciated, the possibility of rain most welcomed let it happen when she was home. She didn't want to battle a wet road on this day as well. She didn't want to face the sudden change of wind that could be quite dangerous.

She was driving as quickly as she now could, given the condition of the road and the wind. It was now a matter of timing. The sun's ray suddenly becoming less intense, quite noticeably, she looked left to see why. She discovered the invading clouds had started to attack the sun. It was a fight the clouds were bound to win. Maybe time was not with her.

The tedium of the day, the disappointment of no library books or watch, not a chance of any real social contact because to the day's urgencies, still a long way to home, tiredness started to take a toll on her mood. With now this added threat of the change the day's stress was not going to ease. All this created a negative mood. All that was left was hope.

All there ever was, was hope. Hope for rain. Hope for no breaks downs. Hope for a good market. Hope for better roads. Hope for better windows. Hope for something different. Hope for a better life. Their lives were built on hope and their aims to fulfil them. But fulfilment? Never totally. Strategies, however well planned, however well worked, could never defeat an enemy called chance. That foe knew no rules. That foe knew no reason. That foe could never be beaten. The chance factor teases them with hope. It is like chasing the horizon. It was never going to be reached. While ever there was this hoping, there was never going to be success for there would always be hope. Contentment and true happiness was always going to be over the horizon. Chance dictates it thus. Complete power over their fate was never attainable while ever chance lurked.

All that she could do was to keep driving. Do what she had to do in an effort to combat this megalomaniac called chance. Deal with each situation as best as she could, in order to survive. Was that all there was, just survival? Was this the answer to the Why? question she asked herself continually?

She could feel the sun's rays ever decreasing. The advance line of clouds now covered more than half of the western sky. The sun was lost. Heavier clouds were now forming as a second wave. Hope that it might bring rain, after she arrived home. She noticed a small mob of sheep to her left, moving slowly east, away from the invading weather, as they do. It was not a good sign. They were searching the red dust for any skerrick of nutrition as they moved. Yet they did not look too poor. Merinos are great scavengers, they could seemingly exist on nothing. They had been bred to survive this wilderness. Their contentment was assured. They knew how to accept this space. To them, the Why? question was not necessary.

The horizon to the front was expectedly changing. A milestone was about to be achieved. The unmistakable line of trees which, after this day's experience, would always bring back the memory of being broken down. Of being stranded in the middle of this lonely wilderness. As she slowed down to negotiate the gully she glanced at the log where she sat waiting for help. Waiting to understand this place where she was. Trying to establish an acceptance. Trying to feel the thoughts she had had at this place, hoping for chance to remedy the situation. That time had now passed, her thoughts were different. Thank goodness for Charlie otherwise she might still have been there, as she had seen no other vehicles on this road. Coming out the other side of the gully it was all, but now a memory. A memory decorated by the surrender she endured whilst waiting and the acceptance that event had created.

The landscape reverted back to normal. She had more of the normal to encounter before the next visual milestone, the farms of Coolagy. At that point, like seagulls to a mariner, home was just beyond the horizon. Being well after five by now, the children from Wymere would nearly be home by now, another day of being bussed into school at Wallabra. Neville, who now runs a bus service, often stays out in a little residence at Wymere so he is ready for the next day. He's done very well out of this school bus, he is even thinking of starting a bus service into Worthton every week. He used to do the mail run out to Coolagy. Shirley and Marg both knew him to be reliable, enterprising and more importantly, a teetotaller. When the battle for the school bus was in full swing they approached him about taking on the school bus and he has never looked back.

The clouds had now entered into the eastern section of the sky. It was devouring all the blue as it passed. To the west the sky was looking much darker. The wind still howled from the northwest, but for how much longer? At some stage, sometimes without warning, the wind will change. Sometimes with more force than the north westerly, sometimes with rain, sometimes with nothing much at all except hopefully cooler air. The race was well and truly on. Her wining post was her home. The weather's winning post was undefined. At least she was now passing the turnoff to the Coolagy school and community hall.

The Coolagy School was still operating although the numbers had slowly dwindled. Mr Plummer now teaches in Worthton and the current teacher wasn't much chop apparently. The community still held as many functions at the hall as they ever did. There was a dance night on next Saturday night. Sue was president of the CWA this year and Marg the secretary. The differences in opinions they encountered during the school bus episode had been filed into distant memory. They now accepted each other's views. There was no room for grudges. They were all in this place together. Their army had to be united against the elements. They needed each other's company. The status quo continued. At the last meeting Ursula said that she was having trouble with the urn so Polly, who was going to Worthton the next week, said that she would be able to get one. It is now a school project for the children to water the gum trees in Buff's old paddock and the Oleanders at the front of the school in an effort to help them through the drought. Buff now enjoyed his retirement on a vast and open plain. The Gilmores had now acquired a better car. The old one was still being used to run the children to the bus stop. It was teaching them all to drive.

Not far to go now and in familiar territory. Next milestone was the crossroads. She had done well, but time had not stopped. Even though the sun was now obscured, it was still obvious by the fading light that evening was approaching. The time of the day when another danger would emerge from their day time slumber to graze: the kangaroos. As the sun is setting there's that period where eyes are changing from sunlight to headlights and the surroundings are difficult to make out, that is the time they are most prevalent.

She knew them to be silly things. They react first and think second. Trouble is their reaction is so erratic and very difficult to predict. Marg would hate to hurt one, but it would be unavoidable. Worst of all they make a mess of the car. A few months previous they were worse than what they were now. Because the road is fenced off the natural pastures can grow uninhibited. In a drought this is the only feed left so the kangaroos feast on it. However since the drought continues and the graziers are running out of feed on their properties the temptation of the long paddock is too great. Mysteriously front gates get left open and the sheep escape onto the road, it then takes the graziers a very long time to get them back into the paddock. Hence the roadsides were now as barren as the paddocks they guarded. The kangaroos have been very disappointed.

By the time the crossroads were in view the gloom of the evening had set in, so much so that the headlights were now needed. Although she did not have any idea of the time, it seemed that the evening was happening before it should've. Surely it hadn't taken her that long to traverse Wymere road.

Turning left onto Coolagy she realised why. The cloud cover would've had a lot to do with the disappearing light, but as she looked at the western horizon she discovered another threat that explained the disappearing light much more logically. She had seen this sight before on similar such days. It was a sight she had learned to dread. This time, being in the car, it was a perilous sight.

The now thickness of the cloud cover was always going to hide the reds, the oranges, the yellows of a summer sun set. Yet the whole western sky had a bank of reddish brown hue advancing is a straight line. It advanced much quicker than the higher clouds did during the drive home. This threat was coming in like a blitzkrieg.

There was only fifteen miles to go till she reached the safety of home, but she knew, by its sudden, unstoppable advance, that she had one more battle to fight. The change, in the form of a dust storm, was about to hit.

# CHAPTER 31
## LORRY'S DAY. FEBRUARY 1965.

The bucket had proved to be very handy for Lorry to bring water to those sheep that couldn't make it to the drums. Realising that if he took the tractor, and the water it carried, to the weakened sheep he would have the whole mob following him as they were now trained to realise the tractor meant water. Instead he parked the tractor in the usual position, began the syphoning into the drums and cheated some water into the bucket and snuck away.

The dogs, at first were a little puzzled by the bucket of water. This puzzlement upon the logic of humans was a common pass time for the dogs, but they would watch with interest as they would wonder how their questions would be answered. They knew that they always would be. They soon cottoned on to what Lorry was doing.

In anticipation, as Lorry would lift up each animal's lifeless and disinterested body, place its head close to where it could smell the water and feel interest return as they drank, the dogs sourced the next one lying on the ground. Occasionally the threat of the approaching dogs would stir life into them. The sudden flight of fear would lead them to the mob where they found water. Other times the animal was too far gone to be worried. Upon discovering these, the dogs would sit close to that animal as if to signal to Lorry where to come to next.

Even when Lorry would return back to the tractor to refill his bucket, the dogs would wait by the stricken animal. Eventually, unbeknown to the dogs, the tank would run out. They learnt that the signal for this was the tractor starting. This signal meant their duty of parting the sheep out of the tractor's path was once again required. Another trip back to the house was now in progress.

Back at the house Lorry was surprised not to see Marg returned from her journey. The wind had not abated and the heat, despite now being later in the afternoon, had not decreased. He had observed the progress of the clouds filling in quickly from the south west. The change was on its way.

The question still beckoned in him and had now become quite a concern, "Where was Marg?"

She should've been home by this unless there was something amiss. Refilled, to the dog's disappointment, expecting the return journey to the sheep, Lorry stopped by the house. As they observed Lorry entering the house yard they resigned themselves to a quiet moment in the shade of the landing. Lorry proceeded into the house careful to brush off as much of the red dust as he could and taking his boots off. He was not intending to stay long. A phone call to Kelly's was the only item on the agenda.

After several attempts on the phone it was obvious that it was not working. Frustrated, there was nothing that he could do. No way of finding out what had happened to her, nothing he could do to help. Where was she?

There was still light in the sky. There were still sheep that needed water. Maybe she would be back when he returned.

Another journey to the sheep completed. Another tank full that had been emptied, more sheep had attained their feet after being bucket fed water, the return journey commenced. It was now obvious that the light was quickly diminishing. The clouds had thickened. The sun was lost, but not yet set. Twilight had arrived ahead of time, spreading a gloomy hue as though a precursor to an imminent threat. Beyond the rushing of the wind, the noise of the tractor, an uneasy calm was infiltrating the scene. The dogs interrupted their rhythmical pace to look about them in an attempt to try and understand this strange phenomenon. Lorry too could sense the change in the atmosphere. He also looked about him to try and see this new threat.

He did not have to wait long for the answer. To the south west he could see the signs. He had seen them before. They were unmistakable. The reddish brown mass underlying the clouds was conclusive. A dust storm was on its way.

It was also realised that this weapon didn't give much warning. The dogs picked up their pace as they reacted to the higher pitched tractor indicating greater speed. He wanted to do another refill, just in case, and it would be handy if it was done before the dust cloud hit.

By the time they had reached the house the threatening mass had filled half the western horizon. The light had decreased to such an extent, headlights were now needed. Of greater concern to Lorry was that there still was no car. Marg had still not returned. The thought of her being stricken in the middle of this poison of red dust encroaching, filled him with real fear for her safety. Worst of all was that he felt so useless.

Before the refill, a quick stop by the house and a hurried entry, but still no phone. He made sure the light in the landing was on to act as a beacon.

Upon setting the tractor up for the refill he noticed the north westerly wind which had barraged them all day suddenly retired, succumbing to a greater force. A worrying calm descended, the light vanished abruptly, time to be ready for the attack. The dogs stayed close to the tractor as they sensed a danger.

The quiet was disturbed at first by a soft rumbling which could not be distinguished. Then it grew louder to reveal itself as a wind of such fortitude it seemed to move the whole earth. The leaves on the gums trees around the house suddenly rustled to a higher pitch.

As it hit the tractor Lorry had to hold onto whatever he could so as not to be blown over. With his other hand he covered his face to try and strain the dust out of his lungs. The dogs now realised that their fears were not in vain. They moved and sat close to the tractor tyres for shelter.

The defence to this weapon was endurance. It was the same strategy as always. They were used to it. Only this time there was the added concern for Marg.

# CHAPTER 32
# LOTS OF RED DUST. FEBRUARY 1965

At first Marg thought she might be able to beat the dust storm home. It is what she wanted as a victory against the foe. But with still fifteen miles to cover and realising the speed at which it was advancing, it had probably already hit their property. This soiled mass heading rapidly towards her was possibly their farm, in soil, coming to meet her. She was going to have to fight against this terrifying insurgence. A plan of defence had to be incorporated.

Realising all the windows in the car were open and that she couldn't close the back ones whilst driving, she had to stop. She wasted no time in closing them and hopefully the lever that read "vent". Although by the dust that always filtered into the car, open or closed, she doubted its worth.

With the headlights on, trying to pick up speed, endeavouring to get as many miles done before the storm, watching out carefully for kangaroos, the journey continued. Knowing that when the storm hit her visibility would be severely lessened, she wondered if she would be able to see the turn off into their property. She wondered if she would be able to see anything. If she could get to the gully before it hit, she knew how far it was to their entrance from there. A check of the odometer at that point would give her an indication.

With the encroaching cloud of dust, evening had quickly turned into night, a dark and sinister night at that. Visually, the headlights were all she had left. She strained her eyes to the sides of the road for the sudden movement of a kangaroo, whilst also hoping for the first sight of the gully. She did not fancy coming upon that depression amongst a catechism of swirling dust and possibly falling branches.

After much hoping the top edge of the headlights revealed the road descending. The gully had arrived. Slowing down to negotiate the rough crossing, she rejoiced in a small victory attained. Her satisfaction did not last long. As she ascended from the gully she could hear a great noise as though it was Armageddon itself. She thought she could hear a branch from one of the trees snap. Confirmed by the almighty crash it made upon landing. She had been very lucky to have reached the western side of the gully before it had landed.

Quickly focusing her eyes on the odometer she was not prepared for what she would encounter beyond the gully. As the car surfaced from the gully it was hit with a force much stronger than Marg had ever anticipated. Instantly she became disorientated and panic filled her thoughts. It felt as though the car had been encapsulated into a mass of whirling matter, like being drawn into a black hole, a lightless infinite sphere of dimensionless chaos. The windscreen was a mass of colliding particles. It took a bit of getting used to.

Where had the road gone? All she could see was dust and an invisible force pushing her in a direction that could only be dangerous.

The car rocked and swayed like a boat in rough seas. She searched for some semblance of road, but could only see confused matter of soil heading anyway. She felt like she was being dumped by an enormous wave with no up or down, no direction at all, just chaos.

The road had to be found. The headlights, as they were, only revealed reflected rubble. She tried switching the headlights to low beam and suddenly could make out what appeared to be a solid surface, hardened by tyre tracks.

The road's definition was faint and intermittent. The wind gusted with some of the gusts bringing extra dust which for a moment would obscure the track from view. At these moments all she could do was to keep the steering wheel straight and hope for the road to return. She also had to hope that no kangaroos would appear. The catechism happening outside the car would be spooking them. At which point their common sense would not be operating. Also hope that there were no other cars on this section of road. She was having enough trouble seeing any road at all let alone be on the alert for anything else. Hope the car would persevere in its task. Hope that she would actually make it home. Only her skill and chance were the determining factors.

Nerves on edge, always totally alert to any stimulus, worried, she had slowed down considerably, staying in second gear. This, and endurance, were the only defence. Her only contact with reality amongst this particle cosmos outside which seemed to be eating away at the fabric of the car in an effort to compel her to become a part of this atomised existence, was the odometer. It alone gave her hope that she was progressing. She found herself glancing at it more regularly.

She was becoming used to the external forces, the effect on the car and her eyes had trained themselves to be fixed on what road she could find. It was now just a test of endurance and good fortune.

She cursed her luck that on such a day as this had been, with all its mishaps and given the urgency of the whole trip, that she would be stuck with a dust storm at the end of it. It was another test that had to be overcome in this land and existence of constant and differing examinations without ever a pass mark to be attained.

All she could do to be positive was to imagine that this whole day's toil would soon be over. The odometer was ticking over. She could start to fantasise about that shower she was going to have and how clean she was going to feel afterwards. Certainly a vast contrast to how she was at this moment. She had discovered the vent didn't close. The red dust had found the weak point and was now consuming the interior so much that she could feel the need for a severe cough. There was nothing for it, but to fight back. She opened her window a little bit. Being on the windward side it was not going to let any in, but should let a lot out. It worked and a little victory attained. All she had to do was hang in there and keep watching where the headlights go.

The miles ticked by slowly. According to the odometer she should be now within a mile of the entrance to their place. Through the dust she was starting to strain to see where the track from their place broke onto Coolagy road. She didn't want to go past it as that would be very easy to do given that she couldn't see very much outside except for what the headlights revealed.

Then she saw the opening off this road. It was most recognisable not because she had a clear view of it, she did not, but by the fact of instant recognition after years of repetition. She didn't bother indicating as she turned into their place. She was on the last mile to home.

At last and what a day it had been. All to do now was to front Lorry who would be wondering why it has taken her so long.

# CHAPTER 33
# INTO THE NIGHT. FEBRUARY 1965

The dogs were puzzled again. Why was Lorry standing near the gate into the house yard, with the tractor going, headlights on and facing the wrong way. The tank was again full, they had all had their bodies refreshed by the water, why this inertia?

They waited beside Lorry as he stood firm against the wind, the dust, the heat like troops waiting for the onslaught. The dust storm had curtailed the trip back to the sheep for the time being. Maybe Marg would arrive home while he was waiting. He kept straining with his eyes and ears hoping for some sign of Marg's return. Reluctant to go back inside the house for fear of letting in too much of the red dust, he contemplated chancing it. Maybe the phones were back on and he could get some information.

So they stood, with the elements tearing at their bodies, worrying about the purpose of Lorry's existence, Marg. The dogs twigged first. Suddenly their ears pricked and they stood more upright. Watching and listening with extreme interest. Lorry noticed this and thought maybe this was the sign. He was not disappointed. Suddenly the dogs rushed off and they could all see a pair of headlights forcing their way through the dust.

The track from the main road to the house travelled

south. Marg had gained experience of the wind forcing the car in a different direct. It did not take her long to be bored of the exercise in preference to finding the house. Knowing that the track would veer to the right near the house she watched anxiously for the turn.

Then she spied something different to the mass of dust clouding her windscreen, a faint light struggling like a harbour light in a rough sea, through the swarming dust and unorganised matter. It could only mean her journey was coming to an end, she steered towards the light. Help was at hand.

It was confirmed by the darting figures of the two dogs exploding out of the darkness like a rope to a drifted boat. They startled her and she stopped suddenly not wanting to run into them. With the car now stopped the dog's surprise, excitement and joy expressed itself by jumping onto the driver's door anxious to greet the inhabitant.

Not appreciated by Lorry who had now joined the scene and less than politely ordered to them, "Get down from there."

They knew that had done wrong and had to now wait for Lorry, who was progressing to the driver's door to open it, so their greeting could continue.

After being encapsulated inside the car, the sudden force of the wind now caught Marg off guard. She was pleased that she had gotten home before she had felt its real power. Alighting from the car their relief upon being together again was expressed not in words, but in a passionate embrace. The dogs waited in turn.

"I'm sorry I've taken so long Lorry, I've had troubles," she said.

"I've been worried about you," he said. "What happened?"

"I did a fan belt about half way to Wallabra on the way in and there wasn't a spare in the car."

Meanwhile the dogs gained ample pats from Marg and were well satisfied. Even in the dust and wind they kept their happiness and excitement.

"Bloody Joe Clements has had one on order for ages."

"Well he had one when I got there."

"He kept that a secret, then. How did you get on?"

Lorry may have been out in the weather for quite some time, but Marg, having emerged from the shelter of the car, was still not used to it, nor did she want to be. This was not the time or place to tell such a long tale.

"I'll tell you about it later," she said. "Here's the part you are after," reaching into the car to retrieve it.

In the half-light which the tractor and car transmitted through the still blinding dust, he opened the parcel and was relieved to see its contents.

"Well done."

Marg could see that he was keen to put the part into practice. Even in the horrid dust storm and no light. She looked at the faint light of the landing calling to her to shower and rest, but by Lorry's appearance, he too had had a trying day.

"You are going to fix it up now?" she asked knowing the answer.

"Yes," he replied.

"Do you need a hand?"

"Wouldn't mind," he replied. "I'll need all the light I can get so I thought if you could bring the car down, I'll go down in the tractor and we'll use both the lights off them plus the torch. Do you want a drink or anything?" He asked with consideration.

She could see a chance looming to go into the house and freshen up a bit. She could do with that, until he suggested,

"There's a water bag on the tractor."

"Have we got everything that we will need?" she asked, resigned to the fact that the day was not yet over. She grabbed a drink before the next excursion.

"Yes and there's an old coat here for you as well."

Mounting their machines for one final battle on this day, they set off into the darkened threatening wilderness. Lorry led the way with the two dogs scouting in front. Marg was grateful for the shelter of the car and having a guide through an atmosphere composed of earth. Marg felt lost in a place that she should've known very well.

Fixed in a trance of watching Lorry and the tractor in front she was very receptive of the hand signal he gave to stop. Through the light the tractor emitted she could see the familiar gate into the paddock in question. She felt a sense of satisfaction knowing where she now was. To her right she could just make out the sound of sheep bleating and some movement amongst the dust.

After opening the gate Lorry suddenly appeared at her door. She opened the window and felt the force of the wind again.

"Need to close this gate quickly before the sheep follow us in," he said and quickly remounted the tractor to drive through the gate then kept going. Marg figured it was up to her to close the gate, quickly.

There was no time for a motivational talk in fronting the wind and the stinging dust, just do it. She could hear the sheep moving towards the gate. Fortunately the dogs anticipated the situation and were confronting the sheep, stopping their progress. They had to wait until Marg had closed the gate before they received her gratitude.

By the time Marg had made it across to the bore Lorry had set up the tractor in the position that he wanted. She found his figure through the dust near the bore with his hands directing the angle he wanted her to place the car. Upon seeing Lorry the dogs rushed over to him expecting praise for their effort with Marg at the gate. Lorry was unaware of the feats, but gave them a short pat anyway. That was enough for them. They perched themselves in their overseeing role as Lorry began to work on the bore.

At first Marg was quite content to wait in the car. Her job of bringing and positioning the light had been done. She felt secure and safe in the car sheltered from the wind and the dust. It was quite noticeable that the temperature had cooled. Her dress no longer had wet patches. The longer she stayed in the car the more tired she became. Minutes must have been ticking past although there was no way of knowing. The night and the dust hid any indication of time passing. It was all the same. But then the boredom created impatience. It was noticeable that the wind too was now dying. Stillness was starting to insist its presence. She hoped this might be the precursor to rain. It often happened that way. There was no way of knowing as the sightless night offered no clues. The air was thinning, the wind abating, she no longer felt threatened by them. Perhaps outside the car she could smell the approaching rain if there was any. Besides, she might learn something of what Lorry was doing so the next time she had a broken fan belt she might be a little more skilled.

"Anything I can do?" she asked, approaching Lorry.

He paused for a moment, as though he was lost in his project and had to plan beyond the task.

"There are a couple of half forty fours where the sheep are. I'll need them here so the water can pour into them before it goes into the dam. That way they drink from the drums and not go into the dam and get bogged again."

"You want me to go and get them?"

"If you could, you'll have to go on foot. I don't want them coming in here yet and some of them will be at the gate."

It appeared that her lesson in mechanics was put on hold. The new errand was not to her liking. Venturing out into the darkness, the hidden, the abyss that was this wilderness looking for drums that she wouldn't be able to see. She now wished that she had stayed in the car.

"Where exactly are they?"

"You'll see them. There'll be a fair few of them hanging around them and the light from the tractor should be enough," he said pointing vaguely in an obscure direction.

Nothing for it, but to take a deep breath and do it, hopefully she would find them and hopefully she could carry them across. As she was climbing through the fence she felt the tension suddenly tighten on the wires, which didn't help. The dogs, satisfied that Lorry had his job well in hand decided Marg's venture would prove more interesting, hence the tightened wire as they jumped through it. Certainly they found where the sheep were and that did help.

As the sheep were dispatched from their place by the dogs, she noted where they had been. The faint light from the tractor helped her distinguish objects out of place on a flat landscape. She found the drums and one by one carried them over to the fence, placing them over it.

About to get back through the fence again she tactically paused for a moment. Her dress, although very dirty, had passed the day unscathed and at this its last danger of being torn she was not going to take any chances. Her caution was well founded, the dogs, upon seeing her at the fence instantly jumped over it or through it, thus making her clamber through less confusing and safer.

When she got back to Lorry with the first drum she was rewarded by the sight of water pouring out of a pipe coming from the bore. Their day's anxiety dispersed like the fading wind and the settling dust. Soon after it was filling the first drum as Marg retrieved the other one.

It was one of the attributes Marg admired in Lorry, his ability to get things done. He had a way with machines, animals, farming which was very much – can do. He made her feel safe.

Syphoning hoses attached to the second drum, dogs rewetted and shaken, tools packed, all that was left to do was to instruct the sheep. Surely then this day would end.

"I'm going to leave the tractor here with lights on so they'll know where to come. We will then take the car to open the gate. If you and the dogs could get the main mob through, I'll take the car and scout around for any stragglers."

The wind had died considerably as Marg alighted from the car near the main mob. It was now much cooler as the change had taken its effect. She was glad of the coat. Lorry whistled the dogs who bounced into action, instantly knowing what to do. It did help that many of them were still at the gate and when it opened filed through. As sheep will follow sheep the main mob sensed what was going on.

As many of them progressed through the gate they could then smell the water which increased their motivation. Worried that some of them might go to the dam instead of the drums Marg headed to position herself between the drums and the dam. She heard a whistle from Lorry and heard the dogs rush off towards the sound.

Standing near the dam Marg had a chance to reflect. She watched the progress of the car's light wandering around the next paddock. Stopping for a while then moving on. The shepherd was tending to his flock. The protector was guiding his charges to safety. The toil was continuing. Just like it had done for years and will be doing for years. The constant battle against the elements was never going to cease. Their lives were fixated with survival. The question, Why? was always going to be present.

The wind had dropped to a cool breeze. The day's weather drama had passed, with only the wind burnt skin as remnant. A silence, the silence distinctive of the Australian outback, was encroaching. A force of peace was invading, a feeling of acceptance. Of being a part of what was always going on. She felt as though she was a collection of particles, like the red dust, inhabiting this space. It was to be appreciated. She could feel a great calm overtaking her. The same calm as when she was stuck on the side of the road with the broken fan belt, a feeling of the inevitable, of surrender, of acceptance, of being mixed with this environment. Fighting against the current was always going to be a trial, better to go with it and use its energy to find a solution.

It sometimes followed that this calmness, after a dust

storm heralded rain. She looked towards the sky, above her it was overcast, but as she looked towards the south west she could see stars starting to emerge. There would be no rain this time. All those hopes that the day might turn out positive after all the extremes had passed, were dashed, like most hopes are out here.

Although no water fell from the sky, they did now have water for the sheep who were revelling in it. Their desperation when they arrived at the gate into this paddock had changed to a quiet contentment as many of them, now with a belly full of water, found a place to lay down, amongst the red dust, in readiness of the next day's search for food. They were happy now. Their wants were satisfied. They enjoyed the peace. The sun will surely rise again tomorrow and it will ring forth its trials, but right now the night's peace created contentment. It was enough for them. It had been enough for Charlie to be a part of this great landscape in an accepting union. They hoped for nothing else, but was it enough for Marg?

For solace, Marg looked upon the flock with satisfaction. The day's dramas had now come to a successful conclusion. A victory attained and the enemy retreated. The travelling, the heat, the wind, the breakdown all now made worthwhile by the sight of the sleeping sheep. The effort had been rewarded. That contentment was to be enough for most, but was it for Marg, who still hoped for more.

Her mediation was broken by the light that had zig zagged across the paddock passing through the gate. Lorry was returning, this day's end was going to happen, hopefully. Then she could see the light was preceded by a small mob of sheep who were being guided to the drums by the dogs. She watched the car stop near the drums. She observed the dogs bouncing around the car in expectation of the next task. Her moment of reflection passed. Need was about to interrupt her capitulation to a timeless land.

The dogs were at first startled by the figure appearing from out of the dark, but were quickly overjoyed to discover it to be Marg. Marg, however, was not too impressed by the sight she was beholding. Lorry had obviously found some of them who were too weak to walk. Since the car was all he had and that there was space within the car, he had managed to place the sheep where ever he could in the car. Some were in the boot, some on the back seat, and a couple in the front. Marg shuddered to think how much of a mess there would be in the car, not to mention the smell she would have to endure driving it back to the house. She also wondered where he had placed the esky with the shopping in it. Somewhere safe she hoped. Annoyed, she accepted the situation and realised that it had to happen. It was what happened out here. Besides, wasn't the car dirty enough as it was, it had been subjected to all the dust the wind could level at it during the day. Charlie's aroma, all the supplies she had transported to Wallabra, the dried sweat which still made the seats sticky, the sheep only added to what already was disgustingly dirty. Surely the driver's seat wouldn't be as bad, since Lorry had to use it to drive to this place.

As best as she could, she helped Lorry drag them to the water, one by one. Satisfaction was attained to see them drinking. Another life saved. A job successfully concluded. This was to be enough.

Another test successfully passed. Another battle won.

They could both draw breath. There was nothing else they could do for the sheep. For a moment Lorry and Marg stood motionless and speechless, there was nothing that needed to be communicated. The peace that the night provided and the operation now concluded needed no words, just inner satisfaction which was obvious to both. The dogs waited, anxious for their next directive. Eventually the hope of a warm shower, being clean and a well-deserved rest overtook their thoughts. The day was over, surely nothing else could go wrong.

"Is there anything else?" Marg asked.

Lorry was hesitant in his reply as though she had broken his similar moment of peace, but then replied, "No that's it."

They gave each other a little kiss and headed towards the vehicles.

"I'll see you at the house," Lorry said as they parted.

The dogs were confused. They had figured that home was the next destination, but which vehicle were they to escort? Which machine would be first? Marg viewed their dilemma and feeling sympathy and respect for their day's toil decided to give them a treat. It was never a common practice for obvious reasons, but since the car was already a complete mess and given that they had had a very busy day, Marg decided they deserved a special treat. She caught their eyes and pointed to the inside of the car. They needed no second opinion, they knew what this meant and they were not going to pass up the opportunity of travelling in the car, the soft seats it possessed, the distance that didn't need their energies to be expelled.

They returned her kindness with such gratitude as she

climbed into the car for the last time on this day, she had to speak to them in a toned voice to settle them down. The excitement of a trip in the car had overwhelmed them.

Engines started. They left the sheep to their rest sleeping on the red dust, the night to its peacefulness and the country to its beauty. They were heading to their world of lights, electricity, shelter and a shower.

Marg was grateful for the company of the dogs, although their constant licking of her arms, tasting the salt from her day's sweat, caused her to speak severely to them again. Certainly the car was quicker than the tractor, so Marg took the lead. She knew the way. The dogs were ecstatic, but yet they had possibly had the most difficult day of all. Not needing any reason, without the constant nagging of the Why? question, they just did it with delight. As with all the humans and animals out this way, they were used to the fight, it was all they knew, they rejoiced in being a part of what had been going on successfully for thousands of years.

What's more they were happy doing it. They had what they wanted, although it wasn't very much, there was no need to hope. The dogs were now seated neatly on the front seat, panting with excitement, absorbed by the country the headlights presented to them. Most of all, as Marg observed, they had smiles on their faces. Perhaps there was something to be learnt by the dog's behaviour Marg thought. Yes, there had been no rain out of this change. She had had a dreadful day. She felt dirty, tired and bothered, but on this day she had learnt acceptance of this existence, an understanding that it was always going to be like this.

It was always going to be a battle against an unbeatable enemy called chance, but they had a weapon this enemy could not combat. One thing she and all of them shared was love. This was their constant weapon to fight off the elements. Love of her husband, of her children, of the community, of the farm, of their life, this was as constant as the land they inhabited. This was to be enough. With this there was no need for the Why? question. There was no need to hate the enemy, just learn to live with it. She did have a choice, the choice of attitude towards her situation.

This land will provide, it always has, she just had to have patience and time is something that there was plenty of out here. The timelessness and the peace this land permeates is this country's beauty.

If there was to be hope, let it be for her children, for good health, for the odd good crop, hope to be happy. Perhaps one day, she hoped, when the boys were educated, they might move to somewhere that was a bit closer to her sisters, a bit closer to better rainfall, a place where there wasn't so much of the red dust. With the house now coming into view, journey's end, she also hoped that the windows in the house had kept out the red dust.

With the ignition key now switched off, Marg knew from experience that the door needed to be opened quickly so as to save herself from the dogs clambering over her in their effort to get out. They do that. She flung the door open and felt their paws use her body as a launching pad.

The wind had died to a zephyr and all was very still. It was very dark, perhaps a little too dark. Shouldn't the landing light be on, it was when she arrived home from

Wallabra. Hurrying along the path, esky and handbag in hand, she was anxious to find out why. As dark as it was, she knew the way to the light switch. It was in the "on" position. Perhaps it was just a bulb. She tried the light in the bathroom. Nothing there, it was a blackout. The promise of a warm shower was now dashed. No power meant no pump, it was going to be a bucket job from the rain water tank into the bath. This had happened many times before, a routine had been formalised. She knew where the candles and matches had been placed for such an occurrence. Firstly though, the dogs had to be fed. She found the metal container that the dog biscuits were kept in. They wagged their tails excited in expectation. As she reached into the pile of hard pellets she realised that tonight their meal was going to be a hot one. Perhaps like a Sunday roast for them. The day's furnace was still in the container. They didn't mind.

Although a shallow, cold bath by candlelight may not have been ideal she was relieved to feel her body clean and refreshed. It made her feel civilised again. Fortunately the limited light hid from her the colour of the water after she had finished. It would have been very red. With the towel wrapped around her, candle in hand, she entered the house. It didn't take long for her worst fears to be realised. There was an unmistakable film of red dust on everything in the house, especially, as it seemed to her, their precious furniture. Although the weak candlelight couldn't show the full extent, she could feel it on her fingers. Obviously the force of the wind in that storm had pushed the red dust through the cursed louvre windows. She cursed the dreadful windows and hoped they could get some more modern ones that actually did keep the dust out. Maybe they will, after the drought breaks when all will be much better. But for now she too had to share the red dust, as if they were the same as the mob of sheep in the paddock.

A cup of tea was out of the question. Fatigue had caught her. There was nothing more to do, but sleep. The bedroom was as she had left it only now everything was covered in the red dust. The thought of finding fresh sheets and clean garments by candle light after such a day was beyond her as the thought of sleep was conquering all. She resigned herself to be sleeping amongst the red dust.